LOVED BY THE ALPHA

THE ALPHA KING'S BREEDER BOOK 2

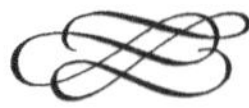

BELLA MOONDRAGON

For Carl

CONTENTS

WHAT NOW?

Isla

I AM ashamed of the fact that I am crying when I get back to my room. I want to scream and break something. I think about how it was when I first arrived at the castle and that old witch, Mrs. Whateverthehellhernamewas got mad at me for accidentally running into something. Now, I want to pick up an antique and toss it across the room.

I can't believe what's happening! Not only did my own sister refuse to answer my questions about where we came from, King Maddox just described me as a friend to a very, very pregnant little girl.

I lay down on my bed and pull a pillow over my head, angry sobs coming out. What in the world have I gotten myself into?

How the hell did I think I could actually stroll into the castle and mean something to the king?

He's the KING, after all, and I'm nothing. I've never been anyone.

Even if my parents truly were once the king and queen of Maatua, they certainly aren't now. That island has been described as cursed by everyone who has ever heard of it.

It seems to me like my entire family is cursed at this point. My parents, having to leave their homeland, my brother's illness, my kidnapping and near-death experience.

And falling in love with the cruel king who obviously doesn't mind making little weaklings like me think that he has feelings for us when he really doesn't at all.

Hearing footsteps behind me, I flip around, pulling the pillow off of my face far enough to see who is in my room.

Thankfully, it's not Maddox. It's Poppy, and she looks concerned. She sits down next to me, and when I roll back over and put the pillow back in place, she rubs my back.

"Didn't go well, huh?" she asks me after a few minutes, which actually makes me laugh.

"You can say that again," I reply. I'm not bawling and crying anymore, but I am still upset. Her hand is soothing in a motherly way, though.

"I'm so sorry," she says, still smoothing her hand down my back. "Did you speak to your sister?"

I sit up, pulling away from Poppy as I move my pillow aside and lean back against the headboard. I try not to think about the times I've actually hit my head on this headboard while making love to Maddox.

Poppy hands me a wad of tissue, and I swipe at my eyes. "I spoke to her. She wouldn't tell me anything. It seems pretty clear to me, though, that we are from Ma–that place. Everyone says it's best not to even say the word."

Poppy snickers. "I didn't take you as the superstitious sort, Isla."

I shrug. "Yeah, well, I need to be more careful. Things aren't exactly going well right now."

Her smile becomes even more sympathetic. "You're alive. That's something."

"I guess that's true. Goddess, my emotions are all over the place, though." I sniffle a few more times and wipe my nose.

"Well, dear, you were poisoned. Your body is probably trying to adjust."

I nod. Maybe she's right. "Anyway, King Maddox came back as I was leaving his office. And he was pissed that I was in there."

Poppy's eyes almost bulge out of her head. "Seriously? Why? He said you could use his phone. As far as I can tell, he has no business being mad that you were in there if he wants to keep getting in there." She gestures with the top of her head at my lower body, and I want to laugh.

But it's too much of a sore subject for me to laugh at the moment.

Instead, I sigh. "I'm not sure that he does," I say. "He had some… girl with him."

"What?" Her eyes are so big now, they look like cereal bowls with pupils, and her mouth hangs open after she's said the word.

"Yeah. She was young, too. Way younger than me. And… super-duper pregnant. So it seems I've been relieved of my services. In fact, considering her baby was about to pop right out of her, I guess I wasn't ever needed in the first place."

"Shut up!" Poppy insists, dropping her hand on my leg, hard. I know she didn't mean to smack me, not that hard anyway, but it stings a little. "No fucking way!"

I can only shrug again. "I'm just telling you what I saw, Poppy."

She is shaking her head. "I can't believe he would do such a thing! I mean, it's not like he has been a saint since the Luna passed, but I can't imagine that he would sleep with someone who isn't even old enough to be his... sister."

I don't know what that means. I think she's just so flabbergasted she doesn't know what to say, and I am right there with her.

"Anyway," I say, "I may as well figure out what to do now. I have no reason to stay here. I guess I can go home, but I'm not sure my mom wants to see me right now."

"You can't leave!" Poppy blurts. "I don't want to be the maid to just any old whore!"

I raise an eyebrow at her. "As opposed to me? An extra-special whore?"

She bursts out laughing, but I'm not sure what's so freaking funny. "That's not what I meant. You're not a whore. You've only been with one man."

I am glad I can amuse her. I slowly shake my head. I didn't intend to be with any other man either, but now... well, if I'm ever going to have a family or anything, I'll need to find someone who will love me.

And here I was thinking perhaps King Maddox was my fated mate! Maybe the Moon Goddess had it in her heart to give him a second chance mate, and that could be me.

The idea almost makes me laugh aloud.

But I bit my tongue. There wasn't anything funny going on here, except for whatever the hell Maddox was up to with that little girl.

"Don't decide anything now," Poppy says, patting me on the leg where she smacked me a little while ago. "You have plenty of time to decide what you want to do."

I hope she's right because I don't want to leave right this very minute, but I also have to wonder what I will do if Maddox comes storming into my room and demands that I leave in the same tone he used when he found me in his office.

"I'll go get you something to eat," Poppy says. "You've got to be tired after everything you've been through."

"Thank you," I tell her, feeling bad that she's even waiting on me. I don't think I need a maid when I am likely no longer the Alpha King's Breeder.

I'm just a glorified guest in the castle who might be asked to leave at any moment, and honestly, I don't want to give Maddox the satisfaction of tossing me out on my ass.

And if he does tell me to leave, I guarantee he'll take back the credit card he's given me, as he should, as well as the little amount of cash I have.

Why would he pay me for having sex with him? That wasn't what I was supposed to do here. I was supposed to have his baby, and he doesn't need me for that anymore.

Poppy gives me another sympathetic look and then leaves the room, leaving me lost in my thoughts.

Eating something fattening and going to sleep sounds tempting. But I'm not sure that's what's in my best interest now. If I have to leave the castle, I need a plan in place....

I'll have to go somewhere.

I think of the cufflinks. I think of the mystery surrounding my homeland. I think of the curse....

Maybe I know where I'll go after all....

Maddox

Sydney is sitting in the chair behind my desk, sobbing, as she speaks to her mother on my phone. I am angry. At a lot of people. Including her.

I'm not mad that she was in an awful position and got herself knocked up by her aunt's husband. I don't think that was the girl's fault, even though I can tell by the one-sided conversation I'm overhearing that she wasn't taken against her will by Alpha Bryant. He wasn't her first. This was the problem that had sent her to her aunt and uncle's house to begin with.

Little Miss Sydney had spreaders disease–the inability to keep her knees together.

But she was only nineteen–a little older than I had thought–and she clearly didn't feel like she was loved at home.

I'll let her stay in the castle until her child is born, and then, after that, we'll reevaluate the situation. Perhaps she can work here as a maid or something.

Beta Seth comes in and says, "Her room is ready. It's on the bottom floor, like you asked, so she won't have to climb stairs, but in the opposite wing as your room, so no one will assume anything is going on."

"Thank you," I tell him, glad I have a Beta who is reliable. "Did you assign her a maid and tell Mystica to come and check her out?"

He nods. "She's on her way, so Sydney might need to get off of the phone."

The girl looks up at his words, and it's clear she's heard him as she manages to tell her mother goodbye. It seems like Sydney loves her mama even if she's disappointed her time and time again.

I will need to have my phone de-snotified before I use it again with all of those tears and mucus flowing out of the girl. She plucks a tissue from my desk and heads toward us.

"Beta Seth will take you to your room," I tell her.

"Thank you, King Maddox," she says, and I think she's actually batting her eyelashes at me. I recoil in disgust.

I want to say she's too young for me, but that's not true since she's basically the same age as Isla, but the fact is, Sydney is far too pregnant for me to even consider what she might look like not pregnant, and she's obviously wild and immature.

Besides that, I'm not interested in anyone other than Isla.

Isla.

I've fucked up.

Again.

After Seth and Sydney leave the room, I sigh and wonder what I should do.

I shouldn't have yelled at her. Thinking back, I'm pretty sure I told her, or at least gave her the impression, that it was fine for her to use my phone. I was just angry when I walked in.

And I honestly didn't want her to see me with Sydney. I didn't want to explain something that had no explanation because I hadn't done anything wrong.

I know what I need to do. With a deep breath, I head down the hallway toward Isla's room.

When I arrive, I stop and stare at the closed door for a moment, gathering my thoughts.

The door to her antechamber is unlocked, so I walk in, but when I reach her bedroom door, I pause again before knocking.

She doesn't answer.

"Isla?" I call.

Again, it's quiet.

"Isla, it's Maddox." Like she wouldn't know that. "Can I come in?"

She says nothing, and I notice I don't smell her like I usually do. I don't sense her.

A bit of panic wells up inside of me as I remember how terrified I was when I discovered she was gone before.

I try the door, and it's locked, but I am better prepared this time. I pull the keys out of my pocket and unlock the door.

My heart stops.

Her room is empty.

FLEEING THROUGH THE WOODS

Isla

WHAT THE HELL do I think I'm doing?

I can't answer that question because if I pause to ponder the absurdity, I will turn back immediately.

Who in their right mind sneaks out of the castle after sunset when some crazy woman who has already tried to kill her is on the loose? And I don't even have a fucking clue where I'm going!

But... I keep running anyway.

Because... at this point... do I even have a choice?

As soon as Poppy left my room, I tossed a few items into a backpack that I knew I could carry on my back in my wolf form. I'm not used to shifting. I've only had my wolf for a short amount of time. Most of us don't get them until we are fifteen or sixteen.

I got mine at eighteen.

And there was never any reason back home to shift. I was always too busy working in the factory or wherever, and that requires thumbs.

I have shifted a time or two in my life, but I've never really let my wolf run. Now, with the darkness of the forest enveloping me, I run as fast as I can.

Sneaking out was easier than I expected. I guess everyone was out looking for Zabrina and Alpha Jordan or whoever was still missing. I didn't even know if they'd found anyone that day, other than Maddox's pregnant lover.

I'd gone out the door closest to the garage, the one I'd been dragged out of by Private Wylie a few days ago when I didn't understand why anyone would want to take me, when I thought perhaps Maddox was hurt, but I didn't know....

I'd run right out as fast as I could, looking for guards that never appeared. Then, I'd shot across the castle grounds to the fence and managed to climb over. It wasn't that hard. If Zabrina could do it, then so could I.

Once I was in the woods, I'd undressed, stuffed my clothes into the backpack, and shifted. I put the bag back on and took off.

All I have with me now is a couple of outfits, whatever cash I had in my wallet, and a few pieces of jewelry I thought might be worth something.

I didn't take Maddox's credit card. I felt bad about taking it, for one thing, and the other reason was I didn't want him to be able to chase me down. The cash, I didn't mind so much. After all, I had done some work for him. It wasn't like it had been my idea to quit trying to be his breeder. He'd made it clear to me that I was no longer needed.

Now, as the woods narrow in around me, the brush growing thicker and reaching out to snare my light-colored fur, I have to wonder where the fuck I think I'm going.

I'm running away from somewhere, not toward somewhere.

I don't know if I should aim for my hometown or if I should try to make it to the port and see if I have enough money to catch a boat to Maatua. Do boats even go to Maatua? I have no idea.

What I do know is I can no longer stay in the castle and see Maddox, even if it's just from time to time, and pretend that it doesn't bother me that he no longer wants me. I love him too much for that.

This way is better for all of us.

I continue to run, knowing the castle is growing smaller behind me, and the world is growing larger and scarier in front of me.

All I can hear is the sound of my own breathing, the rustle of the leaves around me, and the call of the nightbirds to one another.

And... maybe the sound of paws hitting the ground in the distance....

MADDOX

I AM SPINNING around in the center of Isla's bedroom trying to figure out what the fuck is going on when Poppy walks in with a serving tray in her hands. She doesn't even bother to tip her head to me anymore, we've grown so used to one another over the last few days with the adventure we went on.

But she does look confused. "Where is Isla?" she asks me.

"I was going to ask you the same thing," I say. "Do you know where she went?" My heart is beating a million miles a minute as I wait for the maid to respond. I am hoping this is all some sort of misunderstanding. Perhaps Isla has gone into Poppy's room to rest because she is angry at me and doesn't want to speak to me.

Poppy hastily sets the tray down on the table and rushes over to Isla's chest of drawers. She pulls open the top one and yanks out a credit card. I recognize it as the one I have given Isla to use. I am confused, but I take this as a good sign. The fact that the credit card is still there makes me think that she hasn't left the castle. Surely, if she was going to attempt to run away, she'd take that with her.

"Shit!" Poppy says, dropping the credit card on the top of the dresser like it's made of lava.

"What?" I ask, not understanding.

"She's gone!" she exclaims.

"I know. But where is she?" I ask, thinking it's obvious that she's not in the room.

Poppy shakes her head and gives me a look that makes me feel stupid for the first time in many years. "No, Your Majesty. I mean she's *gone!* She's taken off."

"How the hell do you know that from finding a credit card?" I ask, not convinced.

"She took her wallet, all of her cash, but left this." She picks it up again and waves it at me. "It makes sense that she wouldn't take your credit card. You can track that!"

I suddenly realize that the maid is right. I hadn't been giving Isla enough credit. Of course, that would occur to her.

"Where the fuck do you think she went?" I ask, panic washing over me again.

Poppy shakes her head. "I don't know, but she was so upset when you yelled at her and brought that little pregnant slut into the castle! Please tell me that's not your baby, Alpha Maddox!"

I want to growl at her. Since when do I have to answer the questions of the maid? "No, I did not impregnate that girl!" I say, snarling at her. "Are you saying that Isla thought that I was the one who knocked the girl up?"

The maid stands her ground, folding her arms across her chest and shrugging. "What else was she supposed to think?" she wants to know. "You yelled at her for using your office, something you'd previously given her permission to do, and then you stroll in with a little girl who's clearly about to pop."

"Son of a bitch," I say, dragging my hand down my face. I know that Isla was upset at me for losing my temper, and I don't blame her for that. And I can even see her questioning who the father of Sydney's baby is. But I can't imagine she would ever think that I would do something like that!

But then... Isla hasn't known me that long. She's only been here a short time. She might've thought that I had used other breeders, despite everyone telling her otherwise. She might've even thought that I'd inadvertently gotten another girl pregnant, and even though Sydney looks even younger than she is, she isn't that much younger than Isla.

"I don't have time to continue to stand here and argue with you, Poppy," I say. I turn around and head out of the room, but before I get very far, I stop and turn around. "Do not use the mind-link to try to find her!"

"Why not?" Poppy wants to know.

"Watch. Your. Mouth!" I snarl, lifting my hand. Not that I would ever hit her, but she doesn't know that, and she recoils. "Because I fucking said so!"

"Yes... Your Majesty!" she spits at me.

I turn and sprint down the hallway, sniffing the air. Where did she go? I can smell her everywhere outside of her door now, and I know some trails are stronger than others.

I pick up on her scent headed down the hall that leads to the door that exits near the garage, and I pick up speed as I follow it. As I run, I call out to the guards on duty. Has anyone seen anything? Did anyone spy the door opening or someone climbing over the wall?

I get an answer as I open the door and fly outside. "Yes, sir. We have footage of a girl climbing over the wall around the castle grounds," one of the guards tells me.

Thank the Goddess some of our cameras are still working!

He tells me it was fifteen minutes ago and gives me the coordinates of where she was when she made her exit. From her description, I know for certain, it's Isla.

I shift mid-stride, tearing my suit into a thousand pieces and not giving a fuck. When I reach the wall, I leap up and over it, despite the fact that it's ten feet tall. My wolf is tall, strong, and fast.

And I can smell her.

Over the scent of the pine, the wet ground, the fallen leaves, the animals, and everything else that hits my lungs as I take off running at full speed through the forest, I can smell Isla's scent.

Then, something else hits my nostrils, and another ripple of fear pulses through me.

"Seth!" I shout using the mind-link. "I need reinforcements, and I need them immediately!"

"Of course, Alpha," he says in my head. "I know where you went over the wall, but you're so far ahead of anyone I can send. The guards that are on duty have been detached. But... what's the situation so I can warn them?"

I don't have an answer for that. But in the forest around me, I can smell other wolves. Their odors are strong, so they have been here recently, and they are still close by, and the further into the forest I run, the more I can hear them.

The more I can sense them.

I could use the mind-link to warn them that I'm coming and they'd better stand down, but if I do that, Isla will get the message too, and I don't want to scare her. Originally, I simply didn't want her to know I was on her trail because I wanted her to feel comfortable, like there was a chance I didn't realize she was gone, so she'd run slower. But now….

Now, I don't know what to do.

Ahead of me, I hear snarls from between the trees. I hear the pounding of a frightened heart.

I feel her ahead of me. I feel her presence.

I feel her fear.

HELP?

Isla

I AM NOT ALONE....

I know that as I continue to run through the woods. My pace has slowed dramatically, though, because it's clear to me that there are wolves all around me in the darkness, and in front of me, too.

Why am I continuing to run from the man who has already done everything he can to save my life into what could potentially be a death trap?

I can't help but think that I am the stupidest woman alive....

Slowing my rate significantly, I peer off into the distance, looking for movement. I think I see a pair of glowing eyes up ahead. With that knowledge, I change my course, heading to my right. I wonder if I could potentially circle back to the castle and get away from these wolves. They could be castle guards that King Maddox or Beta Seth has sent after me.

But in my gut, I have a feeling that's not who they are at all....

The idea that it would probably be a good idea to call for help also comes to mind, but I can't do that, not now, not when I've screwed up so royally already. And Maddox is already angry at me for using his office while he was gone. Why would he want to come out into the woods to help me?

But he might send someone to save me... again.

He is probably getting really tired of having to rescue me every other day or so....

When I change courses, it doesn't help. It's like these wolves around me can see me and know that I've switched my direction. Now, I feel them closing in on me. I finally come to a stop and survey the situation.

Before me, and to my left, which would've been the direction I was running in a few minutes, I hear snarls and growls. I turn my head to my right, so that I'm looking back toward the castle grounds, which are at least fifteen or twenty miles behind me now, I've been running so fast for so long, and I sense that I'm not alone; something is coming from that direction, too.

When I turn to look behind me, I see a flash of movement, and I can barely get out a yelp and bare my teeth before a massive wolf with dark fur is upon me.

I fully expect that he will run into me and knock me to the ground and then rip my throat out, but rather than pouncing, he pulls up to my left and crouches down next to me... waiting.

The question almost forms in my mind but doesn't quite get articulated as my wonderment about what the hell he is doing is answered when, in front of us and to our left four wolves emerge, their yellow-green eyes glowing in the dark as they creep forward.

I turn to see more of them closing in from all sides, and in total there are at least twelve of them. All of them are bigger than me, with mangy-looking fur in dark brown or gray.

"Rogues," I think to myself. They have to be rogues. They're definitely not in good enough shape to actually belong to a pack. Their fur is missing tufts, they're thin, and they have chunks of flesh missing from their ears or other parts of their body. One of them only has three legs.

"Stay behind me, Isla."

The wolf next to me speaks in my mind with a familiar voice, and I am immediately put at ease. Why I didn't notice his scent before, I'm not sure. Perhaps it was because of my fear of impending doom. But... it's Maddox. He's come to save me himself. He didn't even dispatch someone else to track me down.

My heart melts a little, but I don't have time to bat my eyelashes at him at the moment.

We are about to be attacked by a group of misfit wolves who won't give a damn that this is their king.

I know he is giving them commands. I can see them slowing, their ears twitching, sideways glances given to one another. The fact that he is their Alpha King still makes him harder to ignore because he is their leader, but they have been living out here on their own long enough that they don't have to obey like most of us would. It seems that some of the pack Alphas have figured out how not to follow his commands from what I have heard. But then, those are Alphas who are powerful in their own right.

These scraggly wolves do not look like leaders to me. They look like criminals who have been banished from their own packs because they couldn't follow their Alphas' rules either.

They look like savages who are more than willing to rip their own king apart because they just like to terrorize stray wolves who pass through these woods.

Maddox growls so low, deep, and loud that it makes the earth beneath my feet tremble. The advancing wolves around us stop, and it's clear that he's frightened them.

I don't blame them. I'd be afraid too if I thought I was going to have to fight such a large, powerful wolf.

But there are so many of them, I don't think that their moment of hesitation will last too long. I think that they will come at us again soon enough.

The largest rogue wolf, who is standing in front of me and a bit to my right, begins coming forward again now, and he doesn't look frightened. He lifts his head and gives a short howl.

In the distance, a response comes in force. Loud howls fill the night sky, and my heart stops beating in my chest for a long moment as I realize there are far more wolves out there than I could've imagined.

And yet, the reaction of the rogues is not at all what I am expecting. They look up, back toward the castle, all of them except the one larger one, and then in a flurry of fur and claws, they turn around and dash away.

With a gasp, I watch them go. I'm shocked. Why did those howls make them all leave?

All but one….

And he is snarling at Maddox.

But the king isn't scared. He's not waiting for the other smaller male wolf to attack either. Instead, Maddox leaps right at him, knocking him backward onto his haunches, and then he topples over. Maddox leaps on him and begins to tear into his flesh, and the other wolf screams and shrieks. It's clear, he was no match for the king

I want to smile, but then, I feel a gush of wind, and my body slams into the nearest tree trunk, a sharp pain radiating through my shoulder.

Instantly, whatever it is that has rammed into me is pushed away as Maddox whirls around and sends what turns out to be another wolf flying through the woods. I stumble to my feet, wondering if this is all part of their plan and another wolf will be over here to attack me again. I feel blood wetting my fur from a gash in my head the tree has caused, not to mention the searing pain in my shoulder from the wolf's teeth.

A moment later, Maddox is back with me, blood dripping from his mouth. None of it is his. The moonlight reveals the anger in his eyes as he looks at me. Using the mind-link, he says, "Let's go."

"But… the howling…." I say, looking off in the direction of the castle, where the loud howls seemed to be coming from.

He shakes his head. "Those are my reinforcements, Isla. Now, come on."

A sense of relief settles over me, despite the fact that he's clearly outraged at me. At least I don't have to be afraid of all of those howls I just heard behind us.

I straighten the bag on my back the best I can with no hands. It's been knocked about a bit from the blow from the collision with the tree.

Maddox begins to walk back the way we've come, and I trot to keep up with him, but my head hurts so bad, and my shoulder is bleeding. I can't walk that fast.

It's going to be a long, miserable trip back to the castle.

Noticing that I'm struggling, he slows down a little and waits for me. For the most part, we can walk next to one another, but sometimes, we come to a tighter section of the path we're walking down, and he waits for me to go first. I figure that's because he's leerier of what's behind us than what's in front of us.

Within a few minutes, I see the wolves from the castle running toward us. A ripple of fear washes over me, even though I know that they're there to help us.

To help me.

Maddox stops when the reinforcements reach us, and so do I, but I'm confused. A few of the wolves stop behind trees, shift, apparently pull on shorts they've carried with them, and step out.

They have something else with them, too.

A stretcher.

Maddox stays in his wolf form and tells me, "You're hurt. They'll carry you the rest of the way."

I want to argue with him, but he's right. I am injured–again. And need his help–again.

I feel like a foolish failure as I stand still and let the now human guards load me onto the stretcher to carry me back to the castle.

As they hold me still, another man comes over and patches up my shoulder. It's not enough to fix it, but it should keep me from bleeding to death before I get back to the castle. It seems like the bandage must have some sort of pain reliever on it, too, because the sharp sting fades. It still hurts but not as badly.

Before they begin to move me, a woman in a dress tosses a sheet over the top of me, and I bury my wolf head under it. I don't want to see the world at all. Then, the soft rhythm of the stretcher being carried over the uneven ground lulls me a bit, and I'm reminded of being in my mother's arms or in a cradle

But I'm not in any position to feel soothed or calm.

Not only is Maddox angry at me, but he's also got another woman back at the castle, and I have to return there.

I'm not even able to run away without messing it up.

As I start to doze off, one word flutters in front of my mind's eye....

Cursed.

BLEEDING AND DIRTY

Maddox

I WALK AHEAD of the stretcher carrying Isla and try not to pull my fur out. If I had thumbs, I might've already pulled out enough fur around my forehead that I'd look bald.

Images of a wolf with a receding hairline come to mind, and I almost laugh. But nothing is that funny right now.

What the actual fuck was she thinking?

I already know the answer to that question.

As much as I want to blame Isla for all of this, it's my fault. She left because I was rude and dismissive. She left because she was upset with me. What else could it possibly be? She hasn't been feeling well, and I didn't even check on her today while I was gone to look for the missing kidnappers.

The castle comes into view ahead of me, and I'm glad to see it. I'm not as energetic as I was before, so I don't leap over the fence in a single bound. Instead, I call ahead, and the side gates are open when we get there. Using the mind-link, I call for a servant to open the door for me as well, and I trot down the hallway to my own room.

Seth is waiting for me. He unlocks my door, and I mind-link him to say, "Collect the clothes I stripped out of. My keys are in my pocket."

I've got to stop leaving my keys lying around.

"I already got them," he says, and I see them lying on my bed. "Shall I send the healer into Isla's room? Is she all right?"

Grabbing my clothes in my teeth, I head to the bathroom and say, "Yeah, she needs medical attention. Her shoulder is hurt."

"I'll let Mystica know," he replies, and I pause in the doorway of the bathroom.

Something about his words has me on edge. "Seth, stay in there with her while Mystica is there, at least until I can get there."

"Okay." There's a questioning lilt to my Beta's voice.

I don't want to explain to him why I am leery of Mystica. I'm not sure how much of her past he is familiar with, but I don't want her filling Isla's head with things she doesn't need to know about.

Shifting into my human form, I close the door and turn on the shower, hoping I can wash away some of the stress under the warm water before I get dressed. I won't put these clothes back on, but I've got to stop leaving my keys lying around. Even if they don't unlock Rebecca's room, I don't need people going to places where they don't belong.

The warm water sinks into my sore muscles and starts to ease the ache, but it does nothing for the pain in my heart.

I will go and speak to Isla as soon as I can. I have to find a way to fix this, but it won't be easy. She was awfully upset at me to do something like this. I didn't think she was capable of striking out on her own. I thought she'd be too afraid, too timid.

That just goes to show I don't know her as well as I think I do....

Isla

The lights of the hallway have me opening my eyes. We are back in the castle. I don't want to be here. I don't want to be anywhere at the moment, except for maybe in my mother's arms.

I am carried to my room and transferred onto my bed. Mystica is there already and has a sheet spread over my blankets so I won't bleed on them.

"Stay in your wolf form for now, dear," she instructs me. "Let me take a look." She shoos the others out of the room, but Poppy is standing in the corner, and I have an idea that someone else is present, too, behind me, near the door.

I have no idea who it is, but I know it's not Maddox. I would smell him if it were.

I would sense him.

Perhaps he needed to go check on his other breeder–his only breeder, I suppose–to see if all of this excitement has made her go into early labor.

From the looks of things, I'm guessing early would amount to about fifteen minutes.

Mystica is muttering under her breath as she takes my bag off my back and inspects my shoulder and my head. She's already removed my bandages by cutting through my fur. I suppose it doesn't matter. It's not like I shift much. "Your head wound appears to be superficial," she explains to me.

It doesn't feel superficial.

"This bite in your shoulder is more serious. I'll take care of that first. Okay, dear, I need you to shift so I can sew you up more easily without all of the fur in the way."

"I'll step out for a moment." I recognize the voice as Beta Seth.

"You don't need to stay, dear," Mystica calls after him as the door opens.

He says nothing, and once she gives me a reassuring smile, I go ahead and transform back into my human shape, which is a little painful because of my injuries, but I'm okay.

Another sheet comes over the top of me, and then Mystica is back to patching me up.

This time, when the door opens, I'm not at all surprised to see that it's Seth.

"I said you could go," Mystica repeats, a questioning tone to her statement.

"I know," Seth says as he settles into a chair near the table where I usually take my meals.

That's all he says, and Mystica doesn't question him further, so I suppose there must be a reason he won't leave.

And I suppose that it's because he's afraid I might take off again, or Maddox is. I can't blame them. They paid a lot of money for me, at least, in theory. They did forgive the debt my Alpha, Ernest, owed them. So, I suppose it would make me upset if someone who had cost that much left. I should just stay here and become a maid like Poppy or something.

I'm not thinking clearly, but I do know that it would make me unbelievably forlorn to see Maddox every day and have him treat me like I'm just another maid.

I wonder if there are other women in the castle that he has slept with who are just servants to him. Maybe they are stronger than I am, but I couldn't handle that. Perhaps they can put me in a wing of the castle that he never goes to.

The sting of the needle as it passes through my flesh, again and again, has me turning my head to watch as Mystica sews up my bite. It looks pretty nasty, but I don't think there are too many pieces of flesh missing. If the wolf had torn the meat away from my shoulder, I'd be in worse agony than I already am, and while I am certainly feeling torment and torture, it's mostly in my heart, not my shoulder or head.

When she is done cleaning and sewing up my shoulder, Mystica wraps it up with a bandage. "There we go. And your head just needs to be cleaned and wrapped."

"You won't need to shave my head and stitch it up?" The idea of Maddox wanting to have anything at all to do with me if I'm bald makes my stomach twist into a knot. But then I have to ask myself why I'm holding onto this idea that there's a possibility that this is all some sort of misunderstanding, and he still wants to be with me at all?

"No, you're all patched up. All right, dear. We'll let Poppy get you cleaned up and dressed," Mystica says, repacking her doctor's bag. "Take two of these pills for the pain every six hours. Poppy, see that she remembers. They make you a little sleepy."

"When can I get out of bed?" I ask her.

Mystica pats my hand. "I'll come to check on you tomorrow. For now, rest, and dear… try not to get upset." With those words, she turns and looks at Seth and says, "Try not to let people upset her."

He clears his throat, and Poppy is staring at the Beta as he gets up and follows the healer out. "Why do you think he stayed?" I ask her.

"Seriously? That's the first thing you say to me?" she barks. "Isla, I was worried sick! I went to get you dinner, and you're gone when I get back!"

I realize I owe her an explanation and an apology. "I'm sorry," I say as she goes into the bathroom to get what I assume is a cloth to wash me down with. "I just didn't know what to do."

Poppy shakes her head at me and begins to wash me. I want to tell her I can do it, especially since she's being so rough, but she doesn't seem to be in the mood to listen to me.

"After all I've been through with you. I was so worried when you were kidnapped! Now, you run away, and you don't even send me a mind-link to tell me you're leaving!"

She's got every right to be angry. I'm an awful friend.

But then, I'm not used to having friends.

"I am sorry, Poppy."

She finishes getting me cleaned up and drops a nightgown over my head. "Do you want your cold dinner?" she asks, gesturing at the table where it's sitting on the silver platter.

"No, thank you."

She humphs under her breath and gets my pain pills for me and a glass of water. I swallow them, feeling like a child who has misbehaved.

Maybe that's exactly what I am.

Now that I'm no longer bleeding or dirty, she helps me get beneath the blankets on the bed and covers me up. "If you need anything, let me know," she says. "Don't try to get up. Even if you just need to pee."

I thank her again, but she doesn't say I'm welcome.

As Poppy goes to turn off the light and leave the room, my bedroom door opens slowly. There's no knock, no announcement that someone is coming in, but I don't need him to say it's him. I sense his presence before he walks into my room.

"Your Majesty," Poppy says with a dip of her head that tells me she's not happy with him either. I don't pretend to know what he's done to her. Maybe she thinks he's the one that started all of this.

"Poppy," he says. Maddox follows her out of the room with his eyes before he's looking at me, and I feel like a small child again. His gaze is heavy, and I think it might crush me.

I expect him to shout at me, to lay into me right from the beginning, but the first thing he asks me, still standing by the door is, "How do you feel?"

The answer that slips from my lips is uncensored.

"Replaced."

SORRY... AND STUFF

Maddox

I stare at Isla in bewilderment, not sure what to say to her. I should probably be down in the dungeon trying to break Alpha Jordan, trying to figure out where the hell his fucking daughter is hiding, but I came here because I wanted to talk to Isla to make sure she was all right.

Apparently, she is not.

Sighing, I walk over to her bed and sit down next to her, my hip near her knee. "What do you mean?" I ask her. "Replaced... by who?"

She runs a hand through her hair, blonde curls tangling around her fingers, before she grimaces and untangles herself. She likely forgot about the cut on her head. "I don't think I need to tell you," she says, folding her hand in her lap. Her eyes are wide as she looks up at me.

Puzzled, I stare at her for a long time, trying to figure out what the hell she is talking about. Why is she mad at me exactly? I expected her to shout at me for being cross with her about the office. I don't think I've done anything else.

"What?" I shake my head. "Replaced?" I have to say it again. "Replaced."

"Yes, Your Highness," she says in a way that makes me cringe a little. "I left because I could plainly see with my own eyes that you don't need me anymore."

Suddenly, it all becomes clear to me, and I feel like one of those dense men in a movie where the woman says, "Well, if you don't know, I'm not going to tell you!" and it just seems ridiculous that the idiot man doesn't know.

I was that idiot man until about five seconds ago….

Maybe I just don't want to accept that she's mad at me for *that*.

"Isla," I say, reaching for her hand. She doesn't pull it away, but I know she wants to. She's still that obedient, subservient little girl that arrived here not that long ago who was terrified when she looked at me. "You have to know that that girl, I can't even remember her name, is not pregnant with my child."

The look on her face lets me know I have not said enough to convince her. "The way that you brought her into the office, she seemed very important to you."

I can't help the scoff and laugh that comes out of my mouth, which makes her face contort even more. "I'm sorry," I say, and she narrows her eyes. "No, really, I am sorry. She's not anything to me, Isla. She's just… a headache. A girl I'm trying to help. I never even met her before today."

She doesn't believe me. I can tell by the way she's scrutinizing me that she doesn't. She thinks that Sydney is my lover. And she probably thinks she's… thirteen years old.

"So why were you so angry when you walked into your office and saw me in there doing exactly what you told me to do?" She pulls her hand away so that she can fold her arms beneath her chest, and immediately my hands feel cold.

My eyes grow fixated on her chest. I can see the outline of her breasts against the thin fabric of her light-colored nightgown, and it's cold enough in here that her nipples are a little hard as well. I am distracted. She notices and growls at me.

"Sorry! Sorry!" I say. "I, uh…." What had she asked me? I remember. Angry. Why was I angry? "Baby, I wasn't angry at you. I was just frustrated in general, trying to get one problem solved so I could move on to the next, and Sydney wanted to call her parents, so I brought her to my office, even though I didn't really want her in there, and then I ran into you… and I'm so sorry, but I lost my fucking mind for a few minutes. And I really am sorry." I drag a hand down my face, waiting for her to speak.

She doesn't. She just continues to look at me, like she's not sure whether or not she should believe me, like she's not sure if she can trust me.

"Isla, I don't know what else to say. I went to another pack to get Alpha Jordan, ended up killing that Alpha, the one who impregnated Sydney, and brought her here to keep her from getting further harmed. That's all." I take a deep breath. "I haven't heard for certain, but I'm pretty sure that Alpha Bryant is dead.

Her eyes grow wider and wider with each of my confessions, and I know that she is shocked.

I feel a bit embarrassed telling her all of this, and while I'm not surprised by that reaction, I wish I didn't care. I felt the same way whenever Rebecca asked me what I'd done that day and my duties involved killing someone.

I didn't kill people often back then....

I killed more often these days—since I'd killed Rebecca.

"You've had a busy day." Isla's voice is nearly a whisper.

"Yes, we both have."

Her cheeks turn red, and a hot puff of air comes from her mouth. "I was having a bad day before I ran into you."

I reach for her hand again, and she slides her fingers into my palm. I'm not used to listening to other people when they want to talk about their problems, but for Isla, I will push my own concerns out of my mind and let her speak. "Did you call your mom?"

She nods. "I did. And... she didn't answer my questions. She just blew me off."

I can't help the frown marks that form in my forehead. "Questions?" I ask her. "I thought you just wanted to visit with her."

Her cheeks pink even further as she says, "I did. I miss them a lot. I just... wanted to know a few things. When I started to talk about anything other than what I'm doing now and how they are doing, she just... shut down."

I swallow hard and choose my words carefully. The last thing I want to do is make her mad again, but I'm starting to put all of the pieces together, and I'm beginning to wonder if Isla asked her mother about things she didn't want to discuss.

"Did you ask her about... Maatua?"

She nods. "I did. She said she doesn't know anything about it."

I'm not surprised. If Isla and her family came from the same island that the cufflinks she bought me came from, neither of her parents would want to talk about it at all. "Maybe just give them some time?" I suggest. "They may need to get used to the idea of you living in the palace."

She shrugs a little, and I wonder if there's more she's not saying. "Anyway... I was upset. You were upset."

My hand lifts, and I smooth my palm over her cheek. Just touching her makes me stiffen a bit. I want more than just a sweet caress, but she's not up to it, and I don't want to push her, even when she leans into my hand and moans a little.

"Isla," I say, scooting closer to her, "please don't ever leave the castle without telling me you're going again, okay? I have control over most of the wolves in this kingdom, but as you saw, there are packs of rogues, and they would like nothing better than to jump in and rip someone from the castle apart." For years, my men have roamed those woods looking for those jackasses, but they are great at hiding, and it seems like when we get one, two more replace that asshole.

"Okay," she says, but in her eyes, I see something else, like reservations about not wanting to promise me she won't leave. It makes me nervous. I have a feeling that this isn't the last time we are going to find ourselves in this situation unless I tether her to me.

"Did you say you have Alpha Jordan?"

Her words startle me from my thoughts. "Oh, uh… yeah," I say. "He's in the dungeon. Or, at least, he'd better be." I know this isn't the first time I've said those words recently, but since we have all of his remaining guards and servants locked up now, and his manipulative daughter is gone, I don't think he can find his way out.

She nods. "Do you have work to do?"

I sigh. I always have work to do. I want to stay here with her, but she needs her rest, and if I keep touching her, keep looking at her breasts, I'm going to want to do things that probably aren't so good for a woman with a head wound.

"Yeah, probably so," I say on a sigh. "But I can come in later and hold you—if you want."

She looks at me, those wide eyes sparkling slightly. I am not used to people having to think about whether or not they want my company. "That would be nice," she says, and I start breathing again.

I lean forward, intending to kiss her forehead, but she tips her face up, and my lips meet hers. Soft, warm, inviting, I can't help but press her to part those lips, and I slide my tongue between her teeth and tap it against hers, then I slide it even deeper, and pull her closer to me, reminding myself to be careful of her shoulder and her head.

I feel her fingers grazing my cheek as she slides her hand up to feather through my hair. I moan into her mouth. I'm having a hard time controlling myself. Thoughts of taking her onto my lap, of working around whatever she might be wearing beneath this nightgown, if anything, fill my mind.

I pull back, and our lips make a smacking sound. She looks a bit dazed, and I want to apologize to her. I didn't mean to remove myself so quickly, but I was on the cusp of going too far. "I should go," I murmur.

Her bottom lip trembles slightly as she stares up at me and slowly nods. "Be careful," she tells me.

I almost laugh. "I'm not even leaving the castle." But I know that doesn't mean that I couldn't get hurt or killed. It's not like no one has ever died here.

"I know," she says. "But Alpha Jordan will stop at nothing to get what he wants."

I'm not sure how she knows that. She's known a lot of things recently that she shouldn't know.

I stand and touch her nose lightly with my first finger. "Get some sleep." She kisses my finger as I pull it away, wanting to stay.

The urge to stay is overwhelming and uncomfortable as this woman has me completely hard. With one more smile, I turn and go, hoping she's no longer angry at me.

I'll need to find a way to make this up to her.

ANOTHER VIVID DREAM

Isla

I'M UNDERWATER AGAIN.

This time isn't like the last time, though. I know immediately that things are different.

This time, I'm more angry than I am afraid, but I don't feel the same pressure that I did last time either. I feel like I am storming off, running away, riding my white horse off into the sunset....

But I also feel like it probably shouldn't be a white horse. I know I've done awful things, and I know that I've screwed everything up. I'm not the hero in this story....

I'm the villain.

Normally, I'm okay with that. I don't mind being the one who stirs up all of the trouble. But in the back of my mind, I can't help thinking about what might've happened if my plans hadn't gone awry. Perhaps I should've listened to my father and not messed with the situation so entirely.

None of that matters now. Dad drowned. Mom fled the moment she found out what I was up to. I am pretty sure that Wylie is pulverized, and I have no fucking idea where the driver is.

It's just me now.

Me... and my father's allies.

I know I can keep wading through this deep water until I reach pack lands where I will be welcomed, where I'll be safe, where I won't be handed over to fucking King

Maddox. I just have to persevere, keep going, and hope that this goddamn oxygen tank doesn't run out before I get to my final destination.

I keep on going, staying below the surface of the water where none of the bastards who are searching for me will see me. I'm sure they've found Wylie's body by now. I'm sure he's dead because I tried to use the mind-link to reach him and couldn't. Same with Dad. So they might know I'm in a wetsuit, but they'll never be able to trace me in a fucking river.

Eventually, after hours of swimming, I see what I'm looking for; the base of the Wolf Stone Bridge.

I'm in Duster pack. I need to find the Alpha.

My father's friend, Alpha Hayes, will take care of me.

I haul myself up on the shore and look around. It's dark, but my eyes cut through the darkness with no problem, and I don't see anyone waiting for me, so I quickly shed the wet suit and toss it out into the current, far away from where I'm now standing in a skimpy leotard. It'll do. I hope the river's current carries the wetsuit far downstream, so no one can find me here.

I turn around and come face to face with several men in suits. My breath restricts in my throat.

"Look what we have here," one of them says.

I recoil slightly. "I'm Alpha Jordan's daughter," I tell them. 'And my father is friends with Alpha Hayes."

The largest man in the middle snickers and says, "Too bad Alpha Hayes ain't in charge no more, doll."

His laugh is menacing, and I realize now, I'm in a different kind of trouble than I have ever been in before.

I SIT UP IN BED, gasping for air, looking around my dark room trying to remind myself that that was all just a dream.

I'm not on the shore; I wasn't in a wetsuit; and I have never been to Duster Pack.

"Isla, what's the matter?"

The sound of Maddox's concerned, but groggy, voice coming from next to me on the bed has my head whipping around to look at him.

When did he come into my room? I hadn't woken up when he slipped in.

He reaches for me, and I fall into his arms, snuggling my head against his chest. "Nothing, I tell him. I just had a bad dream, that's all."

Was it a dream? Or like the situation with Private Wylie, was it real?

It didn't seem like a dream....

"I'm sorry, baby," Maddox says and holds me closer. Part of me is still upset at the way that he treated me earlier, but he's the king, and I'm just his breeder. Even if he does have feelings for me, who am I to hold a grudge against him?

I remember what he said when I told him that I love him–that I should be careful because that could be dangerous.

Not exactly an "I love you, too."

Not to mention, how many times has he vowed to never marry again or take another Luna? No, I'm not sure what my place is here, but he's my king. I can't continue to feel entitled to anything other than an apology and an "I'll do better" which is what I have.

He smooths my hair from my cheek where perspiration has adhered it, and the cut on the back of my head smarts a little. It's not as bad as before. I'm sure it's started to heal. My shoulder feels better, too, though it's still tender. Maddox is too sleepy to be thinking about that; he's not rough with me or anything, but he's not exactly gentle.

"Do you want to talk about it?" he asks me. I can hear the sleep in his voice. He's not fully awake at this point, and I suppose he's only been in my room for a few hours, so he must've been in a deep sleep when I woke him.

I can tell by his voice that he's tired. "No, that's okay," I say. "Not right now." I will tell him tomorrow. Maybe something I said will be useful to him. "Where did you go after you left my room?"

He sighs and adjusts beneath me. "I tried to talk to Alpha Jordan, but he didn't want to speak. I'll have to make him a little more uncomfortable tomorrow."

"Wait? Alpha Jordan is here?" I ask him. Hadn't he told me that before?

"Yes," he says. "Remember? I went to get him and ended up with what's her ass, too?"

"Sydney," I murmur. Neither of us has forgotten the girl's name.

It's coming back to me now as the sleep wears away and the last fragments of the dream fade from reality.

It had to have been a dream because, when I thought I was Zabrina, I was thinking that my dad was dead, that he'd drowned. So... I must've just been having a regular dream and not a premonition.

But then... Zabrina had said she assumed Alpha Jordan was dead because she couldn't use the mind-link. Maybe she was too far away now or her dad had been unconscious when she'd tried.

My head is beginning to hurt, so I close my eyes again. Something else occurs to me. My eyes fly open. "Duster pack lands don't touch the river do they?" I ask Maddox.

"Duster pack?" He is a little more awake now as he drags a hand down his face and yawns. "Uh... yeah. A sliver, I think.... By that old bridge. Why?"

I don't answer his question. Instead, I ask another one. "Is Alpha Jordan friends with the Alpha of Duster pack?" I can't remember his name right now, and I don't know what Zabrina called him in my dream.

"I think he might be. Isla, babe, what's going on? Are you okay?" He is looking at me with a great deal of concern now.

"I'm okay," I assure him. Most of my brain is telling me to just go back to sleep, but I'm afraid I'll have another unsettling dream, and I can't even determine if the last one could be real. "I just dreamed that I was in a wetsuit underwater again, but this time… it was like I was in Zabrina's body."

I have his attention now. His eyes focus on me, unblinking; the Alpha King is fully awake. "Zabrina?" he echoes.

"Yes, and she ended up near that bridge… Wolf Stone Bridge. When she got out of the water, a bunch of guys in suits were there. They looked like trouble. She said she was looking for the Alpha, Alpha… H-Hay–"

"Hayes," Maddox supplies, and I nod.

"That's right. Him, but they said he's not in charge there anymore. Then, she felt really scared, and I woke up." That's it. That's all I remember. I sink into the mattress like it has taken all of the energy I have left to tell him this story.

He brushes my hair back from my face, but he's more careful this time because he's awake and remembers my injuries.

"It's probably just a dream, baby," he says, but I hear in his voice that he doesn't quite believe that.

"Probably," I say. I wonder if those men will actually help her, once they find out what she's doing.

Or will they kill her?

I don't want that. Even though she's done nothing but torture me since the moment she laid eyes on me, I don't want those men to kill her. I want her to be brought back to the castle to stand trial. I want to stand in the throne room with Maddox in his proper place on the throne and look her in the eye. I want her to have to spend the next fifty or sixty years in a cell somewhere, rotting away, thinking about what she did, not just to me but to poor Private Parker as well.

"Go back to sleep, beautiful." Maddox's warm lips press against my forehead. "You'll have nothing but sweet dreams now."

"All right," I say, longing for his mouth on mine, but I don't have the energy to lean over and kiss him now, and he's right. I do need to go to sleep.

I have never had dreams like this before, not this vivid and real. I've had dreams where I was confused, didn't know who I was, didn't know what was going on…. I wonder if some of them were similar situations where I was seeing someone else's life.

But these two dreams I've had now, they seem so real, and I knew exactly what happened to Private Wylie before I heard of his death.

What was making these dreams come through? Was it the medicine Mystica kept giving me? Was it Mystica herself? Or was it thinking I might be from the mystical land of Maatua?

I didn't have the answer to that. With another wave of exhaustion knocking me backward into unconsciousness, I closed my eyes and reached for sleep, praying that Maddox could use the information I gave him to sort through the situation with Duster pack tomorrow.

He would look awfully silly calling that Alpha to tell him that he had a hunch Zabrina was there if she wasn't.

But if she was... maybe I needed to start asking more questions of the healer.

Could she be the source behind this newfound power of mine to see other people's realities in my dreams?

MAKING UP IN BED

Maddox

Isla's scent permeates every breath as I gain my bearings, doing my best to wake my sleeping mind. I have a vague recollection of talking to her earlier this morning, before I was fully awake.

She'd given me some startling information, something I needed to look into today, though I'm not exactly sure what it was now....

It'll come back to me later.

For now, my hand is resting on her soft, warm breast, and with her intoxicating scent rolling around me, I can't help but keep the hardness I've awoken with growing in length.

The recollection that she is injured comes to my mind, and I know I should leave her be. She hit her hard pretty hard yesterday, and she has a wounded shoulder, but her nipple is hardening beneath my palm, and I can't seem to pull my hand away.

Groggily, she says, "Maddox? What are you doing?" But her voice is sultry, not at all perturbed that I've awoken her by massaging her breast.

"I'm kissing your neck," I tell her as I do just that. My mouth sinks into the warmth between her shoulder and her throat. She moans a bit, and I feel her nipple pebble even more. I nip her with my teeth, and she backs into me, grinding.

She wants me as badly as I want her. It seems like it's been forever since

"

we've made love, though I know it hasn't been that long. When my hand dips below the blanket that's tangled around her waist, I feel the bare flesh of her hip beneath my hand. Her nightgown has also shifted during sleep, and knowing that there's very little between my hand and her tight pussy has me pressing even harder against her

I lift my mouth to her ear, taking her lobe between my teeth and grazing over it as she whimpers. "Are you feeling okay?" I ask her.

She moans a response that lets me know that she is.

"Can I touch you?" I ask between kisses on the flesh behind her ear.

With another moan, she says, "I think you already are."

I can't help but chuckle. "I want to touch you more," I say, letting my breath fan her cheek. "I want to touch you... deeper." Again, I lower my mouth to her neck as my hand finds her thigh already slick as I trail up her body, following the heat until my fingers brush against her mound, and I realize she isn't wearing any panties.

How have I managed to sleep next to this beautiful woman all night with nothing more than a thin nightgown and my boxers between us?

When my fingers begin to explore her folds she cries out again. I take my time, rubbing the length of her, finding her most sensitive area and pressing against it. She begins to buck against me, and I can smell her longing for me.

One finger enters her tight core, then another, and I move them back and forth quickly as she rocks against me. My cock is so hard, I can hardly pay attention to what I'm doing. I've had to pull my mouth away from her to suck in deep breaths because I am groaning myself as I probe deeper and deeper.

What way do I want to take her? Do I want to bend her over and slide into her from behind? Or should I flip her over and climb on top of her? I still haven't decided when she reaches her climax. Her cries are high-pitched and ethereal as she continues to rock back and forth on my fingers for as long as I can keep her there, but now, I need her myself.

I need to push inside of her.

Removing my hand, I push my own blankets off and remove my boxers while she catches her breath. Before she's completely recovered, I lift her from the mattress and sit her on top of me. She spreads her legs wide enough to accommodate my hips and comes down right onto my thick cock.

"Oh, Maddox," she cries out, biting her bottom lip. I take her nightgown by the bottom hem and yank it up before I remember that she has an injured shoulder and head so I slow down, lifting it more gently.

Her breasts jiggle as she moves up and down, riding me, and my palms immediately lift to circle her nipples until she cries out and grabs my hands, pulling them tight. I pinch, pull, and twist them while she makes the sort of noises that will eventually send me over the edge.

Isla leans down to kiss me. I take her warm mouth in mine, my tongue sizzling across hers. I find her clit with my finger, and her mouth pulls away from mine because she needs to cry out. I take her nipple in my mouth instead, swirling my tongue around it before I suck her to twice her normal size. She picks up her pace, riding me harder, fast, taking me deeper. And it's my turn to let out a deep, savage groan.

I switch breasts, having to move my hand from her clit because I need to steady myself. I want to keep from coming yet, but with her moving that way, I am about to blow everything.

"Maddox!" she sings. "Oh, Goddess!" She is there again, at the peak of ecstasy, crying out, ready to come completely undone, and I can't hold off anymore. As she shouts my name one more time, I fill her with my seed. Flashes of what we are trying to accomplish pass before my eyes, and I wonder if this might be the time she becomes pregnant with my baby.

But Isla is more than my breeder. She is my everything.

When I told her that loving me would be dangerous, I did it because I was scared, not because I don't love her back. I do.

It's never been more clear than in this moment as I'm looking up at her smiling, sex-drunk face. I haven't known Isla that long, but I've already forgotten what my life was like without her.

I've already learned that I don't ever want to go back to my life without her.

But it seems like I'm losing her.

On days when she's actually here and hasn't been kidnapped or ran away, I end up saying or doing something stupid or otherwise asinine that drives us further apart.

I have to find a way to stop living my life like an arrogant bachelor bastard and start taking her feelings into consideration.

Isla moves off of me, moving a little gingerly as she finds her spot on the bed next to me. "Are you hurt?" I ask her.

"No," she says with a smile. "Just a little sore."

Immediately, I feel awful. I shouldn't have taken her when she was injured. I should've waited until she was feeling better. "I'm so sorry,"

"Don't be." She trails her fingers down my chest. "I had a good time."

It sounds like something a woman says after a date that took a turn for the steamy, or someone who's resolved themselves to being nothing more than a one-night stand.

It's not something a woman in love says to the man of her dreams, which makes me wonder what I have done.

I can't let those thoughts enter my head at the moment. I have to concentrate on the positive on a day like this when I have so much to accomplish.

Everything she said to me in the middle of the night comes back now. She saw Zabrina in her dream, I'm certain of it, and how she's able to do this, I don't know, but it's clear to me that she saw Private Wylie, and now she says that Zabrina is near Wolf Stone Bridge.

She says she saw her get out of the water, and she thinks that Duster pack has her.

I need to get over there and see what Alpha Hayden will tell me. He's not my biggest fan. Maybe it will give us the opportunity to work through some of our problems.

Or maybe I'll kill him the same way that I killed Alpha Jordan.

Either way, if I get Zabrina back, I win.

"You should rest today," I tell her, reaching over and stroking her cheek. She has the blanket pulled up to her neck now, but she's still the most beautiful woman in the world.

"Okay," she replies in a groggy voice. "But... you remember my dream, right?"

"I do," I say, still tracing her heated skin with my fingers. I feel myself twitch and know I need to stop before I can't control myself anymore.

"Be careful." She reaches over and touches my chest, her hand trailing down to my abs. My dick twitches the closer her fingers get to it.

"I will be," I promise her, though I'm not sure what she's worried about.

"Those men looked like bad news. I know that you're the king and everyone is supposed to obey you, but I got the impression that they don't care about any of that, that they just care about themselves. They do whatever they want and don't worry about the rules."

Brushing her hair back, I roll onto my side. "Believe me, baby," I tell her, "I've dealt with all kinds. I can handle myself with anyone. You don't need to worry about me. But you do need to rest, feel better, and not leave the castle without me, for any reason, okay? I don't care if it's Seth who tells you that you need to go, stay here until I get back."

She nods in understanding, and I think she gets the picture. I can't imagine any reason why she would need to leave the castle without me, unless a war breaks out while I'm away finding Zabrina, and that is highly unlikely to happen.

I have my enemies, but none of them are strong enough or stupid enough to try taking over the castle at the moment.

I lean over and kiss her again, taking my time and letting my mouth linger on hers, reminding myself that this is a goodbye kiss before I go take a shower and get to work, but it's hard... in more ways than one.

I pull away. "Have a good day, baby. Seriously. Rest."

She nods. "I will. Seriously. Careful."

I smirk at her. Only Isla can say something like that to me and make me smile instead of wanting to rip their head off.

I feel her eyes on me as I pull my boxers on and finish getting dressed. I turn around and smile at her one more time before I head out of the room, noting that her scent lingers on my fingers.

I'll carry her with me all day.

WHAT HAPPENED HERE?

Isla

WHEN I AWAKE AGAIN, after Maddox left to go do whatever he was going to do to check to see if my dream was real, it's to the sound of someone moving in my room. It seems like whoever it is is trying to be quiet, but when something makes a loud clatter, and I hear Beta Seth swear under his breath, it's obvious who it is.

"What's going on?" I ask, groggily. I roll over, pulling the blanket up around me, and look at him.

"Oh, I'm so sorry, Isla. I am just… King Maddox wanted me to put a phone in your room so that you can call your parents and they can call you whenever you want. But the phone jack is behind the bed, and getting to it is being a pain in the a—butt." He stops himself short of swearing in front of me, like I am some sort of a delicate flower.

"Thanks, Beta Seth," I say to him, smiling at his kindness. "Is there anything that I can do to help?"

"No, no, I've got it." He grunts a little as he strains and stretches behind the bed for a second and then sighs with a successful smile. "There we go." He lifts the receiver on the phone and holds it to his ear. "Yep. It works. The phone number is written right here."

I look at the phone and see the number is right above the number pad. "Great. Thank you," I say.

He nods and gets up off of the floor. "You should go back to sleep," he recommends.

"I might," I say. "Did you not go with Maddox?"

He shakes his head and folds his hand in front of him, looking down at the ground. "He wanted me to stay here this time, so I can make sure you're safe."

I puzzle over that for a few moments before I realize what Beta Seth isn't saying. He didn't get to go today because of what I did the day before. Since I had to try to run away yesterday, Maddox doesn't trust me anymore, and he apparently doesn't trust anyone else to watch me, other than his Beta.

"I'm sorry," I say, dropping my eyes. "I didn't mean for you to be put on babysitting duty."

"Oh, it's not your fault!" he insists. "No, King Maddox has plenty of tasks for me to take care of here today. So don't even worry about it." He is smiling at me, and it looks more sincere than before, but I'm not sure if I trust that he hasn't had his day ruined because of me.

"Have you heard from Maddox?" I ask him, holding the blanket against my chest as I sit up a little. My shoulder still stings a bit, but at least the back of my head feels better.

His answer is succinct. "He's almost to Duster pack."

"And... he's okay?" I suppose he would've told me that if Maddox wasn't all right, but I still have to ask.

"Yes, he's fine. It's just taking him a little longer than usual because we spent a few hours planning this morning and gathering together the right forces. He wants to make sure that Alpha Hayes doesn't try to come against him when he arrives."

An uneasy feeling takes over my gut, but I just nod again. I see no reason to try to get more information from Beta Seth. He's not there with Maddox, so he doesn't really know what's happening, even if he is getting mind-link info from the team that's there.

I just hope that Maddox is all right. I also hope the information that I gave Maddox that morning proved to be helpful. If it turned out that Maddox got all the way over to Duster pack only to discover that Zabrina really wasn't there at all, I could be putting him and a lot of other people in danger for no reason.

What in the world possessed me to think that I suddenly had some sort of magical powers? It wasn't anything Mystica had said when she was telling me about where she thought my family was from.

Although, she had said we were descendants of the Moon Goddess. Mansina... our real last name....

"Anyway," Beta Seth says, jarring me back to the present. "I'll get out of your hair."

He's not bothering me at all, but I'm sure he wants to leave. "Thank you, Beta Seth," I say, and he nods before he turns and leaves.

I lay there for a moment and stare at the ceiling. I'm worried about Maddox, but I have to trust that he'll be okay. He's the king, after all. Alpha Hayes would have to be an idiot to do anything to harm him.

How do I know that Alpha Hayes isn't an idiot?

I don't….

I haul myself out of bed and go to take a shower. I take my time, letting the warm water flow over me. It dampens the bandage on my shoulder, which I remove. I can still see the teeth marks, but my shoulder looks a lot better than it used to.

When I finally get out of the shower, I go into my room and pick out an outfit from the closet, taking it back into my bathroom to get dressed, brush out my hair, and dry it. I wonder where Poppy is. She's usually around when I wake up, but then, I am up a little earlier than I'd planned to be.

When I walk out of the bathroom, I sense someone is on the other side of the door in my antechamber. I assume it's Poppy, but when nothing happens, the door doesn't open, and there's no knock, my pulse starts to race. What if someone has come to hurt me again?

"Wh-who is there?" I say in what I hope is an authoritative voice, but it's really not at all.

"C-can I come in?" I hear a soft voice say.

Whoever it is, I don't recognize the voice, but I'm also not scared. "Sure," I say.

The door squeaks open, and I gasp in awe at who is standing there.

What in the world does she want, and why is she here??

Maddox

I HAD TAKEN my time that morning making sure we were ready before we headed out for Duster pack lands. I told everyone in my inner group of warriors that I'd received a tip that Zabrina was in Duster pack territory, but I did not tell them what that tip was.

Not that I didn't fully believe Isla. I did. I just… didn't want to have to explain that the woman I was sleeping with, the woman I loved but had no official connection to, had dreamed that Zabrina had come out of the water here, so I believed that she must be here.

At the end of the day, I'm the Alpha King, and if I want to go to Duster pack to investigate a tip, then so be it.

I ride over in the front passenger side seat of the utility vehicle with dozens of warriors sitting on long benches in the back. I have three other such vehicles with me, but I hope that I don't need any of the soldiers I've brought with me, but with someone like Alpha Hayes, a person never knows.

There's a good chance that we could start a war today. After all, this bastard has been itching for an excuse to fight me for years. He's using the excuse that I don't have an heir yet, trying to rally other Alphas around him, saying he'd make a better Alpha King because he already has a Luna and children, and my fated mate passed away without leaving me a child, but I have to hope there are more Alphas loyal to me than to him.

I have no way of knowing that until we cross the line and war is at hand.

If only Seth were here with me. I wanted to bring him. I included him in all of the planning and discussions we had this morning with the other commanders, but I decided, in the end, it was better if he stayed behind with Isla, especially after what happened yesterday.

Granted, Seth was there when she was kidnapped, but he knows better now, I hope.

I know the rogues that chased her won't come into the castle. But I have no way of knowing who all might want to harm her. That's why I had to leave her with Seth. Besides Poppy, he's the only one I can one hundred percent trust not to do her any harm and to look after her so that others don't.

It's never been my intention to pull up to Alpha Hayes's front door with all of these soldiers, so I leave some of them at the border, but they must be close enough to come to our aid if the rest of us get ourselves into trouble.

The commanders in the other vehicles have their orders, and I move on toward the main village where Alpha Hayes's large home is situated.

We pull up outside, and I get out immediately, not letting any feelings of doubt linger in my mind as I stare at his two-story modern home from the cul-de-sac where it is situated. This is not the ancestral home of past Alphas; this is a new home he and his wife built only a few years ago as a testimony to the grandiose lifestyle everyone in Duster pack allegedly lives thanks to the resources they have.

Personally, I know that it's a shame. I see the books, and I'm aware of how much money each pack has to its name. Where the money came from to build this, I don't know, and I've never had the time to deal with it either. If things go well today, perhaps I'll continue to turn a blind eye.

With conviction, I walk to the door and knock. My men fan out behind me, ready to shift at a moment's notice. I intend to tell Alpha Hayes that it has come to my attention that he has Zabrina, Alpha Jordan's daughter, in his custody, and I want her.

No one answers....

Finding this odd, I knock again and ring the doorbell several times. It makes little sense that a staff member at least wouldn't be inside. It's almost noon. Someone has to be up and about.

I am unable to reach Alpha Hayes by mind-link when I try.

Something isn't right….

I try again but get nothing. I also try his wife…. She doesn't answer either.

Cupping my hands around my face to cut back on the glare, I step over to one of the windows by the door, one where the blinds are a bit open. I gaze inside and my eyes widen in horror.

I can't tell exactly what I'm looking at because the view is obstructed, but even with such a narrow glimpse, I'm quite certain of what that dark substance all over the tile by the front door is.

Blood.

HOW TO BE A BREEDER

Isla

"Can I come in?"

I stare at the girl, not quite sure what to say. I'm taken aback that she's even here. What in the world could she possibly have to say to me?

And yet, it's very difficult for me to tell her to leave. She looks so sad, standing there in the doorway, her bulging stomach protruding in front of her.

"Of course," I say, gesturing for her to come over to the sitting area where I have a couple of comfortable chairs in front of the window.

We both sit, and I readjust my skirt several times, not sure what to say or do. Part of me wants Poppy to come in and say she has my breakfast, so I can at least have an excuse not to be able to talk. If my mouth is full of eggs, I won't have to say anything to this doe-eyed girl who is looking at me like she thinks I have all of the answers to whatever ails her.

"I'm… Isla," I say to her, and she nods. I have to assume she already knows that, but since no one is saying anything, I thought it might be a good way to start the conversation.

She brushes her dark hair out of her eyes. "I'm Sydney." Her voice is quiet, a little bit louder than what mine used to sound like when I first got here and was terrified of everything. It seems like that was ages ago, not a matter of weeks.

"Hi," I say. She only smiles at me. I clear my throat, not sure what to say next. "What pack are you from?"

49

"Well, I just came from Hill pack," she says, her hand folded in her lap around her abdomen, her thumbs twisting around one another. "But before that, I was at Mountain Range pack. That's where I grew up. My parents are the Alpha and Luna."

I am actually a little shocked to hear her say so many words all at once. I nod. "That's… nice." I don't know what else to say. I suppose it would be nice to grow up with your parents as the Alpha and Luna of a pack. She was probably the girl with all of the friends that everyone wanted to be like.

From the look of things, she may have had a boyfriend at some point, too, I am guessing, but then, what do I know?

Not much….

She shrugs. "It was okay when I was younger, but the older I got the more trouble I found myself in."

"What do you mean?" I ask her.

"Well… boys, mostly." She gestures down at her stomach. "I guess I had a hard time distinguishing between who really liked me for me and who was just trying to get into my pants."

"Oh." I don't know what else to say. She shrugs again, and I feel extremely awkward, so I say, "I'm sorry."

Is that an appropriate thing to say? I have no idea.

Again, her shoulders are all over the place. It's like her shoulder twitch is some sort of a coping mechanism or way she defends herself.

"Yeah, well… I heard about you from one of the maids, and I thought I should come and meet you. I figured we had some things in common, and I thought, I don't know how long I'm going to be here, but it would be nice to know someone who is about my age."

"Yes, that would be nice," I say, but I'm honestly just being nice. From what she's said so far, Sydney and I don't have much in common. I've never had a boyfriend before, and I'm not sure that Maddox could be called a boy. I'm pretty sure he's not my boyfriend or my manfriend. I don't know what it's like to have grown up the daughter of an Alpha and his Luna. Regardless of what Mystica thinks about my past, if I ever was a princess and lived a life of luxury, I don't remember it, so that doesn't count. I grew up pretty poor, and I only got poorer the older I got, until I arrived here, and while I guess things have been more than adequate since I arrived, regardless of how nice my room and other accommodations are, I'm still a servant here.

The castle isn't necessarily my permanent home.

I don't want to think about that though; the idea of Maddox throwing me out is terrifying–even if I did just try to leave of my own accord. That's different than being asked to leave.

"So… when did you start?" she asks me, her eyes going to the bed behind me. I didn't make it when I got up and Poppy seems to have dropped off the face of the earth, so it looks like it's been slept in… by a couple of people… who didn't care how twisted the sheets got.

Realizing all of this, my face turns a little red.

But I assume she's asking about when did I start working here. "Not that long ago," I tell her. I give her the exact date, and her eyes bulge.

Then she shakes her head and says, "Oh, no, not with King Maddox. Just in general."

Confused, I ask, "What do you mean?"

"You know. As a breeder. When did you start having sex with men to have their babies and get paid?"

My breath catches in my throat, and I'm not sure if I should be more angry or offended. I repeat the same date I gave her before. "I was sold by my Alpha to King Maddox."

"Wait–you've never done this before?" she asks, and I watch her eyebrows knit together.

"No," I tell her. "I've never done any of this before." I hope she understands that I'm saying I was a virgin before I met Maddox.

"Oh." Her tone changes now, and she looks down at her shoes. "Shit."

I don't know what is happening. "Why did you think–or hope–that I'd done this before?"

Sydney takes a deep breath and blows it out, adjusting in her chair. Her stomach is so big, I am afraid she might give birth at any moment. "Well, a couple of reasons. First of all, I was hoping you would tell me the truth about how this baby is going to come out of me. Secondly, I was hoping you could help me get a job doing this for a living."

I stare at her for a long moment. I can't help her with either of those things. "Uhm, I'm sorry. I'm pretty sure that your pack healer has probably got better advice than I do about how babies really come out. I mean, my understanding is that they come out the same place they went in. And as for becoming a breeder… I never, ever imagined myself in this job. I just got sold into it."

A forlorn look overtakes her pretty face. "Well, I know where this baby is going to come out. I just didn't know for sure how. I mean, the healer said she'd do whatever to help it not hurt so much, but the pack healer here at the castle seems a little weird."

I almost laugh at that, but I keep a straight face. "Mystica has been very helpful to me when I've been injured."

Her eyes widen again. "When were you injured?"

I sigh. "It's a long story." I don't have to tell her everything.

"Did the king hurt you?" She leans forward in her chair. "I have heard that he's very cruel. Is it true–what they say–about…." She looks around like she thinks someone might be eavesdropping on us before she whispers, "His first wife?"

Clearing my throat, I take a deep breath before allowing myself to answer. I shake my head. "No, it's not true. I mean, he's never hurt me. He's very kind." I picture how angry Maddox was when I left the office yesterday. Sydney was there. She is already looking at me quite skeptically.

And honestly... I have no idea what happened to Luna Rebecca.

But I know Maddox didn't kill her. He isn't capable of that.

Is he?

"All right. Well, maybe we can still be friends," she says, shifting again in her chair. She grunts a little and puts a hand on her side, and I think the baby might be kicking her. I can't help but wonder what that might feel like, to have little toes pressing into one's rib cage. It probably hurts.

Not sure how to respond, I take a moment. She only wanted to be my friend because she thought I could help her, and we don't have much in common.

But I don't really want another enemy either. I think of how awful it was having Zabrina in the castle. Even before she started killing, she was a menace.

"Sure," I say. "We can be friends." I force a smile to my face.

"Good. And who knows? Maybe someday our babies will be siblings." I'm not sure if that's a smile on her face or something else, something more... devious.

"What?" I ask her, my forehead crinkling.

"Yeah, well, just because King Maddox doesn't seem to want this baby right now, that doesn't mean he might not want it later. Or maybe he'll pick me to have his second kid after you have one for him." The shrugging is back, and this one is a big one. "After all, it is just a job, right?"

How do I answer that? After yesterday, she probably thinks that Maddox treats me like any other servant that works here. She probably thinks he comes in here and we have mechanical, robotic sex every once in a while and that's that.

But he hasn't even had Mystica check to see if I'm ovulating or anything like that.

When we make love, it's not because we are necessarily trying to have a baby. We just... like being together.

I love him.

And even though he hasn't said that he loves me in return, I know he cares for me.

"It's not just a job," I tell her. "It's far too personal to ever be just a job. I mean, didn't you have feelings for your baby's father?"

She shakes her head. "No, and I don't want to talk about that." A dark shadow crosses her face.

"I'm sorry," I say. "I didn't mean to offend you. But anyway... Maddox is more than just my boss, more than just my king. I have feelings for him, and he treats me very well."

A choked laugh comes out of her mouth, like she was trying to hold it back. "Okay then," she says. Then she pushes up from the chair to standing. "If that's what you wanna believe."

"What do you mean?" I fly up out of my chair, too.

"Nothing. It's just... I saw what happened yesterday. No offense, but that sounded like a boss getting onto a worker who had fucked up to me." She starts waddling to the door. "I can't blame you for wanting there to be more there, Isla. But I think... you might be delusional."

I have no words, so I just stare at her.

Sydney opens the door. "I hate to be the one to tell you, but you're just a breeder to him." She gives me what appears to be a sympathetic smile and leaves.

We are not going to be friends.

WHO'S TO BLAME?

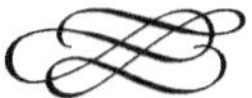

Maddox

BLOOD COATS the floor in the entryway. I could see it before I even kicked in the door. My warriors, still in their human form, join me as I walk into the house.

The body of a young maid, legs prone, arms over her face, is positioned off to the side of the door. This blood is hers. She has bite marks and deep scratches from claws on her chest, neck, and face. I can see that from here, but when I step closer to her and roll her over, I notice that the blood is coagulated. She has been laying here for a while. I'm no medical expert, but I'm guessing it's been a few hours.

I have seen my fair share of bodies on the battlefield from warriors who have died early in the fight, ones we gathered much later, and the blood is similar.

Her cold, empty, green eyes stare up at me. I close them for her, careful not to step in the blood as I walk away.

"Be careful," I tell the men with me. "This is a crime scene."

A whiff of the air tells me that this isn't the only body we are going to find in this house, and that there's a lot more spilled blood seeping into the otherwise pristine wooden floors.

The men spread throughout the house, but I go up the stairs, noticing there are bloody wolf paws on every step. Along with me, one of my most trusted soldiers carefully avoids them as she walks behind me.

"What do you think happened?" Gail asks me as we reach the top of the stairs.

"I'm not sure," I admit. "But Alpha Hayes had a number of enemies. It's possible he owed someone money. Another pack might've done this. I can't imagine it was an inside job."

Alpha Hayes might've been an asshole, but he didn't have any rivals for Alpha in his pack that I was aware of.

At this point, I'm assuming he's dead....

When I open the door to the bedroom, I no longer have to assume.

I see his body, slumped over, but pressed against the headboard, as if a wolf had leaped onto the bed and attacked before he could even get up.

His wife is hanging over the side of the bed, her upper torso pointing toward the light-colored carpet. The pool of blood beneath her is so dark, it looks almost black.

"Does he have... children?" Gail whispers near my left side and still behind me.

"Uhm... he did." I don't know exactly how to answer that question. I can tell that other dead bodies litter the house. But I also know that Alpha Hayes had a large staff. Perhaps, the children, two girls who were fairly young that still lived at home, older children that did not, are all okay. Perhaps the children weren't here when the attack happened.

The idea that anyone could slaughter a couple of little girls has my heart thumping and my gut twisting.

A few years ago, I might've shrugged it off. The closer I've come to my thirtieth birthday, the more important it has become to me to have a child of my own, which means children in general have become more important to me.

Still, I find myself walking down the hallway to the next room. The door is open, and I see that it is a pink room with flowers on the walls. A little girl's room.

The bed is empty, which makes hope spark inside of me. I don't see any blood, but I do smell something as I enter the room.

Someone is here....

A door on the other side of the room catches my attention. I walk over to it and listen.

I hear the thundering of two hearts and shallow breaths.

My own pulse slows as I thank the Moon Goddess, if she exists, for sparing these two little girls. In a soft voice, I say, "It's okay, girls. You're safe. It's Alpha King Maddox."

I hear a slight whimper, followed by a sharp, "Shhh!" and I can tell that at least the older girl doesn't trust me.

I can't say that I blame her. I wouldn't trust me either, not after this. They have no way of knowing that I won't harm them. And Goddess only knows what they heard happening in their parents' room.

Using the mind-link, I tell the others to gather evidence around the bodies as quickly as they can and then get things cleaned up, especially downstairs. When I take these children out of here, I don't want them to see anything.

The Beta is their uncle, their mother's brother. I don't have time to explain to him what's happened right now, so I use the mind-link to tell Gail, who is still standing in the doorway behind me, to contact Beta Ian, tell him there's been an attack, and he needs to get over here quickly.

"Do you want me to tell him his sister and brother-in-law are dead?" she asks me, still through our minds.

"No," I say. "But have Cody meet him downstairs when he comes in." Cody is one of the more sympathetic members of our detail.

"Girls," I say, softly, "I'm going to open the door now, okay? I need to see that you're not hurt."

They don't speak, but I don't wait long either before I gently tug the door open.

The two girls look like they are about five and three, maybe not even that old. I've never been a good judge of age when it comes to children. They have tear streaks down their cheeks that seem to have been there for several hours, and their lips are trembling in advance of more tears falling or screams of fear.

Immediately, I drop to one knee so I am on their level. I don't want to tower over them. I give them a sympathetic smile. "Hello," I say, softly. "I'm Maddox."

The girls look at one another, and the older one nods slightly as she looks back at me. "I'm Kayla, and this is—"

"Haylee!" the little one says in a sweet, high-pitched voice.

"Hi. I guess… something bad happened, huh?" I'm not exactly sure what to say to them, but I want to be sympathetic.

"Mommy was squweamin'," Haylee tells me. "I was scared."

Nodding, I say, "That sounds very scary."

"Daddy told us in our heads to hide," Kayla tells me. "So we ran to the closet. I don't think…." She blinks a few times and stares up at me. "Is Daddy died?"

"Yes," I say. "I'm afraid so."

"And… Mommy's died too?" Haylee is on the brink of tears.

"Yes, your mother has also passed away." They both begin to cry, and all I can think to do is open my arms. Both of them leap up off of the floor and throw themselves at me.

I catch them and hold them close whispering that it's okay, that it's all going to be okay.

But it's not going to be. At least, it's not ever going to be the same. These girls went to bed last night thinking it was just another normal evening, and they'd wake up this morning and have breakfast and do what they usually did.

Instead, they were awoken in the middle of the night by someone storming into their home and murdering everyone but them.

In a way, they are lucky. They are alive.

But as their tears soak through my shirt, I have to wonder how they will get along in life without their parents. Alpha Hayes was a bastard, but that doesn't mean I don't have sympathy for his children.

This is one of the main reasons why I don't want to go to war. When a warrior falls on the battlefield, it's never just that person who is affected. Each of them has a family–wife, husband, children, mother, father, siblings–friends, colleagues… people who will miss them.

People whose lives, like these children, will never be the same.

"Kayla! Haylee!"

I turn my head to see Beta Ian and his wife, Alaina, flying through the bedroom door, dodging around Gail. I assume someone has filled them in on what has happened since I gave that directive, and they seem to know that tragedy has struck.

The girls let go of me and lunge for their aunt who is on the floor now next to me. She holds them close, smoothing their hair, as they all cry.

Ian looks more angry than sad. "What the hell happened, Alpha King?" he demands, as if he thinks I might be the one responsible for this.

"I'm not sure," I tell him. "But… why hasn't anyone noticed your Alpha is missing when it's nearly noon."

"It's Kayla's birthday," he says, as if I should know that. "They were all going to do something fun today. Together. As a family."

I nod. That makes sense. And it's all the more reason to feel awful for the child. "I came to speak to Alpha Hayes because I've heard he may have a prisoner that I've been looking for."

"A prisoner?" I can tell by the genuine confusion on his face that he doesn't know what I'm talking about.

"Yes. Alpha Jordan's daughter. Zabrina," I explain. "She's not here?"

"No," he says. "But I've been out at the river all morning. My scouts reported signs of something odd happening out there early this morning before dawn."

"What kind of oddity?" I ask.

He shakes his head. "Just… vehicles they didn't recognize. There were only two of them, so they didn't investigate. Instead, they called for help. Before anyone else arrived, the vehicles left."

"Did they come toward the village or away when they left?" I ask him, puzzling over who that might've been.

"Away," he says.

I have a feeling, whoever that was came here first to take out the Alpha, to make sure that he didn't interfere with what they were up to. Either that, or Alpha Hayes had Zabrina, but someone else wanted her.

Who would go to so much trouble, though? Only one of Alpha Jordan's allies, which Alpha Hayes was... or someone who knows how badly I want her back.

I open my mouth to tell Beta Ian I'll help him figure it out when I hear a familiar voice in my head.

"Alpha King Maddox, I got somethin' you're gonna wanna get back."

I swear under my breath and drop my head.

"What is it?" Beta Ian asks.

Inhaling sharply, I say, "I know who caused all of this. I know what happened now."

"Well, tell me!" Beta Ian insists, making the girls cry even louder.

I think back over the events of the last few days and know I hadn't done enough. I wasn't careful enough. Hayes was my enemy, but no one deserves to die this way, and his staff and wife certainly didn't deserve to be shredded in their own home.

"Alpha King Maddox, please, tell me!" Beta Ian demands. "Who is to blame for all of this?"

The only words I can say to satisfy him haunt me.

"I am."

PROMISES HE'D BETTER KEEP

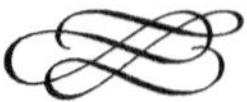

Isla

"So she just waltzed right into your room, had a seat, and proceeded to ask you how to get with your man?" Poppy asks me as I stare at a plate of food I'm probably not going to eat much of. My stomach is still churning, and I don't know if it's because of the odd conversation I had with Sydney or if it's something else.

"Not exactly," I tell Poppy because I don't want her to think I didn't tell Sydney she could come in. And she didn't exactly ask me how to get with Maddox... well, maybe sort of. "She just thought I was a professional breeder or something. She was looking for advice."

"But... what about her current baby? Can you imagine her just hauling that kid around from one Alpha to the next while she tries to get knocked up again? And then she'll do what? Leave a long trail of babies behind her?" Poppy shakes her head and sits down at the table with me, as if she is my friend, not my maid. She is my friend and my maid, but it seems so strange that she's just sitting across from me with her arms folded under her chest, swinging her foot back and forth quickly while I take tiny bites of macaroni salad.

"Maybe that's why she was asking me," I suggest. It's never easy for me to assume something bad about someone. I always think that people have good intentions. It's just that sometimes they don't really give everything as much thought as they should.

A vision of the dream I had last night pops before my eyes, and I think about Zabrina. That's one woman, I have to say, who doesn't have good intentions ever. So maybe I've been too quick in the past to give people the benefit of the doubt. But then, I think most people deserve that at least the first time around.

The second time around, I should know better.

I don't always, though, because I am naive and gullible and hate to be mean or rude to people. The longer I stay in the castle, the more important it is becoming to me not to trust people. In this place, everyone seems to have an agenda. Everyone wants something. So far, the only genuine people I've met are Poppy, Seth... and Maddox.

"Well, I think King Maddox should just take that little tramp back to her home pack and drop her off. Just let them handle her and her bastard child."

Poppy is genuine... but she is also direct. Sometimes I think she is too direct.

"I think she's just scared. I would be if I was her." I can't imagine being in that position where I was pregnant by someone who was dead and no one seemed to want me.

"Maybe she should've kept her legs together." Poppy reaches over and plucks a grape off of my plate.

I think about asking her if that means she's a virgin then, but I keep my mouth shut. It's not my business, and just because Poppy feels like questioning other people's life choices, that doesn't mean I should.

After all, I could be pregnant, and I'm not that much older than Sydney. And Maddox could decide that he doesn't want me. I've already thought that he had made up his mind to let me go once in the not-so-distant past.

Then... what would I do?

I am almost positive I'm not pregnant. I almost died a few days ago. Surely, the wolfsbane would've ended any chances I had of being pregnant

Rather than commenting on Poppy's statement, I decide to change the subject. "Do you know if King Maddox found Zabrina?"

She looks at me for a moment before she says, "I heard that he went to Duster pack to look for her, and she wasn't there." Poppy looks like she doesn't really want to be the one to tell me this. "Sorry."

I shrug. "I'm sorry that he didn't find her, but... I'm sure he will find her."

"Yeah, maybe. I don't know. I just heard it from another maid while I was out helping straighten the rooms Alpha Jordan's nasty-ass soldiers trashed before they either left or were locked up."

"How long ago was that?" I just wonder why Maddox hasn't sent me a mind-link message at all.

"Not long ago. Right before I brought you this," she says gesturing at the food I'm eating sometime between breakfast and lunch.

I wonder how he can even know for sure that she isn't there when he hasn't been gone all that long. How long does it even take to get to Duster pack?

Poppy pushes off of the ground with her feet to move her chair back so she can get up. "Well, I hope that sorry bitch leaves you alone. Who knows what nonsense she might talk you into."

I can tell by Poppy's tone that she's still mad at me for leaving while she was getting my food the other night without even saying a word to her. That's why she's being so snippy—more snippy than usual.

"See you later," I say to her. She gives me a half smile and then she exits the room, and I realize I'm going to have to start doing whatever I can to make it up to her. Poppy is one of the only friends I have in the world, and I don't want her to be mad at me.

Thinking of friends, my eyes go to the phone. I miss Ben....

Maddox

Beta Ian continues to stare at me as I unravel exactly what has happened here. Even with all of the horrible things I've seen in my life, this is one of the worst, and I am having trouble processing the part I played in it.

"What do you mean you're to blame?" Ian asks me.

Shaking my head, I tell him, "I let a psycho know how much I wanted that woman in my custody, and it seems like he went to great lengths to make sure that no one else had her."

"Who is this woman? Alpha Jordan's daughter?" Ian asks me as the little girls his wife is holding in her arms behind him slowly start to stop crying.

"That's right," I tell him. "She caused all sorts of problems for me back at the castle, and I wanted her arrested. I have evidence that she came ashore here, in Duster pack territories, near Wolf Stone Bridge early this morning or sometime last night. My hope in coming here today was to talk to Alpha Hayes to see if his patrols had captured her. But then I found this." I don't see the point in telling him that I have evidence that men in suits collected her at the water's edge.

Now, after the mind-link message I just received, I know that it wasn't Alpha Hayes's men who were there when Zabrina waded ashore.

I just don't understand why anyone would go to all the trouble to attack an Alpha, his servants, and his Luna in their own home when it seems clear to me that the slain Alpha wasn't even aware that the woman in question was in his territory.

But I am on my way to find out exactly why this horrendous act of violence transpired.

"And you somehow managed to get Alpha Hayes killed because you were looking for this woman?" Beta Ian asks.

"Not exactly." I run a hand through my hair and try to cut myself some slack. "I went to visit Alpha Bryant yesterday because he had Alpha Jordan in his custody. While I was there, I discovered he'd gotten his niece pregnant. He tried to blackmail me into pretending the baby was mine. Things got a little out of hand...." Saying it now, I feel a bit disappointed with myself for what happened with Alpha Bryant yesterday, too. How am I any better than the murderers who took out these people?

Well, for one thing, I only killed a mouthy Alpha. I didn't kill everyone else in the building.

"I heard that you killed Alpha Bryant," Ian says to me.

I nod. "That's right. I did kill him, and I'd kill any other Alpha who did what Bryant did. But that being said, Beta Vinny wanted to prove to me that he could take control of the pack and lead it as the new Alpha." I take a deep breath, and my pause gives Ian a chance to speak.

"So you think it was Vinny who came over here and did this? In order to get the girl and impress you? And that's why this is your fault?"

He has leaped to the same conclusion that I have. Of course, my hunch was confirmed when I had a voice in my head telling me that I had been right.

"So... what are you going to do now, Alpha King?"

Ian's voice is snide as he speaks, and I don't blame him. He was already angry enough with me to support his Alpha, his brother-in-law, in a bid for the crown. Now, that other man is dead, and he has to hold me at least partially responsible for that.

"I'm going to go pay a visit to Beta Vinny," I say, certain that my next move will be the right one.

"And, are you going to make him pay for what he's done here?" This question doesn't come from Ian, but from his wife.

I nod in her direction. "I am. But you two need to make a couple of promises to me."

Ian raises an eyebrow, like he doesn't think he owes me anything. "Like what?"

"Like... give me a chance to handle this before you start to organize against me. You may not know the entire story of what was at issue between Hayes and me. You may feel differently about joining an uprising against me."

Ian doesn't make me any promises yet as he asks me, "And what's the second one?"

Again, my eyes flicker to the tiny bodies in Alaina's arms.

"Take care of these girls."

Ian nods immediately. "You can rest assured I will take care of my nieces and raise them like they are my own. And you can also be certain that I will do what is best for my pack." He narrows his gaze at me. "I don't want to fight you, Alpha King Maddox. I always thought Hayes was a little too eager to improve his station. But at the same time, I can guarantee you that if you don't get justice for my family, I will do so myself."

In response, all I can do is extend my hand to him. "I will make sure that the shifters who did this pay for their crimes."

He looks at my hand for a moment before he slips his inside of mine and says, "You'd better."

DID I SUMMON YOU?

Isla

I AM STARING at the telephone, missing my youngest brother, wondering how he is doing, wishing I could see him, hug him, see his smile... when the phone rings, and I jump back into my chair at the dining table, almost knocking it over.

The situation seems a little creepy. Lately, Mystica has been filling my mind with all kinds of thoughts about what could be going on with my mental state–the dreams, the memories, all of that stuff–that when I am looking at the phone and hear it break the noiseless space of my room with its high-pitched chirp, I can't help but wonder for a moment if I did that with my mind.

Shaking my head at my ridiculousness, I get up and rush over to answer the phone before the caller hangs up. I have no idea who would be calling when I haven't given my number to anyone.

My initial thought is that perhaps someone is calling the number wanting to reach whoever had this phone number before, but I won't know until I lift the receiver.

"Hello?" I say, my heart racing. I don't have a whole lot of experience talking on the phone, and the last time I spoke to anyone, well, it hadn't gone well.

"Uhm... is this... Isla?"

My heart leaps into my throat, and my head starts to swim. I lower myself down to the edge of my bed and try to keep my racing thoughts from making me pass out.

Perhaps it's the mix of the injuries I've had recently with all of the emotional turbulence, but that voice in my ear after my last thoughts is making my head feel fuzzy.

"Yeah, it's me. B-Ben?"

"Hey!" he says with a warm laugh, and I can tell the anxiety he was feeling about phoning me has also melted away. It's not like my kid brother has a lot of experience using the phone either. "I'm so glad I was able to reach you. The operator at the castle switchboard said that this was your number, but that confused me. I figured you'd be working."

"Not right now," I say quickly. My initial thought is, "Not this time of day," but I'm not going to say that to my brother who has no idea what my real job is. I'm sure, like Mom, he just assumes I'm some sort of a fancy maid. "I was literally just thinking about you when you called."

"Really?" he says with another rich chuckle that makes me smile.

And miss him even worse.

"Yeah, I really was." I don't tell him I was staring at the phone wishing I could call him because that might freak him out. "Where are you calling me from?"

"Home," he says. "We got a phone. It's really cool. And Mom and Dad are looking for a nicer house, too."

I am so happy to hear that, my smile widens. "Wow. That's great. You must be excited."

"We are all excited, and it wouldn't be possible without you. Mom said that King Maddox gave her a bunch of money that you earned. I never knew maids in the castle made so much money!"

My cheeks flush red. He's fifteen, so he's not a baby, but he's still my brother, and I don't want to tell him how his big sister, his best friend, made all of that money. It's not that I'm doing anything wrong. I love Maddox, and I think he cares deeply about me. But... no one wants to think of their family member doing... that.

"I have a pretty particular servant job," I tell him, thinking it wouldn't be fair for me to leave him believing that working at the castle typically pays as much as what Maddox has handed over to my parents.

And that's not even including the debt he forgave to Alpha Ernest.

"When I get older, maybe you can help me get a job at the castle!" he says, already going where I didn't want him to go.

"Uhm, maybe." I see no reason in discussing it now when he won't be eligible to work at the castle for another three years anyway. "You should think about going to college, though. You can do that now. Mom and Dad can afford it."

"Nah, none of us really want to go to college. We just want to be warriors. I was thinking I could start out as a guard at the castle, and then, I could join the castle defense or the king's guard. You could help me with that, right? You know the king pretty well, don't you?"

I choke on air as I process what he's asked. "Yeah, I guess you could say that."

"So you can help me get a job at the castle then, right? Pull a few strings?"

He sounds so enthusiastic and excited, I want to tell him yes, but there's no way he can come to the castle and not know what my job is. "Probably. Let's just see how things are when you graduate from high school." I look at the clock. "Why aren't you in school?"

"It's a holiday," he says, his tone implying I should know that he wouldn't just skip school. Even when he was super sick and was in and out of the hospital, he never missed school unless he literally couldn't get out of bed.

"Where's everyone else?" My mind jumps to the conversation I had with my mom the other day and the one that I had with my sister. I want to ask him what he thinks about where we came from, but the last thing I need is for my mom to know I haven't let it go. She thinks I should just accept that we aren't from Maatua.

"Mom and Dad are at work, and the other guys are out playing basketball with some friends," he says.

"Why didn't you go with them?" I already know the answer to that question, but I want to encourage him. I hope I'm not doing the opposite with my question.

I hear him sigh loudly. "You know, sports aren't my thing."

Ben has been so sick his whole life, he never really got into any sports. He's twig thin and tall, but his weak lungs make it so that he can't run very fast. My other brothers tease him quite a bit about it, and I used to be the one to tell them to stop, but now that I'm not there, I'm wondering who is doing that for him now. Probably no one.

I decide not to bring up our history right now. I don't see the point. Ben wasn't even born until we were in Willow Pack. He won't remember anything. "So... have you started packing yet?" I ask, changing the subject completely.

"No, not yet. We haven't found a place to live. Mom says she'd like to live in a two-story house. She said something about never finding a house like their old one, but it would be nice if they could at least have a house with a dining room. I don't know what their old one was like, but it sounded like it might've been nice from what she was saying."

I don't know if she meant the first house we had in Willow pack, which was pretty nice compared to our current one, or if she's talking about the house we used to live in before.

If they really were the king and queen of Maatua, I'm guessing they lived in a pretty nice house.

Would their home have been anything like the castle I lived in now?

Ben continues, "Oh, but I did hear mom say something to Dad about it the other day. She said we needed to make sure we brought *everything*. I thought that was so weird. What would she be talking about, I?"

Sometimes Ben calls me I, and it's confusing to people because they think he means himself, which often doesn't make sense in the sentence.

I think about his question, and it took me a second, but an idea came to mind. "Ben, you're sure no one else is home?" I ask him.

"I'm pretty sure I'd know if they were here. This house is the size of a shoebox."

I almost laugh. His feet are huge, though, so that might be true. "Could you do something for me?"

"I don't know. What's in it for me?" he teases.

I laugh. "Uhm… a new house?"

"Sure, sis. What do you need?"

A knot forms in my stomach as I think about what I'm asking him to do. Ben is a good kid. I'm supposed to be a good girl. What I want him to do is not something obedient children should be doing.

"Can you go into Mom and Dad's room and see if you can get that board that's loose up out of the windowsill?" I have no idea if Mom still hides stuff in the window like I hid the cufflinks, but I am wondering if Ben can find any proof of where we're from. I've gone from not wanting to tell him anything to using him as a spy. I'm an awful sister.

"Hold on," he says, and I hear him walking into the other room. I am guessing the phone is cordless. He makes a few grunting noises and says, "I think they might've fixed it. It's not working."

Irritated, I ask, "Are you sure? Maybe you should set the phone down."

He mutters something under his breath and I hear him set the phone down. The struggle continues before I hear a crash, and I have to assume the phone fell from wherever he sat it. Ben curses in the distance, but then I hear a squeaking sound–and he curses again. This time, he doesn't sound angry.

He sounds astonished.

"Hey, sis, it's not the window, but the floor just opened when I dropped the phone. There's a space down here."

My heart begins to pound in my chest. "Is there anything in there?"

"Yeah… hold on."

I do my best to stay calm as I wait for him. I wish he'd hurry up.

"There's… a file of old papers, a box with a necklace in it, a few cards, oh, and another jewelry box with… those are weird earrings."

I really want to know what's on those papers, but something else catches my attention first. "Earrings?"

"Yeah, it looks like it would be painful to put these in your ears, and the backs are on super tight."

"What do they look like?" I ask, envisioning some giant hoops or something.

"They're wolves," he says. "Golden wolves."

My heart leaps into my chest. "What?" I ask him. "Is that it?"

"No… they've got jewels on them, Like their eyes. But they don't match. One has emeralds–"

With my heart hammering, I finish for him.

"And the other has rubies."

DON'T DO SOMETHING SO STUPID

Maddox

I DON'T BOTHER to answer the voice in my head. I'm too angry, and I don't want him to know what's coming for him.

Instead, once I've secured the crime scene, had my people take pictures and gather evidence, not that I need it because I am the law in this land, I move out, headed straight over to confront the idiotic asshole who'd decided to take matters into his own hands and cause all of these problems to begin with.

Hill Country pack.

The rest of the passengers are deathly quiet as we make the drive. My eyes focus out the window. If I remembered the images of all of the dead bodies I'd seen in my life, my mind would be full of ghastly figures, twisted, ripped open, covered in blood and gore.

Only a few of those ghosts haunt me still. One soldier who was particularly close to me that I'd gone through my training with had died during an insurrection a few years back. He was a huge warrior, muscle-bound, fierce, and loyal.

Somehow, he'd gotten himself into a situation where he was too far in advance of the rest of the troops, and he'd ended up trying to fight off ten or twelve of the rebels by himself. He was a talented fighter, but even he wasn't capable of holding them off.

When I'd found him, Stephen had been mutilated. I wouldn't have even recognized him except that our enemies had been kind enough to leave his back left hip intact where he had a distinct birthmark that showed even in his wolf form, a patch of white-blond fur. It was tinged pink, but I recognized its shape, a perfect triangle.

The photographic memory of Stephen's body lying in all of those pieces on the battlefield is one image that will never leave my mind.

And so are the images of the Luna I'd just seen hanging over her bed, her blood pooling beneath her, creating a dark patch on the carpet.

Not because I was particularly fond of the Luna in question but because of the way her children looked at me when they asked me if she was dead. Alpha Hayes wasn't a good person; he probably deserved to die one way or another. But their mother? No one should've done that to her.

I think about the other people who died in that house overnight. The staff members who were just going about their jobs or trying to get some sleep so that they could follow their orders the next day without being reprimanded. Why had they all been slaughtered? So that they couldn't call for help?

None of it made any sense. It wasn't as if the warriors from Hill needed to go into the capital of Alpha Hayes's territory at all. They could've just taken Zabrina and slipped into the night. If Hayes had a problem with it, he could've let them know, and they could've faced off about it then.

But it doesn't surprise me at all to know that this monster would sneak in there under cover of darkness and attack people while they were sleeping when they didn't even know the two packs had a conflict.

That's just the way he was.

A weak, conniving asshole.

And I should've shut him down when I had the chance to do so. I was ignorant to think he would do a better job than Alpha Bryant.

And now, this lesson has been learned, and I will be haunted by these images for the rest of my life.

Another body comes to mind, but this one isn't bloody.

Her face is alabaster and serene as she lies on the floor, like she's sleeping, with no evidence of the painful death that just claimed her lingering on her face.

Rebecca....

We pull into the city, and I perk up, knowing I've got business to handle now. I'm not leaving anyone back on the border this time around. We're all going in, and we're all going to rip the hell out of these assholes if I don't get exactly what I want the moment that I want it.

With every vehicle full of men I have with me, as well as a stern message to everyone in this pack that anyone who rises up against us will be put to death sent out over the mind-link, we pull up in front of the Alpha's mansion and get out of the SUVs. Everyone shifts except for me, but I am ready to get in on the action the moment it starts.

I approach the door, knowing full well that Beta Vinny, who has decided that he is taking over this pack after I killed Alpha Bryant, will be living here. Who knows where the previous Alpha's family has been relocated to?

I wouldn't be too surprised if Vinny didn't claim the previous Alpha's Luna, too.

Standing back from the house, I use the mind-link to say, "Vinny, get your sorry ass out here right now, and bring Zabrina with you, as well as anyone who was involved in the raid on Alpha Hayes's home in Duster pack."

I wait for a moment, but I refused to wait long.

Vinny's voice sounds in my head. "I'll be right out, Alpha King Boss Man. You're gonna be so pleased with what I have for you!"

He says this as if I haven't already told him I know what he's done. I say nothing. If I try to speak to him now, even through the mind-link, I will not be cordial.

A few seconds later, the front door opens, and Vinny walks out, dressed in a dark suit. I am reminded of what Isla told me. I'm not surprised to see it because Alpha Bryant and his thugs always dressed like gangsters. Why wouldn't Vinny carry on that tradition?

He is forcing a smile as he comes toward me, alone, and I growl at him, irritated that he's not following my instructions. The closer he comes, the more nervous I can see he is. Sweat beads pop out on his forehead along his receding hairline. His teeth are chattering a bit despite his wide smile that shows off all of his teeth to the back molars. His beak-like nose is even twitching slightly.

"Alpha King Maddox," he says, getting it right for once. "What's all this?" He raises his arms and gestures at the warriors I have brought with me. "This doesn't look like the type of celebratory party I was hoping would come and collect your prize."

"Where is she?" I demand, so disgusted with him that I want to rip his head from his neck with my own hands without even shifting.

"She's here, she's here," he assures me with a nod. "We had a bit of an incident getting her out because fucking Alpha Hayes didn't wanna hand her over, even though I told him that's what you wanted, but we managed to get her for you. I knew you'd be pleased." He flashes a smile at me, but the sun doesn't twinkle off of his canines like he's some kind of a fucking prince.

"You killed him," I say, my eyes narrowed. "You killed his wife, and you killed all of those innocent servants. Some of them in their sleep." I want to scream at him, but I've got to keep the fine grip on calm I currently have. It's about to slip away altogether.

Vinny's eyes widen slightly as he considered what I am saying to him.

"Hey, there, Alpha King Boss Man Sir," he begins, and I bare my teeth at him. "I did what I needed to do to ensure that you got what you wanted." He shrugs. "That's all I was up to."

I snarl. "That's bullshit! Alpha Hayes was asleep in his bed when you burst into his home. So was his wife. You didn't have to do that, Vinny, and I don't recall asking you to go to any great lengths to get Zabrina back!"

"Ah, but you see, that's where you're wrong." He points his finger at me for a moment but when he sees I'm about to chomp it off, he lowers it. "I needed to get her so that I could prove to you that I'm the best person for this pack's new Alpha. We talked about that. So, technically–"

The roar that comes out of my mouth is enough to stop him from talking. "Get the girl out here, now, and every single asshole who was involved in the raid on Duster pack. I want them all, now! And if you don't hand them over, I will hunt them down. If it means I have to arrest every man in your pack, I will find out who did this! You left two little girls as orphans, and you're going to pay for that!"

He stares at me long and hard, his mouth no longer plastered in a ghoulish grin. "They had daughters?" he asks me.

I nod. "Two little girls."

"And… we missed them?"

He said the wrong thing.

I leap into the air, shifting as I do so, and come down in my wolf form, landing on top of him and pushing him backward onto the sidewalk. He hits with a thunk that makes me wonder if his brain is still solid or if it hasn't liquified, and momentarily, his eyes roll back into his head.

Using the mind-link, I demand, "Do you want to call your asshole vigilantes out here nor or shall I bite off your head inch by inch until they're all accounted for."

"Alpha King–please," he groans. "Give me a sec."

I sink my front claws into his shoulders. He couldn't shift now if he wanted to. I'm not giving him enough room. Not that it would matter. He can't beat me.

A moment later, the front door to the house opens and a couple of other guys in suits walk out, blood splatters still evident on their skin. The droplets must've adhered to their fur while they were killing in Duster pack, and they hadn't showered yet.

Between them, they have the prisoner I've been looking for. Zabrina is wearing a T-shirt that barely covers anything. It's clearly not hers. She is bound and gagged and struggling to get away.

"Where are the rest?" I ask Vinny through the mind-link.

He doesn't answer right away, and behind me, I hear a chorus of growls.

"Take her... leave my warriors. I thought that's what you wanted," he coughs out.

"Where are the rest!" I demand, my claws cutting through his suit, through his skin to the muscle.

Vinny screams in agony, and he has to know he can either save himself or he can save his men.

Actually, he can save neither because I will figure out who did this and end them.

Rather than answering me or sending them out, Vinny just lays there in agony, looking like he's about to shit his pants.

But then, I hear another sound, one that's meant to spark fear in me. I lift my head in the direction it's coming from. I'm not scared, but I am surprised

Is he honestly going to try this?

He's going to try to fight me?

The sound of approaching wolves from the rest of the village has my warriors on edge as the noise that drives the last nail into Vinny's coffin is put in place.

Howls fill the air.

So, we're going to fight?

WILL HE PULL THE TRIGGER?

Isla

I SIT ON MY BED, staring across the room at the wall, watching the sun chase the shadows across the painting that hangs there of a woman reading a book. I don't know who she is, and it doesn't matter anyway because I'm not paying any attention to her.

I'm basically as oblivious to her as she is to me.

My mind goes back over what Ben found in the floor. He hadn't been able to look at any of the papers because he'd heard our other brothers coming in the front door and quickly shoved everything back into the hiding place and repositioned the board over top.

But it's fine because I don't really need to know what the papers say in order to put the pieces of the puzzle together.

Those "earrings" weren't earrings at all. They were cufflinks. I could tell by the way that Ben was describing them to me. He said they had weird fasteners. Every detail he mentioned about them told me they look exactly like the pair that I had given to Maddox.

So... that means they both came from Maatua. I have no other explanation.

I do have to wonder, though, if maybe one of the reasons why my parents have had bad luck for so much of their lives is because they are in possession of those cufflinks.

And it isn't as if everything that has happened in the castle since I brought those wolves with the bedazzling eyes through the doors has gone particularly well either.

Of course, things were already going poorly since Zabrina decided she wanted to murder me and take my place, but things seemed to be steadily getting worse now that the cursed objects were here.

Thoughts of going over to Maddox's room and trying to find them come to mind, but I decide against it. He won't want me snooping around in there. I can just wait until he comes back and talk to him about it. I know he doesn't want me to mention Maatua, but that doesn't mean I can't tell him it's okay if he gets rid of the cufflinks.

I run a hand through my hair and let out a loud sigh.

That won't solve all of the problems, though. I need to go back to where I came from. I need to see what has happened there.

How could the place go from a thriving pack territory where gems and jewels were allegedly as plentiful as rocks to a war-torn area that no one dare enter?

Or am I reading too much into the little that Mystica has told me?

I consider calling the healer to my room to ask her more, but I don't think Maddox would like that. He seems so against me asking questions about Maatua, and I don't know why.

Thinking about Maddox makes me wonder where he's at and what went on in Duster pack. Poppy says she heard that he didn't catch Zabrina, and that's making me question everything. What was that dream that I had if it wasn't Zabrina coming ashore near the Wolf Stone Bridge in Duster pack? And if the dream was accurate, why isn't she there?

I can't make sense of it, and trying makes my head hurt. I should probably go outside and get some sunshine or exercise. It would be nice to let my wolf run, but after the last time I shifted, I probably won't be doing that for a while.

My mind hungers to reach out for Maddox, but I stop myself. Whatever he's doing, it has to be important business. It has to be tricky business, and I don't want to be a distraction.

But I do hope that he's okay.

I have a bad feeling in the pit of my stomach that settles into my soul.

What if he's not?

Maddox

Vinny's body trembles beneath me as I growl at him. He knows he's in deep shit. Even with the rest of the warriors from his pack sprinting in to try and fight us off, he's in a position where there's not a damn thing he can do to save himself.

"Are you insane?" I ask him through the mind-link. "What the actual fuck do you think you're doing calling in troops to fight the king's guard while I'm standing on top of you with my claws sinking into your shoulders?"

He shakes his head the best he can with my massive paws next to his neck. "I… I didn't, Your Majesty. I promise! It wasn't me!"

I don't want to believe him because he's in charge here, but even Vinny doesn't seem to be that stupid. My eyes lift to the two assholes holding Zabrina between them on the porch. One of them has a smirk on his face, and I figure it had to be him. He must have dreams of becoming the next Alpha. I suppose he hasn't thought about the fact that he is also right here within my clutches, and his backup isn't here yet.

Unless, of course, this asshole is enough of a cheater to bring a gun to a wolf fight.

I look carefully at him and think he might be packing heat. His jacket is bowed out a bit, and it makes me wonder how this pack got so fucked up.

None of my packs use weapons, ever. I don't care how pissed they are at the rival packs. It's just underhanded and dirty, and I don't want that reputation for any of my packs, even the packs full of assholes like this one.

"Cody, keep an eye on this bastard," I say, walking over the top of Vinny as I slowly approach the porch. Both of the lackeys get nervous. Only one is gripping and ungripping his hand in a fist over and over again.

He's got an itchy trigger finger.

I'm not worried about a bullet or two, but I'd rather not have any silver enter my body. That's painful as hell and not easy to mend. I do have a healer or two with me, but not Mystica, and she's the only one I'd trust to dig out a silver bullet.

"I think you'd better undo what you just did," I say to the asshole through the mind-link.

"I, uh, I didn't do nothin'," he argues.

I narrow my gaze. The howls are getting closer. I know if I turn my head, I'll actually see the wolves entering the block where the Alpha's mansion occupies most of the land. "Then undo nothin'."

He opens his mouth to speak, but no words come out. I take a few steps closer as my warriors spread out, all but Cody who is holding Vinny down. The temporary Alpha still can't shift, and he'll be the first to die.

Well, if this bastard doesn't answer me with an affirmative, Vinny might be the second.

The other guy who is holding onto Zabrina asks, "Did you call for them?" and gestures at the other wolves flying toward us.

"Nah, nah, it was Vinny," he says, but even his friend doesn't believe him.

"Shit! This is the king, you dumbass!" he says. "What the fuck are you thinking'?"

"It wasn't–"

I take advantage of the distraction, and before the fucker in question can even finish his sentence, I launch off of my back feet and pounce on him.

Zabrina screams as he's ripped away from her, knocked backward, his head hitting the side of the house with a sickening crack as my teeth snap down on his throat.

He didn't get a chance to use those silver bullets I'm certain he's got lodged in his gun.

"Oh, fuck!" lackey number two shouts as blood squirts everywhere. Zabrina is still screaming.

"Stop! Stop!" Vinny is shouting, Maybe the other wolves don't hear him because he's not using the mind-link. He's too nervous, I guess. But they keep coming, and my most bloodthirsty warriors meet them before they even get to the edge of the Alpha's yard.

They're coming from all directions, though, and we are grossly outnumbered.

"This is the king!" I tell all of the wolves within a hundred-mile radius. "I command the wolves of Hill Country pack to stop their attack this instance! Anyone who continues to fight against the king's guard will die a painful death!"

Most of the wolves immediately back away and lie down in a subservient position. I'm guessing they were told it was someone else they were attacking. A few bodies are sprawled on the ground, their crimson blood covering the grass.

A couple of my warriors are injured, but none of their injuries look too serious.

I shift my eyes to the suit still holding on to Zabrina. "I want everyone who was involved in the raid on Duster pack out here now, in their human form, ready to be arrested. You get them here, and I'll go easier on you." My mind-link directive is clear. No one is compelled to obey me simply because I am the king, but if they know what's good for them, they will.

He nods. "Yes, Sir, Alpha King Maddox."

I order a couple of my warriors to shift and take Zabrina, not caring at all about their nudity. She is crying as she is loaded into a paddy wagon I've ordered brought here from the castle.

I'm taking everyone who was involved in Alpha Hayes's slaughter back to the castle, and they're going to wish they'd just died out here on this lawn.

It takes about thirty minutes to get everyone loaded up. In the meantime, I shift and get dressed in a change of clothes I've brought with me. I hear

Vinny's voice filtering through the paddy wagon as he begs to be released. He's the guiltiest of all of them. He will pay the highest price.

Four of the attacking wolves were killed. Two of my warriors are patched up by healers. Zabrina has hyperventilated from crying so much. Maybe I'll get lucky and she'll somehow suffocate on the way back to the castle so I don't have to deal with her anymore.

But then... I definitely want the opportunity to punish her the way that she tortured Isla and killed Private Parker.

Once we have all of the prisoners loaded up, I realize Hill Country pack doesn't have an Alpha now, and I have no one in this pack I can trust. So I will have to put it under martial law. I decide to leave Cody and Gail there with a detail and will send more to help them put things in order. I think we've taken out the leaders of the group of troublemakers, so I hope they will all be fine.

Sitting in the passenger seat in the front of one of the SUVs, I give the order, and we head back home, mission accomplished, though it's nothing like I had thought it would be when I left home earlier in the day.

Once we are closer to the castle, I take a deep breath, lean my head back and close my eyes. I have a call to make.

ANTICIPATION

Isla

M̲y̲ ̲s̲t̲o̲m̲a̲c̲h̲ ̲i̲s̲ ̲t̲a̲n̲g̲l̲e̲d̲ in knots as I stare across the room at the tray of table Poppy has brought me. She keeps bringing me things to eat that I'm too nervous to touch.

Poppy putters around the room, rehanging clothes, moving things from one place to another that don't need to be moved. She's cleaning the same surfaces over and over, too, as if she has nothing better to do but also doesn't want to leave me alone.

Her sources, the other staff in the castle, have let her know that Maddox left Duster pack a few hours ago. Where he was going, they weren't certain at first, which made me very nervous.

Then, Beta Seth came in to check on me, and I could tell he was nervous. He'd tried to play it down like everything was fine and he was just there to make sure I was doing well, but eventually, I got him to tell me the truth.

Well... part of it anyway.

Maddox had gone to Hill Country pack, the same place where he'd picked up Sydney and ended up killing the Alpha. I asked Seth what Maddox was doing there, praying it was just to check on the situation and not because the pack was stirring up trouble again, but he wouldn't really answer me. He just shook his head and said not to worry about it.

I was worried about it, though.

"He hasn't sent for reinforcements that I know of," Poppy says off-handed as she puts one of my dresses back on the bar. "And I normally hear about such things."

I want to say that's good to know, but I would be more surprised if he had sent for them because the castle is so far away from that pack. What would be the point?

"He did ask for a paddy wagon, though," Poppy tells me.

"A paddy wagon?" I repeat, pondering why he would do such a thing.

"Yeah, you know, for prisoners." She closes the armoire.

I nod. "I know what one is, I just wonder why he needs that." Why would he need an entire paddy wagon for just Zabrina? None of this is making any sense to me. I try to tie it to what I'd seen in my dream, but I just can't make the leap.

So I continue to sit there, my knees pulled to my chest, my arms wrapped around them, wondering if Maddox is okay.

I think I would feel it if he wasn't. Whether or not I am his second-chance mate, I think I would know if he was in pain or if he was... no longer around. I can't explain why, but I feel it in my heart. When I am a bit older, I should be able to find my mate by scent, but because I'm not old enough yet, Maddox wouldn't be able to tell if it is me–assuming he has a second chance mate.

I know that he's said he'll never take another Luna, but I have to wonder if he might change his mind if he felt the pull....

My thoughts are interrupted by Maddox's voice in my head. I almost leap up off of the bed with excitement and relief, as he sounds strong. He sounds uninjured.

"Hi, Isla."

"Maddox!" I'm not sure one can actually scream through the mind-link since it's just in our heads, but I feel like I am shouting his name. "How are you?"

Poppy has said something I missed and is looking at me funny. "Is the king in your head?" she asks.

I nod, and she smiles at me, but then I give all of my attention to Maddox who is responding to my question.

"I'm fine," he assures me. "We are on our way back to the castle."

"Thank the Moon Goddess," I mumble. "You're not harmed?"

"No. no, I'm fine," he tells me. "I'll be home soon, and then I'll tell you all about it, but you don't need to worry about me. We don't even have any casualties."

I inhale deeply and then let it go. "Thank the Moon Goddess," I say aloud and in my head this time. "When will you be back?"

"I'll be there in about twenty minutes, but we have prisoners, and this time, I need to make sure they don't get out of the dungeon."

I know what he's speaking of. It makes no sense that so many people that he had in custody have managed to get away recently.

Curiosity overcomes me, and I find myself asking, "Did you get... her?" I know he will understand who I am speaking of.

"Yes, we have Zabrina in custody," he says, a confident tone in his voice that sends a ripple of excitement through me I can't deny.

"Good." I don't know what else to say as the tone of his deep, gravelly voice has sent me to places I shouldn't go alone, without him. And I know he'll be busy with actual work when he gets here. So it will be a while before he is available to satisfy my craving... working on the job we are meant to do together....

"I'll see you soon," he says. "Once I get these goons situated."

"I'm looking forward to seeing you." I keep my tone cordial, not letting him know he's ignited a fire in my core.

I hear a chuckle in his voice as he responds, "Oh, I'm looking forward to seeing you, too. All of you." And I know that he has picked up on my desire, even though I was trying to hide it.

I can't hide much of anything from Maddox.

He tells me goodbye and fades from my mind, and I remember the situation with my brother. I feel that I should keep all of that information from Maddox. He will never understand why I want to go to Maatua to see if I can figure out what happened there, but it's so difficult for me to keep anything from him.

And I know I can't just leave without speaking to him about it again. Not unless I have a far better plan than I did last time....

I don't want to do that, just take off and not tell him where I'm going, but I know he will tell me I shouldn't do it, that there's nothing in the islands for me but trouble.

He might be right, but if there are any answers there at all, I need to find them. My parents will tell me nothing. I want to know why they were forced to leave and what happened to our people.

"So...?" Poppy stands at the foot of the bed, her arms spread wide, her palms up, as her eyes bore through me. "I take it by the look on your face that you're done speaking to the king?"

"Yes, I'm finished," I tell her, feeling bad that I haven't told her anything yet when she's always so fast to tell me what she hears from the other servants in the castle.

"What did he say?" she prompts.

"Not too much. Just that he's on his way back. He did get Zabrina, and he has lots of other prisoners, but he didn't tell me who they were, and I didn't ask," I admit.

"Why not?" Her forehead wrinkles up as she contemplates what I've said to her.

I shrug. "I don't know. He seemed busy and distracted. I'll ask him when he gets here."

"Yeah, well, I doubt it will be a priority for you to tell me then when you've got that amorous look on your face." She sighs. "I'll have to go find out what's going on from the other servants. If the king is on his way back to the castle, someone has to know something."

She doesn't seem mad, just curious. But then, Poppy is always curious. "All right," I tell her.

My maid stops pretending to tidy my room and heads out the door, leaving my untouched food.

I ponder going over and eating it now that I know that Maddox is okay. I am a little hungry. But lately, my stomach has felt a little unsettled. I am sure it's because of nerves. I am always nervous about something, and it almost always has to do with Maddox.

Thinking of him sends another electric trill down my spine, and I consider dropping my hand down inside of the white slacks I'm wearing to make a bit of the sting subside. I've never been one to do that, touch myself, but when I think of Maddox, I almost can't help it. I wish his hands were on me, but since they can't be at the moment, perhaps mine will have to do.

A knock on my door has that idea fading away, and a frustrated sigh leaves me.

At first, I think it might be Beta Seth, coming to tell me that Alpha King Maddox is on his way back to the castle. But then I realize that the Beta is probably too busy preparing for the king's arrival with all of those prisoners, particularly Zabrina, to worry about letting me know.

"Yes?" I call sliding down off of the bed and walking over to the door.

It opens before I reach it, and Sydney pops her head in again. "Hey," she says, a meek look on her face.

I hold back my irritation. She's probably the last person I want to see at the moment, except for maybe Zabrina herself, but I see no reason to be rude. "Hi," I say, beckoning with my hand that she can come in. "Is everything okay?"

She stands there for a second, the door ajar, both hands on her abdomen. "I'm not sure. I don't feel so good, and I'm not sure what to do."

"What's wrong?" I ask her, but I barely get the words out before a huge gush of water breaks down from between her legs, spilling all over my carpet and dampening her shorts so that it looks like she'd fallen into a puddle.

"Oh, Goddess!" she shouts, sounding like she may be in a little pain. But when she continues, I realize she's just embarrassed. "I just peed myself! I didn't even know I had to go to the bathroom!"

I can tell that it isn't urine. Not only does it smell different, but she would also know if she had to pee. "Sydney, dear," I say, stepping around the puddle to put my hands on her shoulders. "You didn't pee. Your water just broke."

She looks into my eyes, and all she can say is, "Holy shit."

GET IT OUT!

Isla

THE PUDDLE of water sinking into my carpet is the least of my worries as Sydney is panicking. She grabs onto my arm and squeezes, her nails digging into my skin.

"What? My water broke?" she shouts. "That means I'm having this baby right now?"

"Well, soon," I tell her, prying her fingernails out of my arm. "Come on, let's go back to your room. I'll get the healer."

She starts to walk to my bed. "No! I have to lay down right now!"

The thought of her getting goo all over my bed is unappealing. I know that she has time to get to her own room before she has the baby. After all, I do have a ton of younger brothers, and my mom gave birth to all of them at home because she couldn't afford to go to the hospital.

Grabbing her arm, I pull her back toward the door. "Sydney, there's time," I tell her. "Let's go to your room."

"You can't expect me to walk at a time like this!" she shouts at me, trying to pull away.

Thankfully, I hear a familiar voice at that moment as Poppy comes in the door, stopping in her tracks as I hold up a hand. I know she'll be pissed if she walks through the puddle. "What the hell?"

"Poppy, thank the Moon Goddess," I mutter. "Can you help me get Sydney to her room? And then we need to send for Mystica."

"I can send for Mystica right now. Did her water break?" She sees that Sydney is trying to pull away from me, so Poppy takes her other arm.

"Yes, her water broke, and now I am trying to explain to her that she has time to get back to her own room and that it's not necessary for her to lay down in my bed to have this baby." I say each word with a measured, distinct tone.

Poppy understands my concern and is willing to help me as she says, "Yes, yes, there's plenty of time. Come on, Cindy."

"Sydney," I correct her, but she doesn't acknowledge me as she is pulling the young girl out of my room.

Why is Sydney so insistent that she have the baby here?

Between the two of us, we get her out of my room, and we head down the hallway. Sydney doing a strange waddle that I find alarming until she says, "My pants are soaked!"

"Mystica is on her way," Poppy tells her. "And Beta Seth is going to meet us at your room. Where is it?"

"Beta Seth!" Sydney lurches away from me toward Poppy. "I don't want a man in my room while I'm bare-assed pushing a baby out of my vajayjay!"

"No, he's not coming for that," Poppy assures her. "He's just going to make sure that you're okay, and then he'll leave."

Sydney doesn't seem any calmer, and after a few more steps, she stops and shouts, "Oh, Goddess!" She wrenches her arms away from us and puts her palms on her abdomen. "It hurts!"

"I'm sorry." That's all I can manage to say. I'm afraid she'll go sprinting off toward my room again.

"You're sorry? You're sorry!" Sydney looks at me with fire in her eyes. "Oh, well, as long as you're sorry that it feels like a fucking alien is trying to rip my insides apart, I feel better!"

I stare at her with my mouth hanging open, not sure what to say.

Through the mind-link, Poppy says, "She's just lashing out because she's scared. Just ignore her."

I want to say I think that she's supposed to shout those rude comments to her husband, but she doesn't have one, but I keep my mouth shut. I know better. My dad learned really quickly not to say anything at all to my sweet mother when she was in labor. No matter how kind-hearted my mother typically was, when a baby was about to emerge, she became a dragon monster.

"Where is your room?" Poppy asks again, but Sydney won't budge, and then we see Beta Seth rushing toward us, and I feel relieved. He'll know what to do.

Except, his eyes are wide and big as saucers as he says, "What is going on? Did she have the baby?"

I want to ask him if he sees a baby, but I don't say anything.

Instead, Sydney shouts, "Yes, I did. It was a fucking water baby and it's all over my goddess-damn pants!"

"No," Poppy tells the Beta in a calm voice. "Not yet. Can you help us get her to her room?"

"Is there time for that?" Seth asks.

"That's what I said!" Sydney shouts.

"There's time." Poppy is still calm but obviously a little irritated as well. "Where is her room?"

Beta Seth seems befuddled, but he finally says, "It's this way," and leads us down a hall to the left.

We follow along, nudging Sydney to walk, and eventually, we get there. Poppy insists that Sydney wait while she puts the shower curtain on the bed so that it won't ruin the mattress and then she grabs a nightgown out of one of the drawers. "I'll get her changed. You two wait out there."

Beta Seth and I are more than happy to do just that, and I think that Poppy is a good person to have around when one is having a baby. She's already proven to me that she's a good person to have around during an emergency.

Mystica and a couple of her nurses come rushing down the hallway. "Where is she?" she asks.

"In her room," Beta Seth says. "Poppy is getting her changed."

Mystica doesn't wait. She opens the door. Seth averts his eyes, and I do, too, but I hear Sydney screaming. "What the fuck? Some of us are naked!"

"I'm the healer," Mystica says, and she disappears inside, along with the nurses she's brought with her.

I take a deep breath, thinking my work here is done. I can go back to my room now, even if I have to clean up the mess on the floor myself. I don't mind, as long as I have the proper cleaning supplies.

But then the door opens again, and Poppy is staring into my eyes. "She's asking for you."

I turn around and look behind me, expecting there to be another person behind me.

But no... she's speaking to me. I point at my chest. "Me? She wants me? Why?"

"She says that she wants you in the room while she gives birth and won't listen to anyone who says that it isn't necessary."

Poppy grabs hold of my arm and yanks me into the room, I stumble forward. This is the last thing in the world I want to do.

Taking a deep breath, I follow her into the room. Sydney is on her bed with a sheet over her, and Mystica is giving her some fluids in an IV. I can tell that the girl is in a lot of pain because of the look on her face.

I don't know what to do.

When Sydney sees me, she says, "Thank the Moon Goddess. Get over here, breeder! I need your help!"

I approach the bed, but I am hesitant because I have no idea how to help her. I've already told her that I haven't had any babies, that I'm an inexperienced breeder. I've never helped my mom give birth or done anything other than bring in some towels. I will be more helpful once the baby is born. I have helped my mother take care of the children after they are born.

Nevertheless, I am not one to deny a pregnant woman in labor my presence if it somehow helps her, even if it just means I am about to be cussed at and screamed at until this baby makes its way out into the world.

I sit in a chair next to Sydney and hold her hand, and she squeezes so hard that every time there is a contraction, I think that my hand might be crushed. She is in a lot of pain, and even though I heard Mystica say that she put something in the IV, it doesn't seem to be helping any.

The labor goes on and on for a couple of hours, and Sydney becomes more and more agitated. She's sweating profusely, and it doesn't matter that there's a fan on her and the windows are open.

I see that Mystica and the other healers are whispering to one another, and that's when I realize….

Something is wrong.

Sydney hasn't realized it yet. "Can you please, just… get this baby out of me?" she asks Mystica, and the fact that she's no longer cursing makes me think that she is exhausted.

"We are working on it, dear," Mystica says. She smiles and pats Sydney's leg, but then she whispers something to one of the nurses, and the woman scurries out of the room at a quick pace.

I want to ask what's going on, but I figure, if they're not going to tell Sydney, they're not going to tell me.

Then I realize Sydney is talking to me. "What's happening down there, breeder?" she asks me. "Can you see the kid's feet or what?"

I want to tell her that seeing the feet would be a bad thing, that the baby is supposed to come out head first, but I don't say that. Instead, I get up and peek around the sheet that's held up by her knees. "Uhm, no, I don't see any baby yet." I didn't study the situation as that seems weird, but I do know there's no baby. Not yet."

"Sydney, dear," Mystica says, coming around the side of the bed. "You are a tiny woman, and the baby is rather large."

"Tell me something I didn't already fucking know!" Sydney shouts at the calm healer.

Mystica clears her throat. It's obvious to me that she was about to tell her something she didn't already know.

"We are going to have to do something different to get the baby out, dear,"

Mystica says, still calm. The nurse who had run out is back now with a cart. I can see instruments on it, and my heart starts to beat against my rib cage.

"A different way?" Sydney says. "Wait–if there's a different way, why didn't you just do that to begin with? You think I want to push this kid out through my junk?"

Mystica doesn't react to what almost has me laughing. "The way that we will get the baby out is called a Cesarean, dear. I'm going to have to put you under and then make a small incision in your abdomen."

"You're going to cut me open?" Sydney asks. "Are you shitting me?"

"It's the only way," Mystica says. But Sydney is shaking her head vehemently.

"Nope, nope, nope!" she says.

"Dear, the baby is stuck in the birth canal. If the child continues to work its way down, I won't be able to save either one of you, so please, let me do this."

"Either one of us?" she asks.

Mystica sighs. "I need to hurry, dear."

Sydney looks at me, her face pale, and her mouth agape.

I don't know what to tell her because I have no idea what the chances are that she will survive even if they do cut her open. "You want to save your baby?"

She shrugs. "I don't know."

Mystica says, "If I act now, I have a better chance at saving both of you."

Sydney's head swivels to her and then back to me. "It sounds like you'll both die if she doesn't get him out."

Looking into my eyes, she says, "I'm scared."

"I know," I tell her. "But I'll be right here." I squeeze her hand and try to smile to be reassuring, but I am also scared, scared for her, and I don't even know her–scared for her baby as well.

"Okay," Sydney tells Mystica, but she's looking at me. "Do it."

I glance over at the healer, and I can see that she doesn't look comfortable. I pat Sydney's hand. "It'll be okay."

She nods, but we both know I'm lying.

WHERE SHE BELONGS

Maddox

When we arrive at the castle, I have the pack members of Hill Country who slaughtered Alpha Hayes and his household moved into the dungeon first. I'm glad to see that Alpha Jordan hasn't managed to find his way out of his cell. Everyone who was in the dungeon when I left appears to still be there.

Zabrina is another matter altogether, and I have her moved down by a team of Omegas who I know won't put up with her shit. They're all female, and they don't mind slapping the cuss out of her every time she says something that she shouldn't.

By the time Zabrina arrives in the dungeon where I am overseeing the escorting of the other assholes into their new homes, she is bleeding from her mouth, nose, and one ear.

Something tells me that the ladies were lenient on her after all.

"Put her in that one," I say, pointing at the smallest, dirtiest, darkest cell we have. "Chain her to the wall."

"No, don't do that!" she barks. "My ribs are broken! If you do that, it will hurt like fuck!"

"Do it." I keep the calm in my voice as I tell them to do something they were already doing. Looking the princess in the eyes, I remind her, "You don't give the orders around here, bitch."

"Listen," she says as the guards yank her arms up over her head. "Son of a bitch!" she shrieks, and I can tell it hurts. I almost smile, just thinking about this woman who tried to kill my Isla in pain, "You don't understand, Maddox!"

I was about to walk away, but when she uses my first name like that, I stop and wheel around on her. I get to within an inch of her bleeding face, and in my still-calm-but-obviously-irritated-voice, I say, "You will address me as Alpha King. Nothing more; nothing less. Do you hear me, Zabrina?"

I narrow my eyes at her and watch as her lip quivers ever so slightly.

She's trying to pretend she's just angry, but she's obviously scared, too, and she should be. I intend to do everything to her that she did to Isla and Private Parker—every ounce of torture they had to endure, and then some, she will feel, for just as long—probably longer.

"Alpha King," she says, her voice wavering. "You don't understand. You think I'm the enemy, but it's not me."

I scoff at her. "Oh, really?" I ask, taking a step back, glad to have some space between us as she reeks of urine and blood. "I thought it was you who kidnapped two people that were under my care, drove them out to a cabin in the woods, and tortured them—one of them to death—but, please, if that wasn't you, enlighten me. I'm sure Isla was just confused when she told me that you were the one seated in the car with her."

She takes as deep a breath as she can with her ribs broken, and I see her throat quake slightly as she tries to come up with the correct words, something she thinks I will believe. Something that will still get her off of the hook for the horrors she's committed, but something I might believe to actually be true.

"All right," she says, her voice soft. It's the least aggressive I've seen her since we brought her in. "It's true. I did do that, but you don't understand. I didn't have any choice."

I cock my head to the side and study her face. She has a slight twitch in her upper lip on the right side, and her heartbeat is more erratic than it was before. Tiny beads of perspiration spring to life on her forehead.

She's clearly lying to me. I can tell by those signs alone, even if there was absolutely no reason for me to think that she isn't to blame for what happened.

Yet, I want to hear the story she's concocted. I'm curious. It might be interesting.

Perhaps someday I shall write a fiction book and need some storylines. This might come in handy….

"All right," I say, clearing my throat. "Tell me your tale, Zabrina. But make it fast. I'd like to go see my woman."

I see her eyes narrow at the mention of Isla and how she is mine and Zabrina never will be.

Not in that sense anyway.

"It was… Alpha Grant's idea," she tells me, and I see her eyes widen slightly as the plan begins to come together. Like a black widow spider, she is weaving her web, hoping to catch a male in it and bring him certain death.

Or whatever the fuck it is black widows do to kill.

"Alpha Grant?" I repeat. "From River Crest pack?"

Alpha Grant has always been one of my most loyal followers. He is about my age and has been Alpha there for about five years. He has a lovely wife, Nina, his Luna and fated mate. Nina just gave birth to their second child, a son, the heir to the Alphadom.

It seems ironic that Zabrina would pick him to pin this on, but I am curious now and want to see where she goes.

"That's right. River Crest pack is near my father's territory, you know? Alpha Grant thought it would be more believable for my father to get into the castle and make a deal with you. Originally, the plan was for you to marry me. I'd become your Luna and my father would murder you on our wedding night after I slipped something into your drink. Then, Alpha Grant would take over the kingdom, and my father would be his second in command."

I raise my eyebrows. Zabrina is lucky she's not a movie producer. No one would want to see this film. The plot isn't believable. "But?" I say, prompting her to continue.

"But…." As she speaks, flecks of blood fly from her mouth. She pauses to spit a mouthful of pink saliva onto the stone floor. It mingles and coagulates with all of the other fluid that's been spilled here over the years. "But, my father let him know that it wasn't working. That you had this breeder that you were in love with, so I would never get to be the Luna."

"So Alpha Grant told you to kill Isla and try to take her place?" I surmise.

She nods. "More or less. I didn't want to do it, Mad–Alpha King." She catches herself, corrects her course. "But I didn't have any choice. Alpha Grant told my father that if he didn't go through with the plan, while he was away, he'd burn our villages to the ground, one by one."

"So you had to go through with it?" I ask her.

She nods. "That's right. And that woman, that maid… she was a spy for Grant. She was trying to… kill me. So I had no choice but to kill her first."

"You mean Agatha?" I ask her, knowing full-well that wasn't the woman's name.

"Yes, her." I notice Zabrina is looking around, as if she's trying to figure out if she might be in the same cell now where she murdered the poor maid–Alva–that she'd forced to poison me. She's not–that one was far too nice for Zabrina.

"So… if that's the case, why isn't Alpha Grant burning down the villages in your territory now?" I ask her.

"Well… because… he knows the plan fell apart, and he's trying to look innocent. He probably knows I'll rat him out to you, and he doesn't want to have any reason to look guilty." She tries to shrug and then winces at the pain in her ribs.

"And when your father wakes up, he'll be able to corroborate this?" I ask her.

Again, her eyes widen for a moment as she contemplates how to respond. Does she think she can get a mind-link message to Alpha Jordan in time to tell him what to say? He isn't conscious at the moment. I noticed that as I came through the dungeon.

"I thought my father was dead until Alpha Vinny told me otherwise," she says.

"Beta Vinny," I correct her. "Beta Vinny who is no longer with us."

"Right," she says. "But I think that my father is probably pretty messed up mentally from... the lack of oxygen." Fake tears spring up in her eyes, and I want to slap them away. She doesn't care about her father. If Isla's dream is true, and I see no reason why it wouldn't be since I found Zabrina with men in suits who picked her up in Duster pack, that means Zabrina essentially just left her dad there to die.

No, she's full of shit.

I slam a hand down on her shoulder. "Listen, Zabrina, most of us learn when we are young children that we have to take responsibility for our own actions. Sometimes that is a difficult lesson. Sometimes, children want to do right and please their parents, so they do their best to make them happy."

She is staring at me, not sure what I'm getting at. I continue.

"Clearly, you never learned that you need to fess up when you do something wrong. Admit the mistake, try to correct it, promise not to do it again, and move on. So you just keep fucking up over and over again, and you have no one to blame but yourself."

"But I–" she begins, but I press a finger to her mouth to make her shut up.

"We are done here. You can consider yourself convicted of two counts of murder, one count of attempted murder, two counts of kidnapping, and probably a hundred other crimes that would keep you in prison for the rest of your life." I pull my hand back, letting her speak.

"So... that's what you're going to do then?" she asks me, those tears springing into her eyes again. "You're going to keep me in this filthy dungeon for the rest of my life?"

She's already escaped from here once, and I am so fucking tired of chasing her. I shake my head, and I can see she's not sure whether or not to be hopeful. "No, Zabrina," I say. "I believe the other crimes I didn't list are worthy of earning you a life sentence. But the ones I did list, well, those will earn you something else altogether."

Her lips are trembling again as she asks, "Wh-what's that?"

"Well, you see, first you're going to go through the hell that Isla and Parker went through–the silver, the wolfsbane, all of that torture. Then… well, then I make sure that you never, ever hurt anyone again." I stand up to my full height and tower over to drive home my point.

"H-how's that?" she asks. I think the tears are real this time.

I only have one word for her in response.

"Execution."

LIGHTNING CRASHES

Isla

MYSTICA HAS PUT an oxygen mask of some sort over Sydney's mouth and nose and asked her to breathe deeply. She also gave her something else, something that will make her go to sleep soon. I hold her hand and force myself to smile at her, but as the other woman's eyes grow heavy and flicker closed, I can't help but wonder if she will ever open them again.

I have all the faith in the world in Mystica. She saved my life, and she's treated my injuries more than once. But that doesn't mean she can save everyone in every situation.

Mystica and her nurses begin working quickly as soon as Sydney is out, and I no longer feel the need to sit next to her and calmly hold her hand, especially when I see the sharp instrument that Mystica is about to use to cut her open.

We have a similar thought at the same time as Mystica says, "Isla, dear, you can let go."

Can I, though?

I haven't known Sydney long, and I'm not even sure that I like the girl, but I do feel awful for what is happening to her.

Especially if the gut feeling I have is correct and she doesn't ever open her eyes again.

I pry her fingers away from my hand and then get up from my chair, moving it over out of the way so that the nurses can work, and back toward the door.

I want to step out. I want to open the door, turn around, and run away, fleeing down the hallway as fast as I can go so that I don't have to witness what is about to happen here.

So that I don't have to think about what is about to happen here.

I can pretend, can't I? I can pretend that I never met Sydney? That she never came into my room to ask my advice… to try to steal my man… to see if I could help her become a breeder.

None of that sounded too good on her part, but she is young, pregnant, scared, and had been taken advantage of. I can't hold that against her.

And I can't hold it against her baby.

If Sydney doesn't pull through, this baby will be born an orphan. His or her father is already dead, and the baby's mom is looking paler and paler by the moment.

When Mystica makes her first cut, blood squirts out a bit, and I have to cover my mouth. Once again, I hear alarms sounding in my head.

"What are you doing, Isla? Turn around and run! No one would fault you! Why are you here?" I ask myself, but I have no answers.

It feels like Sydney will know. That she will somehow see me abandoning her, leaving her here all alone to go through this journey through the valley of darkness, when she'd wanted me to stay with her. Even though her eyes are closed and she is under some sort of medication to make her feel no pain and be completely unaware of her surroundings, I feel like she would see me running away from her.

And haunt me for the rest of my life.

But that isn't why I am not leaving the room. I am more afraid of letting myself down than I am in disappointing Sydney. If I leave, what will that say about me? That I can't handle the tough situations in life? That doesn't seem like me.

It certainly doesn't sound like something an alleged descendant of the Moon Goddess would do.

The Moon Goddess….

As the deity's name entered my mind, I catch Mystica's eyes. "Do you think… I can do anything to help?" I asked her as she was doing her best to get to the baby.

"You can pray," she says. "But dear… don't think that you have the power to change what the Moon Goddess has already set in motion."

I look at her, my brow furrowing, not sure I understand what Mystica is saying to me. I'm also not sure she has time to explain right now as I hear a ripping, splashing sound, and then she tugs a purple squirmy blob out of

Sydney's abdomen. It's wet and covered in some kind of white slimy looking stuff.

I realize as the nurse hastily takes the object from Mystica that it's a baby.

It's small and not crying at all. In fact, I think it was more waving around from Mystica's movement than actually squirming.

The nurse sets the baby down on a cart one of them brought in earlier, and two of them immediately start doing something to the child while Mystica is still working on Sydney.

"Why isn't the baby crying?" I ask.

No one answers me because they don't have time. Mystica is shouting things to another nurse, asking for items that the nurse is handing her. What was once a bit of blood has become a lot more, and it's not just coming from Sydney's abdomen either.

It's coming from beneath her legs. It's coming from… where the baby was meant to come out.

Mystica is no longer attempting to sew up the slice in Sydney's abdomen. Instead, she's doing something between the girl's legs, trying to make the bleeding stop, but more and more keeps pouring out.

I had thought I would never see as much blood as I had the time that Zabrina sliced that maid's throat and came down the hallway dripping from the crimson substance.

But I was wrong.

Tears fill my eyes and I have trouble seeing what's happening in front of me. Sydney is bleeding to death, and even though Mystica and the other nurse are trying to save her, I don't think they're going to be able to.

I almost feel like she's already gone.

And the baby… isn't breathing.

One of the nurses shouts, "Mystica! We need another pair of hands!"

"I can't right now!" the healer shouts back.

Without thinking, I hurry over. Still crying a bit, I ask, "What can I do?"

"Hold her like this," the nurse instructs me, and I quickly do as she asks as she and the other nurse do something to try and clear the baby's airway.

She feels too cold to me. She is so still. And her heart…. I can't hear it.

She's just a tiny thing… with dark hair and a beautiful, sweet little face. Her eyes are closed, scrunched, and her little hands are fisted but otherwise limp.

My tears are streaming faster now. I try to keep it together. I can see that the nurses are worried, but they're not crying like I am. I wonder if they've seen other babies pass away. I want to pull my hand away from the little body to swipe at my eyes, but I can't let go of the little body.

Splashes from my tears drip onto her little face, wetting her eyes and sliding down her nose as if the baby is crying, too.

"I don't think we're going to get a pulse," one of the nurses, an older woman with streaks of gray through her dark hair, says, looking at the younger one standing next to me.

Her words only make my tears fall faster. They continue to splash down the baby's face, coating her lips, and landing on her chest.

And then... as the nurses set their tools aside, giving up, there is a loud gasp and an inhale of air before the loudest, highest-pitched, sweetest sound I've ever heard hits my ears.

The baby is crying! She's crying and wiggling and turning bright red! And she is mad as hell, and it makes me laugh because I'm so thankful that the Moon Goddess has spared this little life.

"Holy–" the older nurse says, her eyes wide. "How did that happen?"

"I don't know," the younger one says. "But let's make sure we keep her crying so she can clear those lungs."

The younger nurse picks the baby up, wrapping her in a towel as she rubs her little body, keeping the newborn screeching. I don't understand exactly why they are doing that, but it's not my concern. I'm just so thankful that Sydney's daughter is still alive.

I have a feeling she will make it.

And then I turn around.

Mystica has blood all over her. It coats her arms up to her elbows, and is splashed all over the apron she has on over her clothes. I'm sure it's soaked through and stained the floral fabric of the full-length dress she wears.

She's not hurrying anymore, though. A defeated look sits on her face. I am confused as I move toward her. "Wh-why aren't you... sewing her up?" Sydney's abdomen is still open.

Mystica shakes her head. "I'm sorry, dear, but there was nothing I could do. The baby was stuck in the birth canal. Even though she's not a big child, the mother's pelvis was too narrow. By the time we realized she wasn't going to be able to come out... the damage had been done. I'll need to examine the placenta, but I believe there was a problem with the placenta as well. That would explain all of the bleeding."

I don't know what she's talking about. I haven't read any books about pregnancy yet because, even though I'm a breeder, I'm not pregnant. Not that I know of anyway.

Looking at Sydney makes me want to never be pregnant....

My eyes go to the baby. She's not screaming anymore, and the nurses have her cleaned up. She is wearing a diaper and they are dressing her in a little yellow onesie.

Seeing her makes me want a child, but seeing Sydney makes me want to grab the needle Mystica was using and sew myself up....

"Is the baby's father somewhere in the castle?" the older nurse asks Mystica.

She shakes her head. "No, he's deceased. This baby is an orphan."

My mouth drops open like I want to say something, but no words come out.

The nurse says, "We have several families that will be willing to take her. We'll just have to find the right one."

"Yes, she'll be well taken care of," Mystica says. "But then... I believe the Moon Goddess might've had a different plan for this child."

"What do you mean?" It's the younger nurse who speaks up now.

"Well," Mystica says, "she was stillborn. The child was dead. For several minutes as the two of you worked on her, she was already gone."

"Yes, but we brought her back," the older nurse says, and I remember how she had given up on the baby just before she started to breathe.

"No," Mystica says. "The two of you did a fine job, as you have been trained to do. But it was not your efforts that allowed the child to suck air into her lungs."

"It wasn't?" the younger nurse asks, her forehead creased.

Mystica shakes her head. "No, it wasn't." Then her eyes turn to me, and she adds, "It was you."

WHAT CHILD IS THIS?

Maddox

"You can't do this to me! Don't you know who I am?"

The sound of Zabrina's wailing echoes down the corridor as I exit the dungeon, tired of listening to her scream at me that I can't execute her.

I'm the fucking Alpha King. I'll do whatever the hell I want....

As I approach the stairs, Beta Seth comes from another hallway and joins me. "Did she tell you anything?" he asks me as we take the stairs quickly. I am tired of being down below the castle where everything smells like urine.

With a sigh, I say, "Not anything that's honest. At least, I don't think a damn word she said was true." The fact that she is blaming Alpha Grant for all of this makes me want to scoff.

But then again, stranger things have happened.

"What did she say?" Seth asks me. We reach the top of the first flight of stairs and then walk through the main dungeon, the one where the regular prisoners who haven't killed anyone or tried to assassinate the King's breeder are kept. "Did you get anything useful from her?"

"No, I don't think so. She blamed Alpha Grant," I explain to him.

"What?" Beta Seth makes a noise in the back of his throat that makes me think he is just as skeptical as I am.

"Yeah, she made up an elaborate story about how Alpha Grant and her father were working together to get me to marry her so she could drug me on our wedding night, and then her dad would kill me so that Alpha Grant could be the new king, and her father would be his second." I see the final staircase appear in front of us, and I want to speed up. As much as I need to evaluate this situation with Seth, I also want to see Isla—madly.

"That's ridiculous," he says. "Alpha Grant is completely loyal to you."

"That's what I thought, too," I reply. With another sigh, I start up the stairs. "I think it's probably worth doing some investigating, considering I thought that Alpha Jordan was on our side as well."

I glance over at Beta Seth and see that he is nodding. "It wouldn't hurt, I suppose, sir."

"All right. Let's get one of our best investigators on that. Did you get anything from Vinny's men?"

He shakes his head. "No, not yet. I've just got them in the dungeon now, making them uncomfortable and squirming for a bit."

"That's probably for the best. In a while, go back down there and pick the strongest one and let the others listen to him scream for a while. One of the others may break and give us any information we can potentially use to justify their executions."

I can tell by Seth's wide-eyed expression he doesn't think I should kill all of them, but I've already made up my mind. "They will die for what they did in Duster pack. It doesn't matter to me that Alpha Hayes wasn't an ally of mine. What happened there was barbaric, and it will not happen in my kingdom ever again. If I have to make examples out of these assholes, I don't mind doing so."

"Yes, Alpha," he says, tipping his head, and I can tell he won't fight me on this even though he's still unsure.

"I'll take care of it, Alpha," Beta Seth says. "I assume you're going to check on Isla?"

I nod. "I assume she's in her room?" I hope that she's been able to get some rest while I've been away. She has to be exhausted after everything that's gone on recently. I'm not sure why I assume that Seth knows where she is when he has been busy since I arrived back at the castle, but the face he is making tells me not only does he know where Isla is, something is wrong.

My brow furrows as I step closer to him. "What is it, Seth?" I hear a waiver in my own voice as my thoughts run wild. I told Isla not to leave the castle again without speaking to me first, but who knows what she might've done.

I was getting weary of having to find her....

"It's not Isla," he says, which makes my pulse slow a bit, but whatever is wrong has something to do with Isla. I can tell by the way he reacted to me saying her name. "Then what the hell is it, Seth?"

He takes a deep breath and lets it out slowly, his bottom lip trembling slightly. "She, uh... she's with Sydney's baby."

Confusion sweeps over me as I consider each of his words carefully. "Sydney had her baby?"

His head rocks back and forth as his hands slide into the pockets of his slacks. "About an hour ago."

"How is she?" I ask, meaning Sydney.

When Beta Seth shakes his head back and forth, I understand his meaning without a single word leaving his lips.

That doesn't prevent him from telling me.

"There was some sort of complication with the baby. One of Mystica's nurses filled me in via mind-link around the time that you arrived back at the castle. I guess the baby was too big for Sydney or something, and by the time Mystica realized that, it was too late. That and the... what's it called? Placebo?"

"Placenta?" I say, realizing Beta Seth knows very little about birthing babies.

"Yeah... that was... in the wrong position or something? Anyway, it made Sydney lose a lot of blood, and Mystica just couldn't save her."

I'm not sure what to say about that. I had only known Sydney for a couple of days, but she seemed like a sweet, if extremely misguided, young woman. It was clear her parents cared about her, even if they had sent her to live with the man who had ultimately taken advantage of her and put her in this situation where she ended up pregnant and lost her life.

"I suppose I should call her father," I say.

Beta Seth nods. "He will probably appreciate hearing it from you. But... there is the matter of... the baby."

I stare at Seth for a moment, trying to figure out what he's getting at. It seems to me that the baby will just go to Sydney's parents. Both of the child's parents are deceased. I would assume they'd be the next of kin.

I don't speak before Seth says, "Her parents clearly weren't equipped to raise her, so I doubt they will want to raise the child. Mystica said that there are people here who will raise the girl. But... apparently, the child wasn't breathing for quite some time after she was born, and the nurses couldn't get the girl back. It wasn't until Isla came to help and her tears landed on the baby's face that she began to breathe. So... Mystica has it in her head that Isla brought her back to life. She believes it is a sign from the Moon Goddess."

My mouth drops open as Seth is speaking, and when he finishes, I don't know what to say. Part of me almost wants to laugh because it sounds so preposterous, and I remember some of the other things I have learned Mystica has been telling Isla.

I would've preferred Isla stay away from the strange woman from Maatua, especially since Isla has it in her head that she is from the island herself, which I don't think is possible.

Clearing my throat, I ask, "Where is she?"

"The east wing, third door on the right," he says.

With a nod, I thank him and head in that direction.

I head in that direction, walking quickly, barely acknowledging the servants who pass me and nod in respect as I go. Normally, I would greet all of them, but my mind is preoccupied.

As I enter the east wing, I see Mystica coming down the hallway, and I instantly want to shake her and ask her what the hell she is thinking, filling Isla's mind with all of these ridiculous stories that can't be true.

But I have a great deal of respect for the healer, even if she has been making my life more difficult lately.

I see that she has blood on her dress, and her hands look freshly scrubbed but tinged red. "Oh, Your Majesty," she says with a little head bob. "Have you heard about what happened?"

"Yes," I say, my tone grave. "I'm sorry to hear about Sydney."

"I am sorry I couldn't save her. It was not a typical labor, and the baby was just too big for her tiny pelvis. But then… the baby wasn't breathing and–"

I interrupt her. I don't need to hear the nonsense again. "Where is Isla?" I ask her.

She makes a face at me, clearly not appreciating my interrupting her statement. "She's in there with the child." Lifting a hand, she gestures at the third door on the right, just as Seth had told me. "In there. With the baby."

I am not too surprised to hear she is with the baby, but I'd be lying if I didn't think it was odd. My only hope is that Isla doesn't actually think she has magical tears that can bring the dead back to life.

"Thank you, Mystica. I'm sure you did everything you could for the girl. I'll call her parents later." I make a move toward the door, but she reaches out and grabs my arm.

"You can ignore it, but that won't make it false," she says, her tone eerie.

My eyes go from her hand on my arm to her face, and she is unwavering as she stares at me, the look on her face reminding me of the pack elders that used to consult my father–all-knowing.

I manage a smile. "I need to see Isla right away," I say as if that's the only reason for my interruption.

The pack healer clears her throat and releases my arm, and I can tell she doesn't believe me, and she shouldn't. Even though it's true I want to see Isla, that's not why I cut her off.

Once I'm free, I move toward the door again, hoping Mystica will just go on her way. After a moment, she does, but I feel her eyes on me long enough to leave my hair standing on end and an uncomfortable feeling settling in my bones.

My hand fastens around the knob, and I slowly twist it, pushing it open as silently as I can, in case the baby is sleeping.

I walk in to see Isla sitting in a rocking chair by the window, slowly moving back and forth, a tiny bundle wrapped in a pink blanket in her arms.

Our eyes meet, and she draws me across the room, the door clicking closed behind me.

She is as beautiful as ever, and she is holding the baby like a natural.

Like a mother.

But this isn't her baby–it isn't my baby.

I just have to hope she isn't thinking of trying to keep this child because, if she does, it might make her reluctant to have our own, and even though my feelings for Isla have moved beyond mere breeder, I still need her to do her job.

"HI," she whispers. I give her a small smile, not sure what to say. The baby is clearly sleeping. As I come closer, she tips the girl's face toward me. She is a beautiful child.

She is not our child.

"Alpha King Maddox… meet Sydney's daughter…. Her name is… Maddy. After you."

SHE'S NOT YOURS

Isla

MADDOX IS LOOKING at me like he's afraid I've lost my mind. His eyebrows are nearly touching, he's so concerned, and he's keeping his distance. I imagine him bolting out the door and not stopping until he reaches at least the same point in the woods where he intercepted me a few days ago.

I want to ask him why he's looking at me like that, but I suppose I already know, at least to a degree. He thinks I'm crazy for naming the baby after him. He thinks I've grown too attached.

And he's right. I have, but he doesn't understand the situation. At least, I don't think he has. I doubt anyone has told him exactly what happened, but even if Mystica or someone did explain it to him, he can't possibly understand the connection I have to this child.

"Maddy?" he finally says, a lilt in his voice that shows me he's either frightened or overly concerned.

I nod. "Her mom wanted her to be named Isla, but I didn't think that was a good idea." It was something Sydney had mentioned when she was in the middle of labor, that if she had a girl, she wanted her named for me, and if she had a boy, she wanted to name her son after the king.

Maddox is towering over me, and it makes me uncomfortable. I gesture to another chair across the room from me, and he lets out a sigh as he crosses to where it sits, running a hand through his hair. He doesn't just sit, though. He drags it closer to us and then sits.

I look down at Maddy. She's asleep. Her tiny mouth is pursed, and she looks like she's either preparing to wake up and scream or getting ready to blow a kiss. It makes me giggle, even though my heart is heavy because Sydney never got to see her face, and this child will never know either of her parents.

The king clears his throat, and I return my attention to him. The look on his face tells me he is trying to choose his words carefully. He is leaning forward in the chair, his elbows propped on his knees, and he is alternating his glances between the baby and me.

When he begins to speak, I recognize the tone. He is addressing me like I am fragile, sort of like he did when I had almost died.

"Isla," he begins. "She's a lovely baby. I'm glad she made it. Mystica told me it was… touch and go for a bit. You were kind and brave to stay in there with Sydney when you didn't really even know her, and wanting to help this little one speaks to your good heart."

My eyes are glued on his face right now, and even though he's not all that much older than me, only nine years, he sounds like he is my father telling me that I can't do something I've always wanted to do.

"But… you can't keep her."

I don't say anything, only continue to look at him, attempting to process what he's said to me.

"The baby," Maddox continues. "I'm not sure what your plans were, sweetheart, but you know that you can't keep the baby, right?"

I hear his words, and they are registering in my brain, but I still can't speak.

Mostly because I don't know what to say.

It's not that I disagree with him. I know that it's not a good idea for me to try and keep Maddy and raise her as my own. After all, I've never had a baby before, and I'm not the best choice of mother for her. I remember Mystica's nurses mentioning families that would take her in, but after Mystica mentioned that she thought I had saved the baby–with my tears–she'd implied she thought perhaps the Moon Goddess thought that Maddy was meant to be with me.

I had internalized that at some point. I had made the leap from this child needs a family to I love her to I will wrap her in my arms and never let her go.

But now, sitting here, staring at the serious expression on the man I love's face, I realize he is right.

I don't know anything about taking care of a baby, and ever since I became the breeder to the Alpha King, I've imagined the two of us raising our own baby, together.

Yet, he is right. I'm not ready to take care of Maddy… and I'm not ready to take care of our baby either. How am I supposed to be a breeder when I would make such a terrible mother?

It's not like I've never had any experience with babies because I helped my mom with my brothers, especially my younger ones. But she did all of the hard stuff. All I did was bring her their diapers or pick up their toys.

No, Maddox is right. I can't do this.

"Isla?" he says, and his concerned expression looks even more profound. "What is the matter?"

Shaking my head, I say, "You're right. I can't keep her. I'm not fit to be a mother." I glance down at the sweet child in my arms and wonder how I haven't managed to lose her or drop her on her head in just the short amount of time I've been holding her. I am incapable of feeding her, and even though I heard Mystica say she would find a wet nurse, that's not the same as me actually being able to provide what this child needs like a real mom.

"No, sweetheart," he says, reaching forward to put his hands on my arms on either side of Maddy. "That's not what I was saying. I know you'll be a great mother! I have no doubt in my mind that when you and I have a baby, you will be a terrific mother."

I stare at him, looking into his eyes to see if he is telling the truth. He seems to really believe that.

Now, I am questioning Maddox's sanity.

"But that's just it," he continues, letting go of me and leaning back in his chair as he drags a hand down his chin. "You and I are going to have a baby. Hopefully very soon, and when we do… you'll need to give all of your attention to our baby."

What he is saying makes perfect sense, but now that my moments of panic have subsided, I have to wonder, what will become of this sweet girl? And why can't I take care of her while I am pregnant? And after that, she'll be at least nine months old, probably older, so why can't I just have help? The father of my baby will be the king, after all.…

But I can see in his eyes that he doesn't want to raise this baby. He doesn't want her here. And I wonder if it's because of the deal that Alpha, the one Maddox killed, this baby's father, had tried to bargain with him about this very child.

It's not fair of me to ask him to do something like that, especially not when I know that he will find her a good home with a family that loves her.

I take a deep breath and realize my bottom lip is quivering. "Can we make sure that whoever raises her loves her? And appreciates her?"

"Of course," he says. He leans forward, and he's touching me again, this time on the leg, and it helps. "You can help, if you'd like. I don't want to put it all on you, but you can certainly help. If you want to." Tears begin to cloud my vision. "Do you want to help find her parents?"

I nod, trying to will myself not to cry. "Yes," is all I can manage.

"Good," he says. "It's usually a job of the Luna to help find orphaned children a new home. Rebecca was very good at that."

The way he says the words is confusing to me. It's almost like he's trying to say that it would be good for me to help find Maddy a new home because that's a job of the Luna–as if I might need to worry about the job of a Luna.

I don't know why he'd be saying that. He's already told everyone that he's never taking another wife, never finding another Luna.

But earlier, when we were talking about our baby, he made it clear he intended for me to care for the child. Unlike most breeders who just deliver the baby and go back to wherever they came from or go off to the next man who needs an heir but can't have one with his mate for some reason....

I don't ask Maddox why he said that, but I can see on his face that he is asking himself the same question.

Sniffling a few times, I take a deep breath and try to let it go. I don't want him to think I'm dwelling on it. I never thought he would make me his Luna, and I'm not going to imply that I think that now.

I've never wanted to be a Luna, and I'm pretty sure I still don't want to because it seems like the sort of job a person has to have broad shoulders to carry, and most of the time I don't.

No, I don't think I want to be a Luan.

But... I do want to be Maddox's wife....

And if being the latter means being the former, then I'll have to be both.

Maddox leans forward and brushes a stray tear off of my cheek, smiling at me. "I care about you very much, Isla," he says, and I know that he does.

I also think that means he loves me, but he's too afraid to tell me.

"I love you," I say, and his smile widens.

With Maddy between us, he finds my lips. It's a sweet, gentle kiss, and it makes warmth spread through my chest.

As he pulls away, there's a light knock on the door. He doesn't take his eyes off of me as he calls for the person to come in.

She catches my attention though. A petite woman with dark black hair pulled up in a bun who is probably in her mid-thirties walks in. "Pardon me, Sir," she says with her eyes on the floor. "Mystica sent me for the little one to see if she wants to eat."

"Yes, of course, Blanca." He stands and moves his chair back to where it came from as she approaches me, and I ascertain she's the wet nurse. It astounds me how he knows everyone's name.

I stand and stare at Maddy for a moment. I don't want to let her go, but I understand it's best for everyone if I do. I can't help but think that Mystica is right, though, that we have a connection that will come back to us eventually, no matter what.

Besides, she's not going anywhere just yet. I can see her later.

I lean down and kiss her head, and she grunts in her sleep.

Not knowing what to say, I hand her to the wet nurse who smiles and nods at me, and then I move aside, my arms feeling cold and empty.

Then, Maddox takes my hand to lead me out the door, and the coldness isn't so noticeable anymore.

DID HE SAY THAT TO ME, OR WAS IT A DREAM?

Isla

BACK IN MY ROOM, I can still smell the sting of the chemicals someone used to clean the mess up from when Sydney's water broke.

It seems like that happened ages ago, but it was really only a matter of hours. Maddox still has my hand, and when I pause and stare at the spot where Sydney was standing when she came into my room, he has to stop walking. "What is it, Isla?" he asks me, his tone so gentle, no one would ever imagine he was known as a ruthless killer.

Shaking my head, I try to jar the memory free so it can float away, but it won't come loose. "Uhm, it's just… Sydney. When she came to get me, she was so scared, and I thought she didn't really have anything to be afraid of. But clearly, I was wrong."

He seems to be putting the pieces of the puzzle together now. He must not have known that she was here, that she'd come into my room, but I see his nostrils flare slightly as he catches on that more happened here than he'd first realized. It's not uncommon for my room to smell of cleaner; Poppy likes to keep things spotless. But Maddox's well-trained nose probably picks up on the other very faint odor that no one would even notice if they didn't know that a pregnant woman had been standing here before, and then something had needed cleaning. I don't think I would smell it if I was over by my bed, but I can smell it now.

"I'm so sorry." Maddox pulls me close to him and holds me tight, and I lean my head on his muscular chest, using him for support.

My mind goes to a dark place again. I can't help it, even though I know I shouldn't even allow myself to think of it. Someday, I will be pregnant, if Maddox gets his wish. I will have a baby. What if the same problems arise? I could die.

Even if I didn't die, I had watched Sydney go through a lot of pain before she got the medicine she needed to make the labor pains subside. I can't imagine what her last few hours of life must've felt like. Not only was she suffering, but she was also terrified.

As if he's reading my mind, Maddox says, "It won't happen to you, sweetie." His lips are warm as they press against the top of my head.

I look up at him. "How do you know?" I can't help the question. Ordinarily, I would just nod and pray that he is right, but it sounds bold of him to me to assume he can tell that I will not be one of the unfortunate women who loses her life in childbirth.

Even worse, I can't imagine what it must be like to be one of the women who lives–but loses her child.

As horrible as the first scenario is, the second would be even worse to me.

"I would never let anything happen to you," Maddox tells me, looking into my eyes.

I can't help the soft smile that forms on my lips as I stare into his deep orbs. With every fiber of my being, I want to believe him. But I know that I can't because, even though he might be the most powerful wolf in the entire kingdom, he doesn't have that kind of power.

Before I can say anything in response, he cracks a smile at me. "Why don't I draw you a bath? I'm sure you'll feel much better after a nice, relaxing soak in the tub with all of your favorite… smelly things."

That causes me to chuckle. He has no idea what to call the bath salts and other items in my bathroom. "That sounds lovely," I tell him. "But it would sound even better if you say you'll stay with me."

An eyebrow arches as he considers my proposition. "I'm not sure we'll both fit in the tub," he tells me.

I grin even wider at him. "I know you're a big guy, but I think we can make it work. We've done it before." Has he forgotten we've already bathed together a time or two?

"Yeah, but all of those flowery smells might make it a little harder on me when I go down to the dungeon later to bust some heads." That's the truth of his reservations, I now understand.

"Well, you could always just stay here tonight, with me, and do all of that tomorrow." I lift up on my tiptoes so that my lips are hovering close to his.

"You make a pretty good argument," he says, his warm breath fanning across my lips. He smells like cinnamon, and I want to taste him.

His mouth moves toward mine so slowly, it seems to take ages for his lips to brush against mine, and even then, I'm not quite getting enough of him to satisfy my craving–and he knows it. I can feel the teasing when he lingers just short of plunging in and giving me what I'm longing for. I can't help but run a hand up the back of his head, stretching as tall as I can to coax him closer.

A soft chuckle is muffled by my mouth as he finally gives in, and finally, his tongue is mingling with mine, and I do my best not to devour him, even though my want feels insatiable. He lifts me up, his hands nestles around my waist, and I launch myself the rest of the way, my legs wrapping around him so that we are one unit again, just as we are meant to be.

He continues to kiss me as he moves to the bathroom. It's no wonder he's a terror on the battlefield. His senses allow him to navigate without his eyes and when he sits me down on the counter in the bathroom, it's as if he glided there on air.

I don't want to unwrap my legs from him, and I don't want to let him go, not even just the short amount of time it will take for him to turn on the bath and take off our clothes. He tries to take a step back, but I clench my legs tighter and make a whimpering sound, my lips suctioning to his.

Again, he is laughing in my mouth, and I let him because I don't care if he thinks I'm funny, silly, or even pathetic at the moment. The yearning I have for him is a raging fire now, and allowing even the narrowest puff of oxygen between us will just cause the flames to grow.

Somehow, he manages to unwind himself from me, and I am forced to release his luscious lips. "I've got to turn the water on, baby, and dump all of your… stuff in there."

I have a feeling we will smell like a strange concoction of different floral scents if I let him do this on his own. "Just the pink jar," I tell him as he steps toward the tub. I feel cold in a way that has nothing to do with the room temperature when he moves away from me.

While he is away, I begin to take off my clothing, my fingers shaking slightly on the buttons that prevent me from rushing too much. I hear the water turn on and then the unscrewing of a lid. My nose is suddenly assaulted by the strong smell of roses, and I know he has emptied quite a bit of my favorite bath salts into the tub.

When Maddox returns and sees me stripping, he narrows his eyes slightly and purses his lips. "Uhm, I believe that's my job, young lady," he says, getting a giggle out of me. He comes back to me, catching my lips with his as he finishes taking my clothing off, and when he goes to pull my skirt and panties off of my hips, I lift my bottom for him. Soon enough, I am completely naked in front of him while he is fully clothed. I don't feel vulnerable, though. I feel well taken care of.

He steps back and begins to take off his own clothing, his eyes wandering over my body as he does so. I bite my bottom lip, watching each muscle emerge from beneath the veil of his clothing. When he gets down to his boxers, I can hardly contain myself, I want to feel him so badly. I'm practically rocking off of the counter, my body magnetically pulled toward his.

He wants to tease me, I can tell, because of the grin on his face. But he's also hard as rock. I can see the outline of his cock pressing against his underwear.

So rather than continue to torture me, he finishes with his underwear and then scoops me up off of the counter and moves us both quickly to the bathtub. The water is warm as we sink into it, but all I can think about are his wet hands as they glide up to my breasts.

He leans back against the back of the tub, and I straddle him, my mouth exploring his as if we've never kissed before. He tugs on my nipples, bringing them to life as I move to mount him.

I'm so wet that his entire dick slides right in, and then I have to take a moment to savor the feeling of him, stretching my walls and filling me completely. His hands ripple down my sides to my hips as I start to move, and he moves with me. The water splashes up the sides of the tub, and eventually, it will spill over, but neither of us cares. For that matter, the faucet is still on, but whether or not we will pause to shut it off doesn't even enter my mind. All I can think about is Maddox, my king, my lover, the man who knows how to take me so far beyond the edge I can no longer find myself.

Releasing my mouth, he traces hot kisses down my neck and finds a nipple with his teeth as I moan and rock harder against him, the waves lapping up over my breasts now. He doesn't care if the rose-flavored water gets in his mouth as he continues to suck and lick me.

I'm coming hard and fast and when he senses that, he drops a hand to find my clit and gives it a few sharp rubs. It sends me over the edge, and the rest of the world fades away as all I can think about is him and how he makes me feel so completely… euphoric.

I don't know how long my mind is among the clouds as I pant for air and cry out his name, but eventually, he fills me with his essence as well, and then, we both go still. I collapse, my head cradled between his shoulder and neck, the world quiet around me. I have no idea when he turned the water off. I don't care.

After a while, he begins to wash me with some vanilla-scented body wash. He spins me around and nestles me safely between his legs, his cock, which is beginning to stiffen again, pressed against my back.

I am starting to fall asleep, cocooned by his embrace in the warm, fragrant water. As I drift off, I hear my own voice saying, "I love you so much, Maddox."

His response might have been real, or it might just be a dream, but as I lose consciousness, I think I hear him say, "I love you, too."

STOLEN IN THE NIGHT

Maddox

LEAVING a nice warm bed where I was snuggled up in the arms of the woman who loves me, the woman I have finally admitted I love, too, wasn't the easiest thing I've done in my life, but as I head to the dungeon the morning after we brought in the assholes who slaughtered the innocent people in the house at Duster pack, I know my job is about to get all the more difficult.

I am hopeful that some of the difficult work has already begun. While Isla had slept with her head against my chest, I'd utilized the mind-link to let my most persuasive warriors have a turn or two with the bastards. My hope was that I would find a bunch of broken men who had all confessed to their crimes so that when I had them terminated, no one would feel any sympathy for them.

Dealing with Zabrina would be more difficult, but that could wait.

I take the steps quickly, feeling like the king I am. My mind goes back to the sight at the house, all of the blood, the dismembered bodies, the crying children.

No one who was there deserves to see another sunrise.

"Your Majesty," Blade says, meeting me at the bottom of the stairs. He is aptly named; his father was a strong warrior and wanted to raise a son who would carry on his legacy, so he'd named his child after a weapon—and then he had become one.

I give him a sharp nod in greeting before I ask, "Have they all confessed?" I have no doubt, if anyone in this castle is capable of getting full confessions from the prisoners, it's Blade. The only one more capable of doing so is me.

"Yes, they've all confessed to being present at the murders in Duster pack," he says as we walk down the narrow hallway side by side. Our shoulders are so broad, we nearly scrape along the stone walls as we go, and whenever we come to a light on the wall, he steps slightly behind me. "We do have a bit of a hiccup, though, one I thought you'd want to handle yourself."

I turn to face him, pausing almost at the section of the dungeon where the men are being kept. "What's that?" I ask.

He clears his throat, his eyes twitching just a bit. Even though he's been up all night, I don't see a trace of tiredness on his face, just concern.

Concern that he might let me down, something he's never done before. But he's one of the few I can say that about.

"They say they had no choice," he replies, his hands behind his back, standing up straight and tall, which makes him nearly my height.

I arch an eyebrow. "What the fuck is that supposed to mean?" I inquire. "Of course, they had a choice! Vinny wasn't even their Alpha, not that an Alpha can order anyone to do something immoral and make them follow through."

He shakes his head slightly, his dark hair looking slightly gray in the light as it bounces off of his part. "No, sir, that's not what I mean. Most of them are saying that Vinny had members of their family held in a cell in the Alpha's residency with other guards there ready to kill them if they didn't go through with the plan. Most of them didn't agree to the plan and had told him so before they even left Hill Country pack territory. That's when Vinny decided he'd have to use some of the other guards to help… persuade these men."

My eyes are still locked on his for a few seconds as he finishes speaking before I pinch the bridge of my nose and squeeze my eyes closed, dropping my head so that when I open them again, I'm looking at a blood splatter between my shoes on the stone floor.

"Are you fucking kidding me?" I ask. I don't have to take that into consideration—but it is something to think about.

Blade shrugs. "That's what they said, five of them, all in separate interrogation rooms."

These particular interrogation rooms were less about asking and more about ass-whipping.

Before I say more, he continues, "One of them said that they threatened to kill his two-year-old daughter."

"All right," I say, shaking my head. "Let me speak to him. What's his name?"

"Mike Weaver, Sire." Blade gestures with his hand, and I proceed down the hallway to the third cell on the right.

I look through the window and see a man slumped on the floor against the wall, his clothes covered in blood, one shoe missing, and rips in what used to be a white shirt. He is staring at the ground, but I can see enough of his face to know that he'll likely be permanently disfigured from the beating he's taken since he arrived here.

I gesture for the guard at the door to open it for me and walk in.

Immediately, Mike Weaver tries to get to his feet, but it's difficult for him. He pushes off of the concrete, grimaces, sinks down, and then tries again, but I raise a hand to let him know he doesn't have to get up. Not right now anyway.

Blade takes a position behind me as I look him over. The man is staring up at me, his dark eyes wide, even though they are bruised and bloodshot. His nose, which is rather large, juts off to the side, and his lip is covered in dry blood. One cheekbone is sliced open and the other is misshapen. The way he is holding his left arm makes me think it might be broken, and as my eyes drop to his black slacks, where the right knee is all torn out, I can see why he couldn't get up. His leg is bent at an odd angle.

My guys roughed him up good.

"Mike is it?" I ask.

"Yes, Alpha King Maddox, Sir," he says, his eyes glued to my shoes now as he realizes he probably shouldn't stare right into my face.

"I'd like to hear the story you told Blade about how you came to find your-self in Alpha Hayes's house," I tell him, folding one arm under my elbow as I stroke my chin.

"Yes, Sir," he repeats, clearing his throat. It's obvious his mouth is dry, and I have a feeling, since he's missing a few teeth and the rest of them are pink, his tongue is probably sticky from blood.

With a deep breath, he says, "I worked for Alpha Bryant. I was a member of his guard. When Vinny took over, he wanted to do something to impress you. We'd all heard Alpha Jordan say that he thought his daughter would be looking for help from Duster pack, so Vinny had us stake out the location along the river's edge. He came, too." He blinks a few times, looking uneasy.

"Go on," I insist, rebalancing myself on the balls of my feet.

"Well, sure enough, she surfaced down by where Lou Robb was standing, and he let us all know using the mind-link. Vinny had us move down there, quietly, and I figured we were just going to snatch her up and then let you know we had her." He tries to shrug, but a pain radiates through his likely broken arm, so he sits still.

"But that's not what happened?" I ask, knowing that there was more to it because of the bloody scene. I shove my hands in the pockets of my suit jacket and wait.

"No, Sir," he says. "We did snatch her up and put her in the trunk of one of our vehicles. But then… well, Vinny had us circle back around and move into the village, Duster pack village."

"Did he say why?" I ask.

"Not at first, but when one of the bolder guys asked how come, Vinny said he didn't want the other Alpha coming after what was his. We all looked at one another and knew that he had something up his sleeve, something that was likely to start a war. I was the first to say I wasn't comfortable with that, and then Vinny said, 'I thought you might say that.'"

Mike takes an uneasy breath, and I wait, knowing he'll continue when he's ready.

It takes him a few seconds to continue. "When I asked him what he meant, he said, 'You know where Jessica is right now?'" Mike looks at me, and I see tears filling his eyes. "That's my daughter. She just turned two last month. Of course, knowing what time it was, I told him I figured she's home in bed. But he just starts laughing, and I know I'm in trouble."

I hear Blade moving slightly behind me and wonder if even the assassin is uneasy. He has a little girl now, so I can imagine he might be.

"I tried mind-linking my wife, but I found out later she was asleep. She had no idea anyone had broken into our house and stolen our baby. In the night, the other guards, the younger, inexperienced ones, the ones that had wanted to really impress Vinny, they'd gone all over the village and taken all the kids. All of 'em."

I am puzzled now. "Wait a minute—even the ones that belonged to people who weren't in Duster pack?"

He nods. "That's right, Your Majesty. That's why, when you showed up, everyone came out to fight."

It's my turn to stare wide-eyed as the breath leaves my lungs. "What? That bastard still had the kids in a cell?"

"That's right. They've been released now that Vinny's dead. A lot of the guys you killed in the battle were his arrogant bastards, too. Anyway, last night… we didn't have any choice, Sir. We had to kill those people at Alpha Hayes's house. If we didn't… our kids would've been killed. And even those of us who didn't have any kids, they didn't want to see any of our kids die." The tears slip from his eyes now, mingling with the blood from his cheeks to form streaks of rose-colored water that further stain his ruined shirt.

It seems Vinny, even in his death, has left me in quite a conundrum. Can I punish his warriors for doing what they were told to do while Vinny had their family members held against their will and was threatening to kill them?

Did that make taking other innocent lives okay?

It didn't. But at the same time, I don't know what I would've done in their place. If someone was threatening to kill Isla if I didn't destroy a rival, would I do it?

"We didn't have a choice," Mike says between sobs.

I haven't made up my mind yet, but I do know one thing for sure. In a deep growl, I remind Mike, "You always have a choice."

Now, the choice is mine....

LET'S NOT ARGUE

Isla

MADDOX WAS GONE when I opened my eyes. I shouldn't have been surprised. He told me last night that he had a lot to do, but I insisted he stay with me, and he did.

I had fallen asleep on him in the bathtub, so he probably didn't have much of a choice.

Now, I am sitting at the dining table eating my breakfast while Poppy fake dusts because she doesn't need to keep dusting.

"I just feel really bad for that baby," she is saying. I take a piece of toast and break it apart before putting a small piece in my mouth.

I haven't gone to check on Maddy yet, but I will. Not because I want to keep her. I understand now that Maddox is right. It's not a good idea. I'm trying to come to terms with the fact that I'm expected to do everything Sydney just did yesterday soon enough–except for the dying part. That I'd like to avoid.

"I feel bad for her, too," I manage between bites.

"I mean, in this day and age, now does that happen?" Piper continues. And I don't have an answer for her. "Was Mystica really trying?"

"Yes." That's all I can say in response to that question because I have always had such amazing faith in Mystica, but she was struggling yesterday, and I have to think it's just because the situation was so dire.

"Well, I think it's terrible. I heard that the bed was so bloody, they had to take the mattress out last night and burn it," Poppy says as she runs her duster over some of the trinkets on the dresser.

"That's not true." I don't know why I care what the servants are gossiping about, but I know that's not true. "We put a shower curtain down on the bed to protect the mattress."

"Maybe it soaked through," Poppy adds with a shrug.

I know that it's not possible, but I don't want to argue with her. She's my friend, after all, and it's not worth either one of us getting upset over. The bottom line is that Sydney died, her baby needs new parents, and they won't be me.

No longer pretending to work, Poppy pulls out the chair across from me and sits down, crossing her legs, and balances the duster on her knee. "It's a shame." She pulls in a deep breath and lets it out before she adds, "I never really liked Sydney, but I didn't want her to die. Now, Zabrina, on the other hand." She rolls her eyes.

My stomach constricts, and I'm glad I haven't eaten any of the greasy bacon that still sits on one side of my plate. I'm not sure I would be able to stay here without running to throw up if I had.

The fact that Zabrina is back in the castle makes me super nervous. I know that Maddox will do everything possible to make sure she can't escape this time, but I'm still worried. She's gotten away before. I know that she's not in the same shape she was in before, that she probably won't be able to flirt her way past the guards, but that doesn't mean she won't find a way to get out of the dungeon and make her way up here to torture me.

I'm not the meek little girl I was when I first arrived here, and I know I would fight back, but if she caught me while I was sleeping or in the shower or something, or if she managed to drug me, well…. I'm a bit preoccupied with thinking of ways she might kill me.

"You could keep her."

Poppy's statement comes from nowhere. I have a glass of orange juice in my hand and am getting ready to take a drink when her words hit my ears. I don't take a sip. Instead, I set it down. "Zabrina?"

I know that she isn't talking about my nemesis, but the way the conversation is flowing, it sounds like that's what she might mean.

"No," she says with a chuckle. "No one should keep her. She should die a miserable, painful death. Every one of us who's had a hand in fixing what she's done around should get a few blows in before she bleeds out."

I wipe my hands off on my napkin and push my plate toward the middle of the table. I'm completely over this breakfast. I don't want to get a blow in on Zabrina, but I do want her to be punished. As to whether or not she should die, I waiver on that. I've never been one to think that the Moon Goddess wants evil people to be killed for just anything, but Zabrina is a cold-blooded murderer, and to me, that makes her even more deserving of death than most.

"I meant the baby," Poppy says, going back to the previous conversation. "I know you're going to have your own one day, hopefully soon, but in the meantime. The baby needs parents, and Maddox needs an heir. Why not keep her as a backup in case you can't get pregnant or you don't have a boy?" She says it like it's all just very simple, and I am immediately shaking my head.

"It doesn't work that way," I tell her. "Maddox doesn't want someone else's child as his heir, and besides, if we kept her, that would mean that Alpha Bryant got what he wanted, and someone who acts like him shouldn't be rewarded, even after his death."

Poppy doesn't seem to be too swayed by my words as she reaches over and picks up a piece of the bacon I haven't touched and eats it. Between bites, she says, "Well, I'm just saying, it wouldn't hurt to keep her close by. Just in case."

Fighting with Poppy never goes well for me, but I can't help but say, "Thank you for your vote of confidence."

Her eyebrows furrow as she finishes the first piece of bacon and picks up another one. "What do you mean?" she asks. "I didn't say anything bad about you."

"No, just that I might not be able to do my job," I say, my voice still calm and even.

Hers is not as she declares, "I never said that! I'm just saying, she's a baby, and he needs a baby! Geeze, Isla, lighten up." She eats another piece of my breakfast.

The idea that she is my servant and I am her mistress fills my mind, but I bite back that declaration. She has no way of knowing how badly I wanted to keep the baby and how I was frightened into thinking I couldn't and then I realized that I shouldn't even want to.

I say nothing. There's no point. Poppy isn't going to admit that she said something wrong, and I am tired of arguing about it. I am tired of arguing, period, and I am tired of letting the idea that Maddy could be my daughter fill my head. The connection I feel to her is undeniable. But I won't try to convince myself that I'm meant to be her mother.

"Besides…" Poppy continues wiping her hands of bacon grease on my napkin, "you could take her with you. You know, later."

"Later?" I'm not sure what she's getting at. Take her with me where?

Then… I put the pieces together. She doesn't think I'll be staying here.

Poppy—my best friend, or so I thought—thinks that Maddox will use me for a baby and then send me away. Without my child.

"You don't think he loves me?" I can't blame her if she doesn't, I suppose. After all, I'm not completely sure whether or not I heard him say that he loves me the night before or not. I think, maybe, as I was dozing off in the bathtub, he said that he loves me, but it might've been my imagination.

And if I don't know, how can I expect her to know?

Rather than directly answering my question, she draws in a deep breath, holds it, and lets it out before she says, "He's the king. He's said he will never take another queen, never take another Luna. He loved Rebecca, regardless of what happened to her. I don't know how he feels, Isla, but I'm not sure it matters. He hasn't changed his mind about his decision not to marry again in all of these years. Maybe he'll keep you in the castle so that you can see your child. Maybe he'll even continue to see you. But, is that what you want? Don't you want to find your mate? You'll be twenty-one soon, right? You need to be out there looking for him, and you won't be able to do that if you stay here with Maddox, praying that he changes his mind."

For once today, Poppy is making sense. As much as I don't want to hear her words, she's not wrong.

I do want to find my mate someday. I love Maddox, but he doesn't want to marry again. He doesn't want another Luna or queen, and while a second chance mate isn't unheard of, most people who discover their second chance mate find that person in another who has lost their initial mate.

And I have never met my mate, so I can't possibly require a second chance mate.

Am I content to stay here in the castle and continue to yearn for Maddox when he doesn't have feelings for me? Am I content to just stay here on the promise of hope?

No, I already know the answer to that question. I could never stay in the castle indefinitely hoping that Maddox would sometime come around and realize he loves me.

But I can stay here for my child.

I will stay here for my child.

"I think I'd like to be alone for a little while," I tell Poppy. I'd intended to go see baby Maddy after breakfast, and I still will go and see her at some point today. But for now, I just need some time to myself.

"All right," she says. She stands and gathers up my plate and other breakfast items. As Poppy heads to the door, she pauses and turns to look at me. "I didn't piss you off, did I?" She makes a face, like she's afraid she's overstepped.

She has overstepped, but I'm getting used to it, and sometimes, I admire Poppy's ability to speak her mind. I shake my head. "No, we're fine."

She smiles at me briefly and then disappears out the door.

Poppy and I are fine. I have learned to forgive her sometimes hurtful comments, but it's a lot harder to forget the harsh comments of someone else that play around in my mind.

My own.

TRUTH AND CONSEQUENCES

Maddox

I SIT BEHIND MY DESK, silently swiveling my chair back and forth, just an inch this way and an inch that way, but it's enough to keep my mind locked on the issue at hand.

I have a decision to make, and it won't be an easy one.

Seth clears his throat from the chair across from me. That's his way of saying he wonders if I'm ever going to respond to the question he asked several minutes ago.

It's one I don't have an answer for, one that I've been mulling over since before I even told him he needed to come to my office to talk this through. Of course, I don't expect him to have an answer either, but for the most part, Seth is the one I turn to when I need answers. He's level-headed, smart, insightful, and doesn't get distracted easily.

Right now, I am not distracted either, for once. Lately, it seems like every time I try to make a decision, Isla leaps into my mind, and I'm completely sidetracked. Today, even though I am looking forward to relaxing in her arms at some point, but for now, I've got to figure out what to do with these soldiers from Hill Country pack.

"I've double-checked with the families," I say to Seth. He already knows this. I'm just thinking out loud. "Everything I've been told is true. The children really were kidnapped, and those who didn't have children to take had someone else gathered up–a grandmother, a spouse. Not that there weren't some people who went along with it willingly."

Seth nods at me. "I have a list. We have the names of the three who were acting of their own accord without any coaxing by anyone. According to the others, they've always been loyal to Vinny." He reaches into his pocket and pulls out a notecard. Placing it on the desk, he taps it, and I know what it says.

I already know which three are the ones who had no trouble following along with Vinny's vindictive attack.

With a glance down at it, I sigh and say, "You think we should just take these three out and end them? Let the others live?"

He gives a shrug which tells me he wants to do what I think we should do, and while that's how it will be anyway, I would like to know his opinion, though. I would like to know if he agrees with me.

The fact that he's saying nothing usually tells me that he does agree with me. When he disagrees, he usually shrugs and tells me he thinks we should do something else. Instead, he's tapping his fingers on the arm of the chair. "I will support you, whatever you decide."

"And the others? They might not have had much of a choice in their own minds, but they still need to pay for their actions."

He nods. "According to Mike, most of the ones who didn't want to be there didn't actually participate in the killing."

"But they didn't stop it either," I remind him.

Seth half-shrugs. "True."

I drag a hand down my face. I know I need to be decisive. I need to be fair, and I need to be quick to act. If I wait too long, I'll seem weak. If I don't hand out fair punishments to everyone, I'll be weak. If I hand out some punishments to some people but don't follow through with what I've promised will happen, without a reason that makes sense to everyone, I'll seem like I am capable of being swayed and changing my mind.

It's never an easy position to be in, and that's why when these other Alphas threaten to come and overthrow my throne, I wonder if they really have any idea what they're getting into.

I open my mouth to tell Seth what I've decided to do when my phone rings. With a loud sigh, I pause and pick up the receiver.

My secretary, whose office is down the hall, says, "I'm so sorry to bother you, sir, but there's a woman on the phone, crying, and she's begging to speak to you."

Cradling my head in my free hand, I ponder who it could be. "Fine," I say, not sure. I can think of a lot of women who might be calling me and crying right now. It could be any number of women from Hill Country or the sister of the slain Luna.

I hear the phone click over and say, "This is Alpha King Maddox." My tone conveys I'm actually asking the unspoken question of "what the fuck do you want?"

"Oh, thank the Moon Goddess!" a woman proclaims. "I'm so glad I am able to speak to you, Your Highness!"

I catch Seth's eyes, and his brows are raised as he wonders who it is. I shrug because I still don't know. "Who am I speaking with?" I ask.

"This is Nancy Weaver," she says. "I would like to speak to you about my husband, Mike."

I take a deep breath and try not to keep rubbing my forehead, but I don't really want to be speaking to this woman, not right now. "HI, Mrs. Weaver," I say so that Seth's unspoken question will be answered. "I'm sure you're calling to inquire about the welfare of your husband?"

"Yes, sir. I've been speaking to him through the mind-link, and he told me that he had a chance to tell you what happened, about how they took our baby. They took all of the children, you know? All of them. And some people's mothers and grandmothers... even some of the men had their wife taken!" The way she is speaking, it's hard to understand her because she's so upset.

"I have heard that from several of the men that were in Duster pack yesterday," I assure her. "But you do understand that your husband and the others could have chosen another path?"

"With all due respect, Sir, what path? They could've been killed. They could've gotten our loved ones killed. My baby needs her father! Please, Sir, I'm begging you to have mercy on my husband and the others who had their loved ones taken prisoner to persuade them. You must know our pack is in the situation where we've been brainwashed to think of you as a horrible monster for years under Alpha Bryant and Beta Vinny. Showing our warriors who acted in duress mercy would go a long way toward making amends with our people."

I notice that, despite her tears, she is very well-spoken, and the arguments she's making are solid.

Hill Country pack has usually pretended to be loyal to me, unlike Green pack and Duster pack and a few others that have come right out against me in recent months. But I've always known that Alpha Bryant and his minions, Vinny being at the top of that list, would be some of the first to snap my throat if they got a chance.

Now, Nancy Weaver is telling me that she believes I can begin to win their confidence back over if I am merciful to the men who had no choice but to fight against me.

I'm not usually keen on being merciful, but in this case, I believe I can make a decree to the public to explain the situation, and most of them will be accepting of my decision, so long as I punish those who are at fault by taking their lives.

And it will need to be public.

"Very well, Mrs. Weaver, I will consider it. I will let you know my decision tomorrow," I tell her.

"Oh, thank you, Your Majesty!" she says, and I hear a baby blubbering in the background. "I can't tell you how much I appreciate your consideration."

"You do understand that I have already declared that your husband and all of the others should be put to death for their crimes, don't you?" I ask her, not wanting to get too soft.

"Yes, Sir, I understand, but I believe in a merciful Moon Goddess, and I believe that you are a just king. I know that you will make the right decision. And for doing so, the Moon Goddess will bless you and keep you!"

Her words hit me in the heart for reasons that I cannot quite explain. "Thank you, Mrs. Weaver," I tell her. "I'll call you tomorrow."

I hang up the phone before she can further sway me, and I look straight into Seth's eyes.

"She seems... persuasive," he says.

"Yes, she was," I admit with a nod. "So... we will move forward with the plan as we were discussing before. The three who took no persuasion to help Vinny with his devious plan will be executed. The others will serve... ten years."

He takes a deep breath and blows it out slowly, and I know he disagrees with me.

"Too much?" I ask.

"No, I don't think it's too much," he says. "I'm just thinking... Mike's baby will be ten years old before he leaves the prison."

He has a point, but that's a consequence of a number of actions taken by Mike Weaver and others before this came about. "He could've left Hill Country pack as soon as talk about going against me arose. He could've decided not to be a warrior in the service of an Alpha who spoke out against me. He could've done several things differently, made a series of decisions, that would've put him in a different situation so that he wasn't called upon to help kill innocent people."

"Even though those people were also in the service of a man who hates you. Theoretically, they could argue that they were actually trying to serve you." Seth wears a small smirk.

"You are impossible, you know that?" I ask him, and he chuckles. "What would you do? Five years? Two?"

"NO!" he says. "I think... seven?"

"It's an honor to barter with you, Mr. Negotiator," I say, shaking my head. "Fine. Seven years it is. Anything else?"

"No, Sir." He has a winning smile at the corners of his mouth. "Shall I have them set up the gallows for tomorrow? Party of three?"

This time I do not hesitate in my response to him, and any semblance of laughter is washed from my face. "No, not three prisoners for the gallows tomorrow, Seth. Four."

His eyes widen slightly, and then he nods in understanding. "It'll be a first," he says.

"I know. But it must be done. Four."

He gets out of his chair. "I'll see to it. Anything different for… her?"

"Nope," I say. "She can commit treason, murder, kidnapping, and all other kinds of atrocities like a man, she can hang by the neck like a man."

"I'll see to it."

If nothing else, at least I'll have that pain out of my ass tomorrow.

Zabrina.

A FAMILIAR FACE

Isla

I HUM a lullaby to Maddy as I rock her to sleep in my arms. Thanks to the wet nurse, she has a full belly, and I feel blessed by the Moon Goddess to have the opportunity to sit here and watch her sleep.

I've made peace with the fact that I'm not keeping her. In fact, one of the women from the nursery told me earlier today that they'd contacted some family members that are related to Sydney's mother, and they are planning to come and pick her up in a few days. Of course, they will be thoroughly interviewed by the king and myself first. Maddox will allow that, I have no doubt.

I'm not the Luna, and I probably never will be, but when it comes to taking care of the packs' children, I am willing to assert myself. Perhaps spending so much time with Maddox is making me feel more confident in my ability to make a difference for the better in the kingdom.

As I rock and hum, I think about Maddox. I know he's very busy today. He's trying to decide what to do with all of those people who had a hand in the deaths in Duster pack, and I can't imagine it's easy. He isn't the type of person who just kills indiscriminately. I hope that others know and understand that. I say a prayer to the Moon Goddess that the situation is going well for him.

I also think about Zabrina. I hate her, that's for certain. I can't pretend that I don't. Not only did she trick me, kidnap me, and try to kill me, she is ultimately responsible for the death of Private Parker, a sweet guy who did nothing wrong. All he did was try to fulfill his duties as assigned to him by his king.

She's also responsible for Private Wylie's death, and while he made his own choices that ultimately led to his demise, I believe he was brainwashed or at least heavily influenced by the vixen who arranged all of this.

She can try to blame whomever she wants to, but Zabrina caused all of this havoc. Lots of people are dead now because she was greedy and wanted to be queen.

Taking a deep breath, I try to remind myself that it doesn't matter how I feel about Zabrina or what she's done. It's up to Maddox and the others in charge to make sure she gets what she deserves. Whatever he decides, I will accept it. I can't imagine watching her die, but then, I would be lying if I said I wouldn't feel better about going on in this life knowing she can never hurt me or anyone else ever again.

I look down at the face of the sleeping baby in my arms, and I think that she will be safe in a world where there is no Zabrina.

Maddy coos and shoves her thumb into her mouth, and I want to bend down and kiss her little cheek, but I don't want to wake her. I wonder what life will have in store for her. I wonder if her name will stay Maddy or if her new parents will change it.

A tear forms in the corner of my eye and I can't help but think about how sad I'll be when I have to watch this little one leave. But I remember what Mystica said to me, and I do believe that someday, Maddy and I will be brought together again, that even if she leaves the castle soon, that doesn't mean we will never see one another again.

A soft knock at the door brings me out of my thoughts, and I quietly call, "Yes?" thinking it's probably one of the nurses who has come to gather Maddy back to the nursery too quickly.

It is a nurse who opens the door. "I'm sorry to bother you, Miss Isla," she says, her voice just a whisper. "But you have a visitor here to see you."

My forehead crinkles. I can only think of one person, other than Maddox, who would come looking for me, and Poppy would shout in my head that she was looking for me. "Who?" I ask.

The nurse moves aside, and I am looking at a face I haven't seen in months, one I have missed.

"Ben!" I say, forgetting that I am holding a sleeping baby. The nurse comes forward and takes Maddy, and I get up and fly at my little brother, wrapping my arms around him as he squeezes me tightly.

He's never hugged me this tightly in all of the years that he's been alive because he's never been this strong, and I feel so grateful that he's standing here, that he's doing better, that he's strong enough to squeeze me and take my breath away.

"What are you doing here?" I ask him, still whispering as Maddy is carried away from me. My eyes follow her, and I wish that she never had to leave me. But Ben has my attention now as he starts to answer my question.

"I had to come and see you," he says with a shrug. "I have some stuff to talk to you about."

"But… what about school?" I ask him. "Aren't you missing class? Mom and Dad just let you come?"

"Uhm, well, we have a few days off from school for teacher conferences, and I told Mom and Dad I was staying at my friend A'maree's house." He gives me a sheepish look as he knows I don't like it when he lies.

"But how did you get here?" I ask, still confused.

"We have some money now, thanks to you, and the parental units have been giving me an allowance, along with the other brothers. So I saved it up a couple of weeks, and now, here I am." He grins at me, and I don't even know what to say.

Snapping out of it, I say, "Where's your stuff?" He has no bags that I can see.

Turning around, he shows me a backpack that looks like it only has a couple of changes of clothes in it. Leave it to my baby brother to leave home completely unprepared. "I couldn't let them think I was going to be moving out of the house or anything."

I fold my arms. "You're not moving out of the house," I remind him, and he brushes his hair out of his eyes.

"Okay, okay, but I do need to show you some things that I found. I think they're going to be really important to you." Ben's looking directly into my eyes now, and I feel a shiver go down my spine.

"All right," I agree. "But not here. We should go to my room."

He looks around. "Oh, this isn't your room?"

I knock him into the door. "No! I don't live in the nursery!"

"Well, it's not like I don't know what your job is now, sis."

I start to walk out the door with him, and he sort of shrugs.

"Everyone refers to you as 'the breeder' so even if you wanted to hide it, you couldn't."

I take a deep breath. "Just don't say anything to Mom and Dad, okay?" I say. "I don't want them to know the truth. And Maddox and I are–"

"Maddox?" he repeats with a chuckle. "Dang, I guess the two of you are close, huh?"

I can feel my face turning red. "We are." That's all I care to say about it.

Opening the door, I head out into the hallway and he falls into step beside me as I head back to my room, which is quite some distance from where we are located now. Ben has to walk a little slower than usual because his legs are so much longer than mine. It's unusual for me to think of my sickly brother being so healthy, but he's so strong and confident now. Walking beside him now, it seems like he's just a regular guy, and I am so happy for him.

"Man, this place is amazing," he murmurs as we walk past the priceless pieces of art and other masterpieces.

"I know," I say. "Just be careful not to touch anything." Visions of that horrible Mrs. Washingtonshiresauce showing up and pummeling my baby brother haunt my mind as we make it to my room.

"What happens if you touch something?" Ben pauses by the door with one finger hovering over a vase I've almost knocked off of the small table it sits on a thousand times.

I shake my head. "Don't do it. You'll be sorry."

He slowly lowers his finger until he's touching the rim of the gray vase with burgundy flowers that probably costs more than my parents' house, and I shake my head at him. When Ben pulls away, he accidentally hooks the lip on the vase and knocks it off of the table.

I hold my breath as he tries to grab it. For a second, he has it, but then it's in the air again. Ben's hands shoot down lower, and he grabs it, but then it shoots up, into the air, and he fumbles it a few more times before he finally gets his hands around it.

He cradles it to his chest and says, "Phew! That was a close one."

I shake my head at him. "I told you not to touch anything."

"I know. I'm sorry. It won't happen again." Carefully, Ben puts the vase back on the table, and I open my door, stepping inside of the antechamber.

Ben follows behind me, and I turn to say something to him, just in time to see his backpack hitting the vase. I only have time to get a squeal out of my throat as it falls to the stone floor and shatters into a million pieces.

Covering my mouth with both hands, I stare up at him, and my baby brother says, "Oops."

All I can think to say is, "You're lucky Alpha King Maddox likes me!" I have no idea where that vase came from, how old it is, or how much it's worth, but I have a feeling Poppy will be angrier at me about its demise than Maddox will be.

I grab Ben by the lapels and pull him into my room. "What is it you have to show me?" I ask him.

"Oh, right!" he says. He takes his backpack off and tosses it onto my bed. Without unzipping it, he turns to me and asks, "Have you ever seen your birth certificate?"

My forehead crinkles as I ponder that question. Have I? "I don't know," I admit. "Why do you ask?"

"Well, I've seen it," he says, unzipping his bag. "And yours is different than mine."

"Well, yeah, I'd think so since I'm a lot older than you. And a girl," I tease him, knowing that's not what he meant.

Ben pulls a piece of paper out and hands it over to me. Before I even look at it, he fills me in on what he means. "Your last name is different than mine, sis."

My heart lurches into my throat as I glance down at the paper.

He's right. My name isn't Isla Moon. But I'm not too surprised to see what it says.

My name is Isla Masina.

PREPARING FOR DEATH

Maddox

THE SOUND of hammering resonates even though I'm inside looking out at the gallows that are being constructed in the courtyard. It's been years since the last time I've heard that sound, and this is the first time I've ever ordered it myself

But I don't feel bad about it.

This is something that has to be done, something I know will accomplish several goals all at once. It will get rid of these people who have committed horrific crimes against the crown and the citizens of my kingdom. It will show that I mean what I say when I decree that all of the packs are meant to work together toward a specific end. And finally, it will send a message to anyone out there who is thinking perhaps I am making a bad decision or that I am weak that they shouldn't fuck with me.

That's really the biggest message I am hoping to send, and I hope that my enemies both far and wide hear that message and ingrain it into their brains for the rest of their miserable lives.

Seth is quiet beside me, and I know he has plenty of thoughts he'd like to spew out to me, but I don't want to hear them. He's expressed himself already. He has concerns about the prisoners I'm not killing more than anything else.

And he has concerns about the bitch who started all of this.

"It's just… her mother is ill," he says, and I can't help but reach up and rub the bridge of my nose. I have a headache. It settled into my forehead about an hour ago, and now it seems to be sinking into the rest of my head.

The storm that's rolling in is either the cause or pure aggravation of the sharp, shooting pains. Thunder rolls in the distance, and the men with the hammers speed things up. We've had to erect the gallows from scratch because it's been so long since we've had a hanging. They're making good progress, though, probably because they don't want the lightning in the west to make them the first victims of the structure meant to bring instant death.

"I understand about her illness," I say, putting my hand behind my back and interlacing my fingers. I am trying to use this stance to appear calm but inside, I am ready to strangle my own Beta and best friend. "I don't care. Even if she was well enough to come here to petition me the way that the families of the others have come, I wouldn't change my mind. I've got three other mothers, two wives, and a granddaughter in the waiting area demanding to speak with me, and if Alpha Jordan's Luna was here, I would tell her the same thing I told Cody to tell the others. My decision has been made. I will not be swayed. This will happen. They can choose to stay and watch as part of the crowd, or they can go home. If they'd like to have the bodies returned to them, then they can pay for that to be done. Otherwise, they will be buried in a mass grave in the traitor's cemetery in the forest." I shrug and refocus my attention on the hammering as thunder shakes the ground and the wind begins to blow the leaves off the trees in the distance.

Seth says nothing, only inhales deeply a few times. I understand his concern. He thinks I should consider being more lenient, but I'm not here to make everyone like me.

"Sir?"

I hear Cody's voice behind me and pull my eyes off of the men who are nearly done but might need to retire early to make sure they don't get struck by lightning. I silently curse their leader and send him a mind-link message that if they have to wait until the storm passes, that's understandable.

To the young man standing behind me, I turn and say, "Yes?"

He clears his throat, a sign I will not like what he has to say. "I spoke to the families, and they all insisted on seeing you, but I told them that wasn't possible. Eventually, I had to call the other guards to transport them out, and when they started getting rowdy, we threatened to arrest them."

I wait a moment to see if he's going to say more, but that seems to be everything. "Thank you for doing exactly what I asked you to do and then coming to give me the details about doing everything that I asked you to do."

I'm finding it hard to keep my sarcasm to myself. It seems like there's not much of a point to what he's telling me.

Cody's gaze shifts as he says, "There's another woman here to see you. She has a baby. She says her husband is in the prison, and he shouldn't be."

Cocking my head to the side, I stare at him for a moment, thinking that he must be kidding me. Since when do I let people just show up and question my decisions about who belongs in the prison?

But then I realize who it has to be, and I can't help but chuckle. It mixes with the rumble of the thunder and for a moment, both Cody and Seth seem confused as to whether or not I have laughed or growled.

"Does her name happen to be Nancy Weaver?" I ask.

With his eyes wide, Cody stares at me, probably wondering how the hell I knew that. He nods. "That's right."

"Fuck," I mutter under my breath, and gesturing at the hallway that leads back the way he came, I say, "Take me to her."

He nods and turns around, heading back down the hallway, and I know the question in Seth's mind before he even asks it. He's making sputtering noises, and that's enough for me to say, "I'll see her. I'm not killing her husband tomorrow." Then I add, "Unless she pisses me off."

We traipse down the winding hallways to the front office of the castle. I have two offices; one is where I conduct most of my business, the transactions and discussions that are a little more personal or private than others. My other office is at the front of the castle. That's where I conduct all of my more public business and where I see general members of the public. It's near the throne room, but I haven't actually sat on the throne to dictate my decisions ever.

When we reach the front of the castle, where I've instructed Cody to handle today's business, I see a woman who might reach my shoulder in height. She has dark curly hair that she clearly hasn't had a chance to tame today, and she's so rail thin, I think there's a good chance the child she holds in her arms—who is chubby and lively—might weigh more than she does.

Her large blue eyes focus in on me, and even before I execute the full turn into the hallway, she is marching at me, like the little one is light as air.

She is quick, and if I truly thought she was a threat, I might be irritated at Cody and Seth for not stepping between us, but I know she will only attack me with words.

"Your Majesty," she says, tipping her head a bit in what I can assume is meant to be a sign of respect. "I'm Nancy Weaver."

"I know," I say. "And I'm sorry that you've come all this way to speak to me when you could've been told over the phone. Your husband has been sentenced to seven years in prison for his role in the massacre in Duster pack. He will be able to call you in a few days, but no one is going down into the prison until after the prisoners who are set to be executed have had their sentences carried out."

"But King Maddox, please," Nancy says, and I can tell every word I just said has already been spoken to her ten times at least. "It's not fair to give my husband the same sentence as everyone else, not when he's the one who spoke the truth! He's the one that let you know what really happened in our pack. Please, take some time off of his sentence for being an informant!"

The woman has gumption, and I appreciate that. But I'm not about to let her talk me into anything. "Many of the prisoners were willing to talk when they realized they were all going to be executed otherwise. I know it's difficult to accept this sentence, Mrs. Weaver, but trust me, I've already been lenient. I had initially decided the sentence would be ten years." I turn and stare at Seth for a moment, but he doesn't meet my eyes. I shake my head slightly and return my attention to the woman.

I see tears glistening in her eyes. "Please, sir, what Mike didn't tell you is that... he's very sick. He was diagnosed last year with a form of cancer. The doctors say he only has a few years left. Even if he has treatment, he might not live seven years." She swipes at her eyes. "I'm begging you to reconsider."

Seeing her cry does have some effect on me; I'm not a monster. But I'm also not ready to be swayed. "I'm sorry. I have the best physicians in the kingdom here. We'll do everything we can for him. I'm afraid there's nothing else I can do, Mrs. Weaver." Thunder rumbles outside. "You can spend the night here at the castle if you'd like so that you and your child don't have to go back to Hill Country pack tonight in the storm."

Her mouth opens, but she closes it quickly, and I'm a little surprised. I expected her to continue to argue with me.

Cody takes her by the shoulder. "Let me show you to a room." He steers her toward the hall in the castle where we let citizens stay from time to time in situations like this, and as she begins to walk away, I see Nancy Weaver drop her head and begin to cry.

"That went well," Seth mumbles.

I turn and glare at him, and he flinches slightly. "Do you have a fork?" I ask him.

His eyebrows crease. "Uhm, a fork? No. Why?"

"Because..." I say, shaking my head. "I'm done."

A chuckle escapes his lips, and as much as I was trying to lighten the tension in the air, I was also being completely serious.

Turning around, I head back toward my room. Seth rushes to keep up with me. "Where are you going?"

"I just told you," I say. "I'm done. I'm going to my room."

"But—"

"Seth?" I turn and glare at him.

He raises both hands and backs up, and I know I'll have at least a few hours of peace.

I've lied to him, though. I'm not going to my room.

I walk swiftly through the building, ignoring everyone I pass, even the few people who say my name as if they think they are going to be able to speak to me. I growl at one of them.

When I reach Isla's room, I hear her heartbeat from behind the door, and a smile comes to my face. I recognize that she's not alone because there's a second heartbeat, but I assume it's Poppy. I also notice that the vase that used to sit outside of her door is gone and think that's strange, but it always was an ugly thing, even if it was worth a hundred thousand dollars.

Without even knocking, I open the door, trot through the antechamber, and throw open her bedroom door.

The smile falls from my face as I see her wide eyes focused on me as she stares, stunned.

Her arms are around a man I've never seen before, and she's embracing him in a tight hug.

All I can think to say is, "Who the fuck are you?" as my wolf lunges to the surface.

AN ANGRY KING

Isla

"Who the fuck are you?"

Maddox's outburst has me letting go of my brother, Ben, but standing between the king, who looks like he's about to storm right through me and knock my little brother out the window, I put up my hand and shout, "Maddox, stop!"

I hear Ben mumble a curse word I've never heard come out of his mouth before as he drops to his knee. "Your Majesty!" he declares, and I can't tell if he's afraid Maddox is angry because he's not being subservient enough or if my brother realizes Maddox has the wrong idea.

"Who is this asshole, and what the fuck is he doing in your room with his arms wrapped around you?"

The king steps to the side and I have to move quickly to get in front of him. "He's my brother!" I shout.

Maddox looks like he's about to shift, he's so mad, but when he processes what I've yelled at him, he stops mid-lunge, and his eyes widen almost as much as his mouth, his razor-sharp canines picking up the light from the lamp overhead and twinkling–not in an enchanting way.

"He's your what?" he asks me, glancing from Ben, who's still on his knee, back to me, over and over again.

"My brother!" I say, pushing the king back a bit so that Ben can stand up.

Ben isn't moving, so I reach down and grab him underneath the arm and hall him to his feet. "It's all right, Ben," I say. "This is His Majesty, King Maddox."

Ben makes the sign of respect by tapping his chest and keeps his head down. "It's an honor, Sire," he says in a respectful tone.

I am seething as I look at the king. I want to yell so many things at him, but right now, all I really want for him to do is apologize. Not only is Ben my brother, who looks very much like me, should the king have bothered to look before he stormed in, but he's also practically a child. He may look like an adult from a distance because he's so tall, but he's anything but.

Looking at Maddox's face, I can tell that's registering now, and he's embarrassed. But he's also the king, and it's not like he can just say, "My bad."

He clears his throat and says, "Ben?"

"Yes, Sir," my brother says, still speaking in a respectful tone. "It's an honor to be in your presence."

My brother is being so kind after Maddox nearly ripped his head off.

"I wasn't aware that Isla was having any visitors today," he says, folding his arms across his massive chest. I still wanna punch him for being so mean to my brother, but I'm also a little flattered that he was obviously so jealous.

"I showed up unexpectedly," Ben admits. "I had the day off from school, so I decided to come and pay her a visit. My apologies for not... letting you know in advance, Your Majesty."

I can just imagine Ben trying to call Maddox and ask if he could come over to play or to visit or something. I almost shake my head, but I keep my face neutral. I don't want to yell at Maddox in front of Ben.

"I'm glad you could come," the king finally says. And then, he offers his hand. "It's nice to meet you in person. I've heard many complimentary things about you."

Ben's eyes widen as his brows shoot up and he stares at Maddox's hand like he's not sure if he can actually touch our ruler. Eventually, he gets a silly, crooked grin on his face and grasps Maddox's hand. "It's a pleasure to meet you, too, Sir. Isla hasn't said much of anything about you." And then he chuckles, and Maddox is looking at me. I shrug. Of course, I haven't. It's not like I could tell my brother the truth.

Maddox seems to realize now that he's in a precarious position since he has no idea that my brother has already figured out what my job is here. He releases Ben's hand and says, "Your sister... is a fine worker here at the castle."

Ben bursts out laughing and I elbow him, hard, in the ribs. "He knows!" I say to Maddox.

"You told him?" The king is looking at me with shock on his handsome face. It's getting to be his normal expression after the way he burst into the room.

"No," I say. "He just… figured it out. It's not like this is the room of a maid, right?" I extend my arms and model the room like it's on display.

"That's a fair point," Maddox replies, but you could have another important job here. You could be a consultant. Or a secretary. Or an accountant. Or–"

"Yeah, my sister's smart but she has no training in any of those things," Ben says. "I would believe she was a glorified maid before I believed any of those things, Sir. No disrespect intended."

They both snicker over that, and I am left standing with my mouth hanging open, offended that they both seem to think all I can do for a living is lie on my back with my legs spread open. "Hey! I can do lots of other jobs!" I say. "It's not like I didn't work back in Willow pack before I came here." I scrutinize both of them.

"No, you did," Ben says, " and you did a great job of helping support the family and helping pay my medical bills. I wasn't trying to be disrespectful."

I'm not sure what to think of this conversation because he is clearly trying to get into Maddox's good graces, and it's never been like Ben to try to do something like that at the expense of others. So I give him the benefit of the doubt.

Maddox is still smiling but it's starting to fade as he says, "I should leave you guys to visit. Are you staying the night in the castle, Ben?"

He nods. "If that's all right."

"Of course," Maddox says. "As long as your parents don't mind."

"They don't mind," Ben says, and I feel like telling Maddox it's because they don't know, but instead I just glare at my brother for not being completely honest.

"Good, good." Maddox looks at me for a second and I realize that he came in here because he wanted to see me. He's probably had a rough day, dealing with the prisoners and all of that.

"Are you all right?" I ask him.

"Yes, of course," he says. "It's just been a busy day."

I want to be there for him right now, but I also want to see my brother, and it's clear to me that Maddox is not overly enthusiastic about talking to my brother.

And then Maddox spots the piece of paper I'd set down on the bed right before he came in. I'd set it aside to hug Ben, so grateful to my brother for bringing it to me. "What's that?" Maddox asks.

I had intended to tell him, to explain what this meant, to him, but I'm not sure that's a conversation I want to have in front of my brother when I know how Maddox feels about Maatua.

"Oh, it's nothing," I begin, intending to just tell him the truth later.

But Ben doesn't realize that, and I haven't used the mind-link to my advantage to warn him. "This?" he asks, picking it up. "It's Isla's birth certificate," Ben says. He hands it over to Maddox, and I feel my face beginning to set aflame. "It's interesting because of her last name. Also, look where it says she was born."

"Ben–" I begin, wanting to tell him that he should stop talking, but it's too late now.

Maddox's eyes are pouring over the document, and he's reading every single word.

I take a deep breath and hold it, wondering what he might say. When he reaches the bottom, he hands it back to my brother and says simply, "Interesting."

Ben takes it and I can tell by his expression that he is confused. "But don't you see, Your Majesty? Our parents have always insisted that we're from the south, but clearly we're not. This proves it."

With a shrug, Maddox takes a couple of steps toward the door. "Perhaps," he says. "If you'll excuse me, I need to go."

"What do you mean perhaps?" I hadn't intended to address the situation now, but I also didn't expect Maddox to be so dismissive. It's not like I haven't told him before that I think my parents were the king and queen of Maatua.

He clears his throat. "Isla, we can speak of this another time," he says. "I have other business to attend to."

I can feel myself getting a little upset at his attitude. After all, he should know this is important to me, and now is as good a time to talk about it as ever, even if my brother is there. He has other paperwork with him, other items he took from the stash in my parents' bedroom floor.

"I guess your other business is more important than me?" I ask.

Maddox sighs and stops walking. "Isla, please. Not now, okay?"

His remarks irritate me even more. "Sorry. I didn't mean for my very existence to annoy you."

"It's not that!" he insists. "I didn't say that. I just… clearly this is a complex topic, and I don't have the patience or the energy to talk it out right now."

"You don't have the patience or the energy to acknowledge the fact that I was right? That I am from Maatua, that my parents were royalty?"

"No, I don't," Maddox says, his tone a little sterner right now. "I just don't want to argue with you about it again. Not right now. Not in front of your brother and not after the day I've had."

"Argue with me about it?" I repeat. "What's to argue?" I am still several feet away from him, but I have the paper in my hand. "It's right here! In black and white!"

"No, it's not," he says, shaking his head. "That's just a piece of paper!"

"It's a birth certificate!" I shout, and even though I can't see him, I feel Ben stepping away from me.

"It's not real!" Maddox shouts, his hands flailing out emphatically.

"What?" All I can do is stare at him. How can he say something like that?

Pointing at the paper in my hand, with a flash of lightning in his eyes, King Maddox says, "That's not real, Isla Moon! It's a fake!"

JUST A PRINCESS

Staring at Maddox, I try to understand what it is he's saying, what he's just screamed at me, but it's difficult, and I'm not sure I will be able to comprehend it without some sort of a better explanation.

I wait, hoping he will say more, but all he's doing is shaking his head, running his fingers through his hair.

I'm going to have to ask him. "What do you mean my birth certificate is fake?" My lips are trembling as I ask the question. I thought this would be the proof he finally needed in order to see that I really am from Maatua, that I am a princess, but he doesn't even want to accept this government-stamped, issued document.

A loud sigh escapes his lips as he says, "Perhaps we should speak about this another time."

"What?" I blurt out. "No! You can't say something like that and not explain yourself. You essentially just told me my entire life is a lie!"

"Your entire life is a lie?" he repeats, his eyes wide and wild as he looks at me. "Isla, if this document were true, your entire life would be a lie! But it's not. It simply can't be!"

I hate that my brother is standing there listening to us argue, but I don't know what to do about this. It pertains to him, too, so I'm not about to dismiss him. "So that's your great proof that the document isn't real? Because it *can't* be?" I can hear the sarcasm dripping from my own words, and it surprises even me. I shouldn't speak to him like this. He is the king, after all. Still, he's also Maddox, my Maddox, and the fact that he still continues to speak to me in such a manner after everything we've been through is irritating at least, disheartening at most.

"That's not the only reason," he says, and then he makes it clear that he's also annoyed that we're not alone. "Ben, why don't you... go to the kitchen and get something to eat... or something." He waves at the door, and it's clear he's just trying to get my brother to leave.

"He'll never find the kitchen!" I say. I can barely find the kitchen, and I've lived here for months.

"I'll figure it out," Ben says, glad to have the reprieve as he darts for the exit. I thought perhaps he'd like to stay here and listen to what the king has to say about his family's heritage, but it seems clear that Maddox has intimidated him so much, he just wants to run away, and I can't blame him. I would, too, if I was in Ben's position, and I kind of want to know, even though this is a battle I have already chosen to fight.

As soon as my brother leaves, closing the door behind him, I sink down onto the bed, trying to clear my mind of everything that's transpired so we can start over. "I'm just... confused," I say. "Why would my parents have this document, and all of this other stuff that proves we're from Maatua if none of it's real?"

Ben has left his backpack, and I pull out the other things he brought along. I haven't even seen them myself, but I'm not surprised at what they are. A wedding certificate with the seal of the king, a photograph, crinkled and faded, of my parents on their wedding day, clearly taken in a castle of some sort, a book that appears to be something important–like a family religious record–and the cufflinks.

When Maddox sees them, he inhales so deep, I think the room has gotten smaller. He sinks down next to me. I offer him the box, but he won't take it. "I thought I... removed those from your room."

"You mean, you thought you got rid of them?" I ask him, shaking my head in surprise. "You probably did, but this isn't the same pair. These were my father's." I show them to him, and he can see that they're exactly the same as the pair I found in the village and gifted to him. "I guess there's more than one pair."

"You're telling me that your brother found these in the floorboards at your parents' house?" he asks me.

"Yes! All of this!" I show him the other items. "Ben said there was more, but these were the things that seemed most important to him as far as proving where we came from is concerned."

I pick up the photograph and study it. My parents look so happy, and my mom has never been more beautiful. Her white gown fits her so nicely. It flares out at the bottom like a mermaid's tale. Her hair is pulled up with soft ringlets framing her face.

The room they're in seems to be a chapel of some sort, and it's clear that the Moon Goddess is the main focus. There's a large statue of her far behind them, her silver hands outstretched and lifted to the heavens, like she's lifting the entire congregation up for a blessing.

Maddox takes the picture from me and studies it. I wait, wondering if he will have anything to say. He makes a small gasping sound, but that's all I get out of him. So I have to ask, "Do you recognize something?"

He nods slowly, stroking his chin with his free hand as he always does when he's contemplating something. "The banner behind them."

I look at it. The camera is far away from the banner that hangs above their heads in the distance, and I can't read it, though I think I do see a capital M, but most of what it says appears to be written in another language. The documents I have are in the same language I speak, but I know that Maatua has an ancient language as well, and I wonder if that's what is on the banner. Mystica spoke a bit of it. That's how she was able to tell me my true last name.

"Is the banner from Maatua?" I ask him.

Again, Maddox just nods. It's like he thinks if he doesn't speak of this, it can't be true. If he just ignores it, pretends it's all fake.

But I don't understand why. He must truly believe that not only are the cufflinks cursed but anything and everything that comes from Maatua is cursed–including me.

I need him to explain his thinking to me, so I set the cufflinks and the documents aside, and he gives me the picture to place on top of them. I reach for his hands, and he gives them to me. "Why is it so bad that I'm a princess?" I ask him. Maddox scoffs quietly and shakes his head. "Why can't you just accept that I am who Mystica says I am?"

"It's not that I don't want you to be a princess, baby," he says sweetly. "It's not even that I don't think you could be or already are as much of a princess as anyone ever could be. It's simply… you don't know much about this place you're… apparently from. And it's not the best place to be from, that's all."

"Because of the curse?" I ask him. "Maddox, you don't seem like the kind of person who believes in curses."

He scoffs at me quietly. "No, you're right. I don't. I usually would have no time for that sort of thinking. But in this case, the curse is so widespread, so dangerous, that I simply don't want to take a chance on letting it infiltrate my kingdom, that's all."

"So… you don't want me to infiltrate your kingdom?" I hear the sadness in my own voice as I ask the question.

He shakes his head slowly. "That's not what I'm saying, Isla. If this is truly who you are, if you really are the princess from Maatua who disappeared with her parents all those years ago, then I will embrace it, and we will do what needs to be done to make sure that you are well hidden here. But… I wouldn't wish that sort of existence on anyone."

His words settle into my thoughts, and I have to stop and ponder what he's saying for a long moment before I ask, "Well hidden?"

"Yes. It won't be easy. I mean, Mystica and a few others seem to already know the truth, but the fact that your parents were able to blend into Willow pack undetected for so long gives me hope that we can make it work. We will find a way." He pats my hand, and I can tell he's trying to be reassuring, but he's completely missing the mark.

"Maddox, I don't want to stay hidden," I tell him. "That's the last thing I want to do. I want to… figure out what happened. I want to help my people. I want to break whatever curse there is that has brought us to this situation."

"What?" He is looking at me like I have two heads as his forehead crinkles with confusion. "Isla, don't be stupid. You can't do any of that."

"Stupid?" I repeat, offended. I pull my hands away from him, but he grabs them again, not willing to let me get so mad. "It's not stupid. They're my people. How would you feel if you were in my position?"

"That's different," he says. "My kingdom isn't cursed, and I'm the king. You're just–"

"Just what?" I ask, my eyes doubling in size. "Just a princess? A princess who could be queen someday, under the right circumstances. I know that you've always felt that you were better than me because of our stations, Maddox, and I can't blame you for that, not really, but you don't have to talk down to me."

"I have never treated you with anything but respect," he snaps, and while I can think of plenty of times when that hasn't been the case, I'm not going to list them now. "You're third in line for the throne, Isla. And that's assuming your father wouldn't want one of your brothers instead of you. Really, you're turning this into a problem that doesn't have to be yours."

"It is my problem!" This time, I shoot up off of the bed. "It's my problem, they're my people, and I intend to help them!"

"By doing what?" he wants to know, also standing, towering over me in what seems like an attempt to intimidate me.

"By going back!" I say. "By going there and figuring out what the hell happened!"

The room goes silent as he continues to stare at me, his eyes boring into my soul, but I refuse to retreat. I refuse to blink.

And then he says the one word that makes my insides crumble into a thousand pieces.

"No."

WHAT'S WRONG WITH ME?

Isla

"No."

I stand there, staring at Maddox, unable to comprehend what he'd just said to me. I have to repeat the word out loud before it fully sinks into my mind. "No?" I ask him.

"That's right, Isla. There's no way in hell that I'm letting you go to Maatua. Not now. Not ever." He is standing in front of me with his hands folded across his chest, looking down at me, as if his word is final.

Technically, his word is final. After all, he is the Alpha King. He would be able to keep me from going there in several different ways–everything from just ordering me and compelling me to comply so as not to go against the word of the king to locking me up in the dungeon near Zabrina and the other captives he's just brought in from Hill Country pack.

Not that I think he'll go to those lengths, but as I look into his narrowed eyes, I understand that he means what he's saying to me. For whatever reason, this is not up for discussion.

But that doesn't mean that I'm willing to just say, "Oh, okay then," and let it go.

"Maddox," I begin, keeping my tone as level as possible, even though I feel my hands beginning to tremble and my heartbeat increasing. "You have to let me go. I need to understand what happened in my homeland. I need to find my people and make sure they are safe."

"Well, I think you can find out what happened from your parents, and as far as whether or not your people are safe, Isla, I'm sorry… but they're not. They couldn't possibly be. The war that happened there was violent and all-consuming. It was a total war where nothing was spared, and those who didn't escape to other lands before the war broke out are most certainly dead. The island is all but abandoned now. Only a few rogues live there, and it's practically uninhabitable because of the mass burnings that destroyed all of the buildings and the natural resources. So… there you go. Problem solved." He shrugs at me in a condescending way, and for once I wish I was much bigger so I could slug him.

"Oh, okay then." Now the words are coming out of my mouth, but my tone is very sarcastic. "If that's all there is to it, then I'll just go ahead and have my parents tell me all about what life was like there. They seem pretty willing to do that since they've been lying to me for at least the last eighteen years and my mom even lied to me about it on the phone a few days ago. But hey, I'm sure they'll be happy to comply now that they know my brother went snooping in their room, found some stuff there, stole it, and secretly brought it to me here." I throw up my hands and turn away from him.

Maddox says, "Wait–your parents don't know your brother is here? I thought you guys said they did."

I spin around and take a few steps closer to him. "After everything that I just said, that's what caught your attention? The fact that Ben might've lied to them about him staying over at a friend's house?"

Outside of my window, thunder growls and lightning rips across the sky. Sometimes, thunder makes me jump, but right now, I'm too angry to even let it register.

I need answers. I need them from Maddox, and I need them now.

"Isla, I have a lot going on right now," he says, his eyes dropping to the floor where he's toeing the carpet with his boot. "I know you get that better than anyone else except for maybe Seth. Can we talk about this later? Like in a few days? Or a week? Or a month?"

I take a deep breath. What he's saying to me doesn't sound unreasonable. He has had a lot going on lately; for that matter, he has a lot going on all of the time. But a lot of this stuff is going on because of me.

"Fine," I say with a deep breath. "We can talk about it later, but not in a week or a month. I'm sorry to tell you this, Maddox, but I'm going to fight you on this one. You can't just tell me that I can't go there."

"Yes, I can," he says, taking a step closer to me. I don't retreat, even though everything inside of me is telling me to cower to him, to bare my neck and make the sign of respect, leaving myself vulnerable to his sharp wolf teeth. But I don't. I keep my eyes trained on his as he continues.

"I can keep you from going there, Isla. Not because I'm the Alpha or the king or a lot bigger and stronger than you but because I own you."

I feel my eyes bulging from my head as my mouth drops open. He's never said anything like that to me before. In all of the time that I've been here in the castle, never once has he made me feel like I am a belonging, something he can just use and toss aside, something he can command.

Not even when he made me feel worthless the other day when I was leaving his office did he make me feel like a possession.

"You... w-what?" I ask, still staring up at him.

"That's right," he says, nodding his head. "You belong to me. You don't go anywhere without my permission, remember? We just discussed this. You're here to do a job, and you will do that job. After you've done that job, if you care to leave the castle, we shall discuss it then. But for now, as long as you belong to me, you will not leave this castle without my permission. And I do not give you permission to go to Maatua." He leans forward so that his nose is practically touching mine. "Is that clear?"

A wave of nausea washes over me, turning my stomach and making bile rise up the back of my throat. It seems like an odd response to my Alpha King's intimidation tactics, but I suddenly feel sweaty, clammy, like I'm about to throw up–or pass out.

I open my mouth to say something, but I can't get a word out, and I feel my eyes begin to roll into the back of my head as I lose sight of Maddox.

"Isla?" he asks, and his tone has changed. I feel myself tipping backward and hope I am close to the bed so that when I fall, I will land on the mattress, though falling on the artifacts my brother brought is probably not a good idea.

I don't feel the bed behind me when I tip back, though. Instead, I feel Maddox's arms as he says my name again. "Isla? What's the matter?" he asks me.

My eyes roll back to their proper position, and I say, "I'm sorry. I don't feel good."

Without a word, he sweeps me up and lays me on the bed, moving the backpack and paperwork out of the way and placing them on the nightstand. He picks up a glass of water I have sitting there from this morning and lifts it to my lips.

I take a sip and choke it down. It gets stuck in my throat for a second, but then I get it down, along with the contents of my stomach that were trying to come back up earlier. My mouth still tastes sour. I reach for the glass and take another drink as Maddox sits next to me on the bed.

"What can I do?" he asks me. I can hear the concern in his voice. It has replaced all of the commanding tone he was using to address me earlier.

I shake my head. At least I can see him again now. "Nothing, I'm fine," I tell him.

"Clearly, you are not fine. Have you been feeling badly all day, or did this just come over you right now?" He brushes my hair back away from my face, and I can feel how sweaty it is when it bounces back and sticks to my skin again.

"No, I've been fine," I tell him. It's the truth. I haven't been feeling bad at all today. "I wonder if it's just left over from hiding my head on that tree."

"I don't think so," he says. "And the poison should all be out of your system by now. Could it be… what I said?"

Part of me wants to say that it is. It's what he said to me earlier that upset me so much it almost made me pass out, but I'm pretty sure that's not it. "Maybe it's just… too much excitement for one day," I reply. "I'm sure I'll be back to myself soon enough."

"Well, I already sent for Mystica, so we'll have her do a thorough exam," he says.

"Maddox!" My tone conveys my protest. "No, I don't want her to have to come and examine me again. She sees me more than anyone else in the castle!"

That makes him chuckle for some reason. "Maybe that's because you're the most important person in the castle."

I narrow my gaze at him. "A moment ago you reminded me that you own me." I probably shouldn't have said that, but he is always sending me mixed signals. I felt compelled to call him on it.

His smile fades. "It's true, Isla. That doesn't mean that I don't have feelings for you. I already told you that I love you."

"Yes, and I'm sure people who have pet dogs love them, too," I reply snidely.

He shakes his head at me. "You're not a dog, Isla. You're a wolf."

"I'm also a person, Maddox. A person with feelings. And I hate it when you talk to me like that, like I don't even matter."

"Don't be ridiculous." He says it like I'm way off base. "You definitely matter, Isla. More than anyone." He leans down and presses his lips to my head, and while I want to keep arguing with him, Mystica opens the door and walks in.

"What happened, dear?" she asks.

"She almost passed out," Maddox says, getting up and moving aside so that the healer can examine me.

"Oh, dear," she says, coming over to me. "Let me check your vitals and run a few tests. Have you eaten today?"

"Yes," I say to her. "But not very much."

"Hmmm," she says as she listens to my heart, takes my temperature, and then checks my blood pressure. "Everything seems normal. Maybe your blood sugar is low. I'll take a bit and go run some tests, all right?"

"Okay." What am I going to say to argue with her?

It stings a little as she sticks the needle in my arm, but then, she leaves, and Maddox and I are in the room alone together again. He's managed to put the items my brother brought me into the backpack without Mystica seeing them–purposely, I'm sure–and I am beginning to wonder where my brother is.

Before I can reach him through the mind-link, Maddox says, "I'll leave you to get some rest while I go take care of a few things, but Isla, if you start feeling badly again, let me know. And don't you dare try to go anywhere."

Thunder booms outside, and I say, "Don't worry. I'm not going out in the rain."

He looks at me like he's not sure he can trust me but then bends to kiss me, and I let him before he takes off, leaving me all alone with my thoughts.

Now, I not only don't know who I am... I don't know what's wrong with me.

DEALING WITH HER AGAIN

Maddox

WELL, I fucked up again. Obviously.

Leaving Isla alone to get some rest or maybe visit with her brother if he comes back, I head back to my office. Now that I've had the relaxing diversion of arguing with my breeder–or lover–or whatever the fuck you want to call her–I'm ready to get back to work.

I see Seth in the hallway walking at a brisk pace, and the way he's flying down the hallway, practically running, I have to wonder what the hell has happened now. I don't even want to know. But I ask. "What's going on?"

Seth shakes his head. "It's Zabrina," he says. "She's just down there in the dungeon throwing a fit, and the guards want to know if they can sedate her. I told them to go ahead, but somehow, when they went in to give her the shot, she managed to rip it out of the guard's hand with her teeth and plunged it into the guard's face. Now, they're all hesitant to go back in there."

"Oh, for fuck's sake!" I say, wondering how this woman has gotten to be such a pain in my ass. Thank the Moon Goddess she will be dead tomorrow, even if I have to rip her head off myself.

"I'm headed down there to handle it myself now," Seth says to me, and I can see in his eyes he's had just about as much as he can take from her, same as me.

"I'm coming with you," I decide. The work in my office that needs to be done is all trivial shit that can wait, though I know that Alpha Jordan's Luna has all kinds of other Alphas calling me, trying to convince me that Zabrina is innocent, and I'm going after the wrong person. I didn't buy her bullshit story when she pitched it to me, and I don't buy it now. I won't buy it when I hear it on my answering machine from other Alphas who are clearly more loyal to Alpha Jordan than me, either.

As soon as we open the door to the stairwell that leads down to the dungeon, I can hear her screaming.

"Fuck you! Fuck all of you! I'm going to rip your dicks off and shove them down your throats! You might think you can kill me, but I will be back! I will haunt your dreams, I will haunt you every moment of your fucking lives!"

When I get to the space right outside of her cell, I see that she's feeling a lot better than she was when we brought her in. She's practically naked, her clothes in tatters, like she's attempted to shift and hasn't been able to do that, probably because she did have a shot earlier of something that would keep that from happening. But she'd been wounded then, and she's obviously healed herself.

I stand back and watch her as she practically rips her own fingernails off, her hands clamped along the bars as she shakes and screams, banging her head against the bars.

My mind goes back to the first time I met her. She seemed to be a polished, well-educated, sophisticated young woman. I wasn't interested in her one bit, and it was clear that she only wanted to date me–or have sex with me or marry me or whatever–because she wants to be the next Luna Queen.

Now, looking at the wild creature in front of me, it's almost impossible to believe she could possibly be the same person. Her hair is ratted and messy, not the coiffed pinned up, elegant locks I remember. Her face is a mess, with scratches all over and cracked lips. Her eyes are swollen and bruised, and she has dried blood under her nose. She's hit her head on the bars a few times, so she has welts and bumps on her forehead.

I remember the elegant dresses she would wear to dinner. That's a far cry from the rags she has on now that don't even properly cover her. Her exposed body is covered in bruises and cuts.

It's honestly hard to believe this is the same woman.

But... when I stop to ponder all of the horrible things this monster has done to so many people, including killing her own maid and an innocent guard, I have to think this wild version of Zabrina is probably more accurate than the one she'd tried to present herself as when she first arrived at the castle.

"Zabrina!" I finally bark at her. "Shut the fuck up!"

When she realizes it's me speaking, she continues to carry on for a long moment, but then, her wailing fades, and she begins to hyperventilate, sucking in air as she tries to calm herself. Her erratic behavior calms as well, and she stands there, her head resting on the bars in front of her as she gasps for air.

My Alpha King ability to bend my subjects has worked well on her. Sometimes, it's not as easy to get my biggest advisors to do as I say, even with this ability given to me by the Moon Goddess, but considering she is exhausted and mentally drained.

"Zabrina, you're wasting your final hours acting like a fucking psycho!" I tell her. "You're dying tomorrow. There's nothing you can do to get out of it. You may as well calm the fuck down and enjoy the few hours you have left. If you'll stop acting like a crazy person, I'll have the guards bring down one of your favorite dishes, but otherwise, you're going to die on an empty stomach."

Rather than verbally responding, she looks up and meets my eyes, staring right through me for the longest moment before she begins to sob. At first, it's just a few tears as she continues to gasp for air, but then, she breaks down completely in loud, vibrating, deep sobs that fill the entire dungeon with their lamentable sound.

"I don't want to die," she says, over and over again. "Please, please, Alpha King Maddox. I'm too young. I don't want to die."

"You know who else was young?" I ask her, not waiting for her to stop crying to answer me. "Your maid. Private Parker. Even Private Wylie."

She doesn't respond, only continues to cry, on her knees now, her hands over her face.

With a sigh, I move toward one of the guards who was clearly involved in the mauling earlier as he has claw marks across his chest where his uniform is ripped, and the scratches on his face, though crusted over now, look deep.

He is holding the one thing that Zabrina deserves right now. As I motion for him to give it to me, he complies quickly. Zabrina isn't looking at me as she weeps bitter tears into her hands.

I crouch down across from her. Even though her hands are through the cell bars, I'm not afraid of her. She's tired, weak, and distracted. She won't be able to get anything over on me.

I can sense it in her, though, as I get close to her. All of this is an act, and she thinks I'm too stupid to know what she's up to.

"Zabrina," I say, "you've made your bed. And now you'll lie in it."

Her eyes latch on to mine, her tears dry up, and that wild look is back on her face as she reaches for me.

I am faster than her, though. I catch both of her hands, claws extended, in my right hand, holding them together as I plunge the needle I've gotten from the guard into her upper arm and push down the plunger.

"Nooo!" she screams, her fangs protruding from her mouth as she realizes she's not going to be able to hurt me. And now that she's drugged, we can keep her sedated until we take her to the gallows tomorrow. We'll need to let her wake up a little so she can walk under her own power, but there will be no contemplating all of her mistakes tonight. Even before I stand up and release her arms, her eyes are starting to gloss over.

"There you go, bitch," I say as she slowly falls backward onto her bottom. "The next time you wake up, you'll be facing the gallows and then your maker."

"Fuck you, Maddox," she says, her words slurred slightly. "You think this is over, but it's not. It doesn't end with me. I already warned you. I'm not the culprit here. There are others, stronger than me, angrier than me, and more compelled to bring you down than me."

"Then I hope they're a fucking lot smarter than you, too," I say, just to jab her.

She glares at me, and I can see she wants to try to spit on me, but I'm far enough away now that if she does spit, it will land on the floor. "I hate you!" she says. "I will haunt you! I will show up in your nightmares and when you're walking down the hallway at night! You think your fucking Rebecca haunts this castle? You just wait! And if I see that bitch in hell, I'll kill her again!"

She's trying to hurt me, but it just pisses me off. "Rebecca isn't in hell, but if she sees you on the other side, she will shred you to pieces, Zabrina. You have nothing on her. She was a Luna Queen, and you're just a selfish little bitch daughter of an incompetent Alpha." I keep my voice even, my tone unstrained.

"Well, you're forgetting one similarity between Rebecca and I," she says, pausing like I might ask her what she's talking about, but I don't because I don't give a fuck what she's talking about. She continues, "You killed both of us."

The guards and Seth move toward her then, ready to beat her for saying such an awful thing to me, but there's nothing Zabrina can say about Rebecca that can hurt me. I've already accepted the fact that I'm responsible for my wife's death. The words coming out of her vile lips don't make it any more or less the truth.

The guards don't need to pummel her, she's already fallen backward onto the floor, her head making a sick cracking sound on the concrete, and for a moment, I hope maybe she's already dead. But she's not. She's still breathing. I can hear her heartbeat.

Now that my job here is done, I turn and head back upstairs, Seth behind me. "That was… vicious," he comments.

I say nothing. I don't have any words to describe what it was. I'm just glad it's over. I decide to head to my office now since Isla is probably still sleeping, but as soon as I get to the top of the stairs, I hear Mystica's voice in my head.

"Can you come back to Miss Isla's room, please?" she asks me, her tone calm.

"Okay," I say, using the mind-link. "Is everything all right?" Unlike my time with Zabrina, this makes me nervous. I am doing my best to sound calm.

"Well, I'll leave that for you to decide," she says. "I just need you there when I give her the results of the tests I ran."

I feel my heart stop beating and practically have to thump myself in the chest to start it again. "Mystica, what is it?" I ask her.

Her only response is, "I will tell you when you get to her room."

THE GOOD NEWS AND THE
BAD NEWS

Isla

I AM DREAMING AGAIN. I know that it's a dream because nothing I'm experiencing makes sense to me from my most recent memories, and as I puzzle over what I am looking at, trying to put it together, I'm struggling to figure out not only where I am but when I am… as well as who I am.

This feels different than the other two dreams I've had recently where it took me a while to realize that I was dreaming and then to figure out who I was, but I seemed to know when it was happening.

The sensations that surround me as I stand in this meadow and look at this young woman and young man who are obviously in love make me think that this dream is more like the memory I had of getting on the boat with my parents back when we fled Maatua, the dream I had when I was dying.

I know I'm not dying right now. I'm just sleeping. But this does feel like a memory.

The only problem is, as much as I feel a familiarity toward both of these people, I have no idea who they are.

The girl is beautiful, with large blue eyes and long caramel blonde hair that falls to her waist in soft waves. She's wearing a fancy light pink dress, and I think this must be an important moment for her, as she is looking at the boy–or maybe he's more of a man, a young man–and smiling.

He is quite handsome, and in some ways, he reminds me of a younger version of Maddox. He has the same dark hair, but his eyes are a jade green color. His jaw isn't quite as strong, and he's not nearly as muscular, though he is well built. Something about the softness in his gaze reminds me of someone else I know, but I can't place that look.

The suit he's wearing is nice, though the jacket is off, leaving him in black slacks, a white button-down, and a red bow tie. He also has on suspenders that make the whole scene seem a bit old-fashioned. But I know this isn't a memory.

Unless it's a memory from one of my ancestors that they're projecting into my mind from beyond. Could these people be my parents? No, I don't get that impression at all. They don't look like my parents. And I've seen their wedding photo recently, so it's not them.

Perhaps my grandparents? I shrug and step a bit closer to them. They know I'm here, but they are talking to one another in sweet whispers, and I would feel like I am intruding, but they glance at me and smile every once in a while.

They are holding hands, and the golden sun dances on the highlights in her hair. She is a sweet, gentle soul. I can tell by the way she's gazing at him. In a way, perhaps it's her nose or the set of her eyes, or maybe it's her petite figure, she reminds me a little of Sydney, but she looks too kind to be any relation to Sydney.

But then again, if she was brought up by someone else, other than Sydney's parents, perhaps she might be her cousin or something….

They both start laughing at something one or the other of them has said, and then he pulls her in for a quick kiss before they both turn to me. The young man says, "Did you hear? She said yes, Mom!"

"Mom?" I repeat, as confusion washes over me, but then I feel someone shaking my shoulder, and the meadow, the bright golden sun, the two smiling faces, and the feeling of joy radiating from the couple all washes away.

I blink a few times, looking up into Mystica's face. "Hello, Isla," she says with a chuckle. "Sorry to have had to wake you, dear. I have some news."

Groggy, I have a hard time processing the information she's just given to me. I push up off of the mattress to sitting and run a hand through my hair, longing for the happiness I left behind in the meadow. That place seemed so peaceful compared to here.

I take a sip from my glass of water as Maddox comes into the room, and I feel my gut tighten. The last time I saw him, we were arguing, that is until I nearly passed out. Now, here he is with a concerned look on his face, as well as a scowl.

"What is it, Mystica?" he demands, which makes me think she must have summoned him here. I wonder where my brother is. He hasn't come back from the kitchen. Is he lost? I wish he was here to hold my hand and make me feel calm.

Maddox can't do that right now. The king is standing at the foot of my bed with his hands in his pockets as he scrutinizes the healer, his eyes shifting from her to me and back again.

Mystica gives him a look that should serve as a warning that he needs to stop behaving like a beast, and I see Maddox's expression soften just slightly.

"I thought you might want to both know at the same time what I've discovered from the tests I've run," she says. "But perhaps I should ask Miss Isla if she'd like to hear the results alone. You might be the king, but if you're going to continue to act like a menace, she might not want to share her confidential health information with you!"

Maddox's gaze narrows. "Tell us both, now." His voice is a low growl.

Mystica turns to look at me, and I know immediately what my choices are. I can either agree with the king that she should go ahead and tell us what she discovered in front of him, or I can disagree, and she will send him out. If that's the case, he will not go quietly. She will have to fight him, and even though I don't think he'd ever hurt her, it's not worth it.

No, I may as well let him stay, even if he is acting rather barbaric. "What did you discover, Mystica?" I ask her.

She clears her throat and says, matter-of-factly, "The reason you're feeling this way, dear, is that you are pregnant."

My eyes bulge from my head and my chin drops to my chest. "Pregnant?" I repeat, and she nods her head.

I shake mine. "No," I say. "I don't think that's possible. I was nearly dead just a couple of weeks ago. Surely, that would've terminated any pregnancy. And if I'd gotten pregnant since then, you wouldn't be able to determine that yet, would you? The baby would be so small…."

"It's a fact," she says with a brisk nod of her head. "You are about six weeks along. Which does mean that the child was within you when you almost died, though undetectable by any tests I would've run at the time."

Both of us shift our eyes to look at Maddox.

For the first time that I can remember since I've met him, he looks completely stunned–speechless. He is just standing there, his face devoid of any sort of expression and almost as white as the sheets on my bed.

"Maddox?" I cry, wondering if one of us should go prod him. "Are you all right?"

He shakes his head slightly, and I see his Adam's apple bob as he swallows. "Fine, fine," he says. "Uhm… did you say… she's… pregnant?"

"Oh, good. Your ears do work when you're in a trance," Mystica says, chuckling under her breath. "Yes, that's what I said. But here's the thing I need both of you to consider. This child has been exposed to some toxic substances. Not only did the poor baby have to put up with everything Zabrina did to you when she tried to kill you," she says softly as she looks into my eyes, "I'm afraid many of the drugs I used to save your life are not good for wee babies either."

"What are you saying?" Maddox demands as if Mystica is the enemy here.

She gives him another stern look. "I'm saying… there is a possibility the pregnancy may not be viable. And if the child does survive to term, there's a chance he or she may have certain limitations due to what they've been exposed to."

"So you mean a handicapped child?" Maddox blurts out, and I am livid.

"What!" I demand, sliding to the edge of the bed. "Don't use that word in my presence! I don't care who you are!"

Maddox looks at me like he can't believe his question has made me so mad as I storm across the room at him. "Wh–what?"

"My brother had limitations for quite some time! He was wheelchair-bound and suffered all kinds of symptoms from his diagnosis. But now, he's here, walking around, doing everything any perfectly able-bodied person can do! So if you're going to speak of someone's limitations, use terminology that's not so offensive!"

He stares at me for a long moment before he says, "Like… what?"

"Like differently-abled! " I shout at him. "I won't have you calling our baby names!"

"I'm sorry, Isla!" he says quickly, reaching for me. Hot, salty tears run down my face as I try to process all of this. I'm pregnant? But my baby might not make it. And if my baby does make it… they may have a difficult life because of what was done to me.

None of it is fair! All of it hurts.

I can't help but break down, and Maddox lifts me into his arms and carries me back to the bed. "It'll be all right, Isla." He smooths back my hair and then pulls the blankets over me, but I can't even look at him, I'm crying so hard.

Mystica hands me some tissues, and I try to get myself under control. But I'm struggling to breathe. "We'll do everything we can to help the baby," she says. "I have some supplements you can begin taking, and we'll take a peek with an ultrasound and see how the growth is coming along. Try not to worry about it, love. You know the Moon Goddess has a plan."

I think about what the Moon Goddess's plans have been for me so far, and I'm not impressed. Sure, I'm a breeder to the Alpha King, but having to flee my homeland because of war and having to work a million awful jobs because of my brother's illness… all of the trials and tribulations we went through… none of that was fun.

"It's too bad you're not still in Maatua," Mystica says under her breath, and I immediately stop crying enough to look up at her.

"Wh-why is that?" I manage to get out between hiccups.

"Well, because… in Maatua, they have a way to fix all of this." She makes the statement as if it's a well-known fact.

I hear the skepticism in his voice as Maddox asks, "What fix is that?"

Mystica looks him in the eyes and says simply, "The fountain."

TELL ME ALREADY!

Isla

ALL THE INFORMATION that Mystica is giving me is too much for my mind to process all at once. I'm going to need a few moments to get it all into my brain. For now, I'm still stuck on trying to grasp the idea that I'm pregnant.

I'm pregnant, and my child was not only exposed to the wolfsbane that that horrible bitch Zabrina poisoned my body with, but who knows what kind of damage the medications Mystica gave me in an attempt to heal me could cause in a body so tiny and undeveloped?

Maddox is telling Mystica to stop filling my head with nonsense when I finally begin to pay attention to their discussion again, and the healer looks horribly offended. "Your Majesty!" she declares. "I am not filling her head with nonsense! It is about time that you came to understand the truth of the situation. You have to accept the fact that your beloved breeder here is more than just the title you have bestowed upon her! She is, in fact, a princess! She is from Maatua! And she does have capabilities beyond anything you have ever experienced before!"

Maddox glowers at her, but before he can say anything, I intervene, "Mystica," I say, reaching for her hand. "Thank you for standing up for me. I appreciate how you've always been so quick to tell me the truth, to the best of your ability, when it comes to dealing with everything that I have faced–my past included. Maddox and I have discussed the possibility that I am from Maatua, and we will continue to discuss that point, so please don't feel that you must keep imploring him to believe you. Truly, it hurts my heart to see you feel that you must put yourself in such a position to have to argue with your own Alpha King on my behalf."

"It shouldn't, dear!" she insists, patting my hand. "I fully respect the king and the power of his position, but I will never sit idly by and let false information be proclaimed as truth by anyone."

Mystica gets another grunt out of the king, and I hope to be able to prevent her from digging herself into a further hole, but she still doesn't seem to be listening.

My true goal in asking her to drop it had been to get back to what she'd said about a way for my child to be saved from any difficulties the poison and medications may have caused, and I don't know how to get her back to that when Maddox still wants to assert his authority and convince her that she's out of line talking to me about Maatua.

"The fountain?" I blurt out, catching Maddox's eyes as he seems about ready to shout at her. "What fountain, Mystica? Where is it, and what can it do?"

"Oh, well, why even bother to tell you of its great power when clearly everything I know of Maatua from living there for decades is a work of fiction!"

I've heard her get snippy with Maddox several times, but this is the most irritated I've ever heard her, and it concerns me. I don't want him to blurt out something he can't take back. I think back to the gallows I know he was having erected earlier, before the storm. I can see him saying something stupid like she needs to join Zabrina and the warriors from Hill Pack tomorrow for disrespecting the king.

"It does matter," I assure her. "It matters to me, most certainly, and I believe it matters to the king as well. He will want to do whatever is possible to help our child."

Our child. I say the words quickly in context, but as soon as they are out of my mouth, I can't help but look at the king. I am having a baby–another life is growing inside of my body–and Maddox is the father. This new person we have created together is part him and part me. I don't know how anyone can say that magic doesn't exist when they contemplate the miracle of new life.

Mystica is looking at Maddox when she says, "I'm happy to tell you, dear, but at the same time, I'd hate to anger His Royal Highness."

"Mystica," Maddox begins, and I can tell that he's calmer than he was a few moments ago. Perhaps the reality of what I've said is beginning to sink in for him, too, and he knows he needs to at least listen to what she has to say. "That's enough. You don't need to take that sort of attitude with me. Just... tell Isla what the hell you're talking about without taking shots at me."

Mystica is still irritated, but when I squeeze her hand, she decides to do the right thing and let Maddox's earlier statements go in favor of his new, more cool, collected persona.

The healer takes a deep breath and sits down in a chair next to my bed. I get the impression this isn't going to be a simple answer.

"In Maatua," she begins, "nature is not quite as important to the people as the Moon Goddess herself, but it is often a close second. We believe that the Goddess often shows herself through the beauty she brings to the earth, that the majesty of the mountains, the tranquility of the ocean, the white sands of the endless beach all work together to glorify the Moon Goddess. In turn, the Moon Goddess uses nature to bring blessings upon her people."

"You mean like the blessings of a war where nearly every citizen died?" Maddox asks, folding his arms across his muscular chest and rocking back and forth, changing his weight from one foot to the other.

Mystica glares at him. "No! That was the doing of a nonbeliever! One who let his lust for power grow so strong, he would do anything to become king, including destroying is own country and betraying his own family."

I know she is speaking of my own uncle when she talks, but I say nothing, wishing that Maddox wouldn't either. I know how Mystica is, and if we allow her to speak at her own pace without interrupting, it could take an hour for her to get to the point.

I attempt to move her along with what I hope is a well-phrased question. "So the fountain was a gift from the Moon Goddess?" I ask her.

She nods, her eyes softer as they fall on my face. "Yes. It was discovered in the forest near the foot of one of the most sacred mountains near the capital city hundreds of years ago. A child was picnicking nearby with his parents when he was bitten by a deadly viper. No one had ever lived from being struck by this sort of snake. His mother used water from the fountain to wash the wound, and not only did the child live, but within a few moments, he was revived to complete health as if he'd never been bitten before!" Mystica smiles and claps her hands before raising them both to the heavens. "Hail thee, oh, sacred Goddess of the Moon."

Another grunt came from the foot of the bed. "What if it just wasn't a poisonous snake?" the king asks.

Mystica opens her eyes and narrows her gaze at him. "The story is true! You can ask anyone who has ever lived in Maatua."

"Even the dead people? Why didn't they just carry everyone who was wounded in battle to the fountain so they wouldn't die?" I don't like his sarcastic tone.

"If you must know, the battles were waged in the city, far away from the fountain!" she replies with a bite to her tone just as venomous as the snake, I imagine.

Maddox only shakes his head. I want to tell him to shut up, but he is the king, and doing so will only make the situation worse.

"Throughout the years, many more stories were told of people who had suffered great injuries, illnesses, even death. When they were taken to the fountain, they were always completely healed. The only limitation was that they had to get there within a few hours of their passing, or else the fountain's powers would not work," Mystica explains.

I look at Maddox as I think he is about to say something else snide and unnecessary, but he doesn't speak.

"I believe, if you go to the fountain and bathe in it, even while you are still pregnant, you will heal your unborn child of any afflictions he or she may have suffered from the wolfsbane and other substances you've recently had in your body, dear," she says. "Oh, how I wish I had known at the time! I would've been more precautious."

"If you'd been more precautious, Mystica, Isla would be dead," Maddox reminds her.

The healer sighs, and for once she agrees with him, nodding her head. "Perhaps this is so. But... I feel terrible for the hand I've played in any harm befalling the heir."

My hands go to my abdomen. It's just as flat as it's always been, but I can sense the child within me now. Thinking of myself as the woman carrying the heir to the throne, the next king or queen of our lands, makes tears come to my eyes.

Maddox misinterprets them. "It's all right, baby," he says, rushing to the opposite side of the bed from where Mystica is sitting. "We will find a way to make sure our child is healthy."

I take the hand he offers me, but I shake my head. "You can't know that for certain. It's not as if you believe in the fountain Mystica speaks of. And since you've already forbidden me to go to Maatua, the point is moot anyway."

Before he can reply, Mystica says, "Forbidden her to go? To her own homeland?"

"Mystica, please," Maddox begins. "That does not concern you. At all."

"But it does!" the healer insists. "She is the princess! If she wants to return to her home, how can you stop her?"

"How?" Maddox asks, turning with fire burning in his eyes again. "Easily! I am the king!"

I hope that he doesn't mention owning me again. As much as that might technically be true, it makes me feel very small to hear him shout that, even when he's obviously mad and not thinking clearly.

"Besides, Mystica," Maddox continues. "For all of your talk of the beauty and enchantment of Maatua, you are not mentioning one rather important detail at all! Why is it that you think Isla deserves to know all of the wonderful features of her homeland but not the ugly parts?"

"What is it you're speaking of?" I ask him, feeling my heart rate increase. "What ugly parts?"

He stares at Mystica for a moment, silently ordering her to be the one to tell me. But she keeps her lips pressed together and her chin raised. Somehow, she's strong enough to refuse what is all but a direct order from the Alpha.

"Fine," he says. "I'll tell her." Turning back to look at me, Maddox says, "The curse."

ABOUT THE CURSE

Maddox

THE SHADOWS on the ceiling begin their dance again, and I suddenly feel all alone, like I used to just a few months ago that feels like a lifetime ago. I watch as tree branches turn to fingers, beckoning, pointing, accusing. I would shift my position and look at the wall, but it wouldn't make any of the problems and responsibilities weighing me down go away.

Isla wanted to sleep alone tonight. She said that she needed some time to process everything, and she still wasn't feeling well.

I believe her on both accounts, but it makes me sad. My arms feel empty without her wrapped within them. My chest feels cold and exposed without her head cradled there.

I've made a lot of mistakes in the last few months. I can't admit that to anyone else, but I can admit it to myself, at least to a degree. I knew that Isla was special the moment I first laid eyes on her, standing in her bedroom with a towel wrapped around her, and especially when I caught a glimpse of her perfect form in the mirror in the bathroom as she hastily dressed. But once I got to know her, it was clear to me that she and I were meant to be together.

Even if I don't know how that fits into my decision never to take another Luna, she is having my child, a child I must protect at all costs. The idea that there might be something wrong with my baby isn't conceivable to me. I am the king. I should be able to command everything to be well with my child, but I can't. I have no power over such things. It's difficult for me to accept the fact that there are things even I cannot speak into existence.

My mind goes back to Isla and how I have treated her recently, how I refused to listen when she tried to tell me the truth about who she is, where she came from. That place… I don't even want to think about it, but now I have no choice. As much as I don't want to admit it is the truth, I know that she truly is the Princess of Maatua.

Turning over onto my side, I look at the window. The curtains are parted slightly, and I can see a full moon hanging in the sky, its silvery light bathing the tops of the trees in the garden.

I think of Isla's face when I told her she couldn't go to try and find this ridiculous fountain Mystica told her about. "The curse," I'd told her. "You can't go because of the curse."

Her eyes had widened, and she'd demanded to know what I was talking about. "How can you refuse to believe in the magic of the healing fountain," she'd asked me, "but readily accept the notion that there's an island with a curse on it?"

I'd sat down beside her on the bed and said, "It's not that I believe the curse is necessarily real, but I don't see the point in toying with it either if it's not necessary. I mean, I'm pretty sure I could get bitten by a poisonous viper two miles from the castle and run back in time to get the anti-venom, but I'm not willing to take the chance."

She'd narrowed her eyes at my analogy. "And you don't think potentially saving the life of your child is reason enough to take the risk?"

"I don't think there will be anything wrong with our child," I said. "I trust in the Moon Goddess, and I know she wouldn't give me a child at all if she was only going to take the baby away." I'd tried to sound confident.

But Isla's next words stung like the bit of a venomous viper.

"So… why would the Moon Goddess give you a fated mate if she was only going to take her away?"

She'd said the words in a calm tone, not an antagonistic one, but it had hurt–deeply. I think my response was too raw for her.

"The Moon Goddess didn't take Rebecca from me," I'd told her. "I lost her myself."

She'd taken a deep breath and stared into my eyes before she said, "You still haven't told me of the curse."

I'd looked at Mystica then, thinking she'd be better able to tell the tale of her own land, but the healer had shaken her head. "By all means, Your Majesty," she'd said with a flourish of her arm. "Speak your truth."

I'd glared at her for a moment before I'd returned my attention to Isla. "The story I've heard is that when two brothers were warring over the crown, one of them turned to the mountains and to an evil mage who's said to have lived there for hundreds of years. He asked the mage to unleash a spell upon all of the people so that those who stayed but did not turn to him as their new ruler would die, and only those who would accept him would be spared. Because he was evil, and the hearts of the people of Maatua were good, everyone perished except for a very few people who dropped to their knees in order to spare their lives and declared he would be king."

"So…" Isla had said, her mouth pursed as she mulled over the story. "Wouldn't that mean that he would still be there and be ruling as king over the very few people who accepted him?"

"No," I said quickly with a shake of my head. "Because six months after the war ended, there was a violent earthquake that shook the entire island. Most of the dwellings that had survived the fires that had been started during the fighting fell to the ground, including the palace. Only a small part of the castle remains intact today–the Temple of the Moon Goddess. The rest crumbled, including the throne room, where King Antonio was holding court. He was killed. It's said that when the few survivors came looking for him, they found his head severed by a large chunk of marble that had fallen from the ceiling."

"Antonio?" she had repeated. "Uncle Tony?" Her eyes had gone to Mystica.

The healer had nodded. "If the curse is true, he would be the one who went to the mage. The other brother was, of course–"

"My father," Isla had supplied. Then, she was looking at me again. "Do you believe, then, that the earthquake was part of the curse?"

I'd shrugged. "Isla, all magic has a price. Tony wanted something, and he got it, but then he lost his life. It's said that people who have gone to the island to gather valuables to sell or trade end up dying within a few months of returning from there. People who purchase those items have also been known to die. You almost died on the day you did so." I'd had to point that out to her, even though it clearly upset her.

"And I was saved by someone who learned to heal people while she lived on the island," she reminded me. "I don't understand, Maddox." She'd reached over and taken my hand. "If our baby is in danger of dying or having a horrible disease, why wouldn't we at least go try? If I have this baby safely, and then something happens to me, at least my baby will be alive."

I'd immediately shaken my head, unable to think of the possibility of losing her. "No." Once again, I was unable to tell her anything more than that. My decision was final.

I'd gotten up and walked to the door, my hand on the knob as I'd said, "We are not going there. You are never going there. And when your brother leaves, make sure he takes everything with him that came from Maatua." I'd stormed off and hadn't seen her again all evening, but as I'd closed her bedroom door, I'd heard her begin to weep.

Sighing, I thought about how I'd tried to lose myself in work after that but been unable to. I'd really made a mess of everything, not because of the decisions I'd made–I didn't regret telling her she couldn't go–but because of the way I'd ordered her about. She didn't deserve to be spoken to that way, like she was a helpless child.

Now, I am contemplating going to her, sneaking into her room and wrapping my arms around her soft, warm body, pulling her to my chest, kissing her sweet lips, and falling asleep in the only way I ever can now–nestled up with her.

It was my pride that got me into this situation where I am sleeping by myself, and it is my pride that is preventing me from fixing it. Once again, I roll over, this time to face the wall, and bury my face in my arm.

I close my eyes and try to picture a happy scene, Isla and I in a meadow, a picnic blanket beneath us, children laughing and running around us, the sun highlighting their golden hair. Each of them reminds me of their mother with hints of me in their facial features.

That doesn't help for long, though, as the smile that momentarily lit my face slides away, and I grimace again at the weight of everything I must carry on my shoulders.

Thoughts of what will transpire tomorrow come to mind. I need to have my wits about me to perform the first public execution ceremony in many years, the first one ever where the daughter of an Alpha will be put to death. If I'm not rested, it will show, and I will appear to be weak and flustered. No, I must find a way to go to sleep–but I'll have to do it here, on my own.

Somewhere in the distance, a wolf howls, filling the night air with the mournful tones of a creature out in the darkness reaching for an unattainable goal, an object that will always be far beyond their limitations of achieving.

That's how I feel now, not about Isla or my baby or what is about to happen tomorrow but about restoring peace and prosperity to this kingdom so that no one has to be concerned anymore about the threat of war, about being slaughtered in their own home as they sleep, about being poisoned and dragged from their loved ones.

But peace may as well be as distant as the moon, and I feel I'll never reach it. As my eyelids begin to flutter, I have to wonder, maybe it's not just Maatua that's cursed.

Maybe I am, too.

CONFIDING IN THE WRONG FRIEND

Isla

"I JUST DON'T UNDERSTAND how he can be so confident about the existence of this curse but not be willing to budge an inch when it comes to the discussion of the fountain." I take a bit of my piece of toast and shake my head, not sure if I'm actually going to be able to eat much of what Poppy has set before me on the table this morning. All night, I tossed and turned, thinking about Maddox and the discussion we'd had right before I asked him to leave the night before.

"Well, he is very protective of you," Ben says, still chewing. His appetite has definitely not been affected by this situation. He came back to check on me after he was certain Maddox was gone last night, and I'd told him I was pregnant and needed to get some rest. He'd been ecstatic to know he was going to be an uncle again. My sisters have kids after all, but he never gets to see them because they live so far away, and even though I do, too, now, my brother and I are very close, much closer than he is with anyone else in our family, so he knows he'll be a part of my baby's life.

It wasn't until this morning that I decided to fill him in on everything else that had gone on, how Mystica had been worried about the baby, and Maddox didn't want to listen when she talked about the fountain. It's all just too much, and I find myself wishing I was in a position to make this sort of decision for myself.

But I'm not....

"He is protective of me," I agree with Ben. "Overly protective," I modify.

"It's aggravating how he can go from making me feel like I'm the most important person in the world one minute to making me feel like a purchase he regrets making in the next."

Across the room, Poppy clatters some glass together as she's dusting my dresser, and I look over at her. She's glancing over her shoulder at me, and from the looks of it, she has something to say. Her forehead is puckered, as are her lips, but I have no idea what her problem is, and when Ben begins to speak again, Poppy makes another loud noise with her duster.

"He might change his mind," Ben suggests with a shrug. He's cleaned his plate of bacon, eggs, and toast now, and I see him eyeing mine. He's always been so thin, but he can eat like any growing boy.

I slide my plate over to him, only keeping my toast. My stomach is twisted, and I don't think it's only because I'm pregnant. I think I'm also too upset about Maddox and the baby's health to eat.

Ben digs into my food, and I consider what he's said. It is possible Maddox might change his mind, but I don't think so. Still, I don't want to argue with anyone. "Maybe," I acquiesce.

"Sorry the breakfast I brought you is so disgusting you can't eat it," Poppy says, coming over to stand behind the chair next to me. "Would you like me to bring you something else?"

I glance at the plate Ben's almost done clearing. "Oh, it was fine, Poppy," I say in as pleasant a tone as I can. I don't know why she's acting this way. "I'm just not hungry. I have so much on my mind right now."

"You mean... like your pregnancy? And the fact that your baby might be unhealthy? And how you got Maddox to confirm that he thinks you could actually be a princess? But he won't let you go home to Maatua? Not even to find a special fountain that might save your baby? Because of the curse he does believe in?"

I stare at her a moment longer, waiting to see if she's finished yet, and it seems that she is. I finally say, "Yes–"

She nods sharply, and before I can say more, she replies, "Sorry to be eavesdropping. It's a small room." Then, she turns to walk away, heading toward the bathroom, adding, "I wouldn't intentionally want to know any private information that doesn't concern me without you wanting me to know." When she reaches the bathroom door, she slams it pretty hard.

I suddenly realize what Poppy is so upset about.

"Oh, shit...." I can't help but hang my head and shake it.

"What's the matter?" Ben asks, his mouth so full of food, it's hard for me to understand him. "Oh, shit what?"

"You didn't hear all of that?" I whisper, inclining my head toward the bathroom door where I can hear what sounds like furious bathtub scrubbing of porcelain that's already clean.

"What? The maid? Guess I wasn't listening. Though I do think it's pretty cool that you have a maid now." He is finished and places my empty plate on top of his empty plate before picking up his glass of orange juice and taking a big guzzle.

I sigh. "She's upset that I didn't tell her any of this before I said anything to you. Or right when I found out, for that matter."

His forehead creases. "Why would you tell the maid you're pregnant?"

"Because she's not just my maid!" My volume is a lot louder now, and I don't care if Poppy hears this part. "She's also my friend! A good friend. She helped save me when I was kidnapped."

"Oh." He doesn't seem to get it still. "I guess you're lucky Mom and Dad don't know about that. They'd be freaking out."

And... Ben has changed the subject. I realize he is a teenage boy, and it really isn't the strong suit of most males to notice things like this like what's going on with Poppy, but it would be nice if he would just stay on the subject.

"I need to talk to her," I say on a sigh. It's the last thing I want to have to worry about right now. I do realize that Poppy is acting a little selfishly right now. If she really cared about me as her friend, she wouldn't be so hung up on the fact that I didn't tell her and would be thinking more about the fact that I am struggling with a lot of issues right now. So why am I now feeling bad about offending her instead of continuing to work on my own issues?

"Talk to who?" Ben asks, wiping his mouth with a napkin. "The healer lady? Mom?"

I grumble. "No, Poppy!" I am back to a harsh whisper now.

"Oh, right." He shrugs. "I don't know. I'm not good at stuff like that."

"I hadn't noticed," I say with an obviously sarcastic tone. He only smirks at me. "Listen, I'm really glad you're here, especially when I needed you most, but I think you should probably go home now."

Ben's eyes widen as it sounds like Poppy is throwing stuff in the bathroom. Ben doesn't seem to notice that. "Leave?" he asks. "But I just got here."

"But Mom and Dad don't know where you are," I remind him.

He shrugs. "I'm sure they're fine. I can call them and tell them I'm still at my friend's house."

"Ben... you're lying to them," I remind him, and he starts laughing hysterically.

"Yeah, you're right. I'd hate to lie to Mom and Dad after they've always been so honest with us."

I feel my ears turning red with heat because he's right, and it makes me sad. And a little angry. "They're still our parents, and they deserve our respect."

He shakes his head. "I don't think so, but I will check in with them."

Before I can say more, his chair screeches across the floor, and he goes over to the phone by my bed. He apparently has their number memorized because he dials it quickly. "Mom?" he says. "Hi. I'm fine. No, nothing's wrong. Just making sure you're not worried about me. I know I don't spend a lot of time away from home. Okay. Yep. I will. Okay. Bye."

My little brother turns and looks at me. "We're good," he says.

My mouth opens and then closes again. They haven't figured out that he's not where he says he is, so... "Fine," I say. "Stay, but only until tomorrow. I don't want to have to tell them about all of this right now, and I don't want their stuff to be out of the house any longer than it has to be."

He makes the sign of respect to me, and I know he's being a smart ass.

Thinking about the stuff makes me think about the curse, and I can't help but groan as my stomach tightens. But Ben doesn't notice. "Guess I'll go get ready," he says with a smile on his face.

"Ready?" I don't know what he's talking about. He's not leaving until tomorrow.

"Yeah–for the executions. Did you forget?"

I have another reason to groan. "Yeah, I did."

He gives me a sympathetic smile now. "I'm sorry. I know one of the people they're executing is the lady that tried to kill you. That's gotta be satisfying, right?"

I want to say that it is, but it's not. I don't want to watch Zabrina die. I don't want to watch anyone die. But I have to be there. Maddox did mention that to me yesterday before I kicked him out. He said he'd need me to be there with him during the ceremony. I know he's nervous about it. I would be, too. It's been a long time since we had a public hanging at the castle, at least as far as I know.

"You should get ready, too," Ben tells me. "You need any help? Getting your clothes out of the closet or anything?" It seems like an odd question from my brother, but he does know I don't feel well. He wouldn't help me dress and couldn't help me with my hair or makeup.

Before I can reply, Poppy comes flying out of the bathroom. "No! She does not need your help, Ben Moon!" she shouts. "I am here to help her, not you! I'm here to be the one she turns to when she needs something–not you! You should go, Ben Moon! You should go right now!"

I stare at Poppy, unblinking, shocked at her outburst. I'd like to say I'd never seen her act this way before, but it wouldn't be true. Still, this is probably the angriest I've seen her, maybe ever.

I look at Ben and he looks at me. "Bye," he says, sliding out the door, and I turn to Poppy.

"We need to talk."

YOU LOOK LIKE HELL

Maddox

Seth shakes his head at me as he walks toward me in the hall. I narrow my gaze at him, but I can hardly be mad at him when what he's saying is absolutely correct. I'm sure I do look like hell. I probably look like hell twice warmed over.

He has my morning protein shake in his hand, and rather than chastising him for making fun of me, I say, "Give me that."

"All right," he says, handing it over. "But I'm pretty sure it's not gonna help with… whatever's going on here." He raises a hand toward my face and moves it around a bit as if to indicate which part of me he is mostly talking about.

I literally growl at him and take the drink, sipping a bit of the vanilla-flavored concoction as I glare at him over the top of the glass. "You're so helpful," I mutter. "Thanks."

"Maybe we should call in Willa?" He sounds hesitant to say such a statement, and he should be. I groan in disgust. "Oh, come on! It's her job, Maddox."

The hallway is empty. I know it must be for him to so casually speak my name. He doesn't do it often, not anymore, not since the last time he accidentally did it in front of a dignitary from another land, and I almost bit his head off–also literally–but that's Seth's way of telling me that he is concerned about me.

"Willa?" I repeat, still complaining. "You know how much I hate wearing makeup."

Willa is the woman we keep staffed at the castle to make me presentable. She's a professional and very good at making the bags under my eyes and the placid, grayness of my skin dissipate. There was a time when I needed her services almost on a daily basis. Back when Rebecca had first passed away, I was a fucking wreck every damn day. It didn't matter whether I'd fallen asleep drunk off of my ass or completely sober. When I woke up, I looked like hell.

Most of the time, I'd gotten two or three hours of sleep at most, gained off and on through the night, while hammered. Drinking was the only thing I could do to manage the pain. And while it obviously didn't work, I convinced myself that being drunk was better than being sober.

The fact that my Beta was trying to convince me that I needed to go see the miracle worker now was alarming. Did I really look that bad now?

If I had slept, just like after Rebecca died, it had been intermittent. A few minutes here and there. Most of the night, I'd laid away thinking about Isla and the huge fucking mess we were in.

"You didn't talk to her?" Seth asks me as I continue to walk toward my office. I had filled him in only briefly after I left Isla's room the night before. He knew about the baby, and he knew about the island. He knew about the fountain, and he knew about the curse. That was about it.

"No." My answer came quickly, sharply. I didn't want to talk to him about not talking to her.

"You know, I bet if you go to her, you can probably–"

"Enough!" I turn and glare at him, and he makes the face he always makes when I scream at him for absolutely no reason. Immediately, I am reminded that I am an asshole. But that's nothing new. I soften my tone when I say, "Let's just get through the ceremony first, all right?"

"Of course," he says, and we make the rest of the trip to my office in companionable silence.

Once we arrive, I give in and give Willa a ring, sighing as I hang up the phone. I know how bad I look. I don't want to admit it, but if I'm going to stand before the people and try to portray myself as a mighty king, one who has his shit together, I am going to need her help. Right now, I look like a derailed train that's bitten off more than it can chew and can't continue to tread water–one huge cliche of ruin.

Seth and I go over the expectations for the ceremony, which will start in less than three hours. He has jotted down some remarks for me to make. I go over it and change a few words so that it sounds more natural to me. "No one says, 'henceforth,'" I say, looking at him across the desk.

"It's an official-sounding word for an official sounding speech." He shrugs his shoulders like I am the one who is being weird.

I shake my head but decide that the rest of what he has written will accomplish my goal.

Willa comes in, and immediately, the middle-aged woman pulls a face. "Eek," she mutters. "So... rough night?"

I stare at her for so long, she tips her head down and turns it to the side, exposing her neck, and I can only mentally think, 'Yeah, that's what I thought.' But I don't reply to her remark. "Come on," I murmur, and she crosses the room, setting her makeup kit on my desk as she does her work.

It takes about thirty minutes, an indication that it is pretty bad. But a great deal of that time is letting the concoction she puts on the bags under my eyes begin to work. When she's done, she is smiling. "There we go. You look a thousand times better, Sir."

Saying anything other than, "Thank you," is likely to get me into trouble, so that's all I say, and she leaves.

"I'm going to go make sure that the prisoners get their last meal and are ready to go," he says. "They'll be moved to the holding pin an hour before the ceremony begins."

I nod. We have about two hours before it's set to start, and I should probably be working on the stack of papers that's begun to accumulate on my desk while I was off chasing Zabrina, but I can't. Instead, all I can think about is Isla.

"The crowd's already gathering," he continues. "I'll make sure we have enough guards around the platform to hold them back."

My brows furrow. "Are they against what is about to happen?" I ask him.

Seth shakes his head. "No, from what I can tell, about ninety percent of them are here out of morbid fascination, that and the need to support the actions of the kingdom. But there are always those who will want to afford change through their own actions, especially people from Zabrina's home pack and Hill Country pack."

"Make sure the people from Duster pack have a good view, especially the families of the servants who were killed–and Alpha Hayes's family." I know that his children will not be here. I've left them in the care of responsible enough people that they would never bring them. In fact, it is against the law for children under the age of twelve to attend hangings. That's a change I made back in the beginning of my reign. Not that we had the weekly hangings like used to take place under the reign of some of my ancestors. Back then, the children of the prisoners would be brought to the front of the gallows so that the criminals–or alleged criminals–could look into the eyes of their offspring as they hung there, swinging, no bags over their heads.

A particularly gruesome hanging came immediately to mind as I thought about the time my father had hanged six men for conspiring against him. One of them had insisted that he was innocent until the very end. He had three small children under the age of ten, two boys and a girl. They stood there with their mother to watch the hanging, as they were required to.

The hangman had made a mistake with the noose, and rather than hanging him, when the floor dropped out from beneath him, the knot severed his head. It was the vilest thing I'd seen at that time.

I'll never forget the looks of horror on the faces of those children.

A shudder goes down my spine as I think about it.

No matter what happens today, it can't be worse than that—can it?

I don't want to find out.

My work blurs before my eyes as I think about Isla. I can't possibly sit here and pretend like whatever the fuck is on these papers is more important than me going to speak to her. I know she kicked me out last night, so she might not even want to speak to me, but I've got to try.

With a sigh, I push up from my desk and head to her room. I hope she's awake and feeling well, but at the same time, if she's still sleeping, that's good, too. I want her to get everything that she needs as long as she is carrying our baby.

My stroll down the hallway reveals the castle is in a flurry today as servants and others rush by, on their way to make sure that the ceremony goes off without a hitch. They are all respectful as we pass, and I nod and let them go on their way.

What am I going to say to Isla? I don't know. I hope when I look at her, the right words will emerge. I do realize that her brother may still be with her. I won't kick him out again, as much as I want to. She doesn't get to see him much, and it wouldn't be right for me to make him leave her.

At her exterior door, I pause for a deep breath, hoping the words form on my tongue when I open my mouth, but when I walk into her antechamber, I freeze.

I can hear the sound of Isla's voice, and whomever she is speaking to, she is doing her best to remain firm and fair; I know that tone. But then, when there is a reply, I almost knock the door down in my haste to defend her.

It is Poppy talking back to her, yelling, and regardless of what has happened, my instinct to protect her kicks in, and it's all I can do to stay on this side of the door and let Isla resolve this issue herself.

She is fully capable of doing so, after all, and I can't expect her and Poppy to get along one hundred percent of the time. Still, that's my woman in there, and she's carrying my baby, and Poppy has picked the wrong day to be a bitch. My hand hovers above the doorknob when I hear Isla say the one phrase that practically rips my heart out of my chest.

"Poppy, I need you to be reasonable right now. You and Maddox can't both be irrational at the same time. I can't bear it."

A sigh escapes my lips as I think about the fact that Isla is right.
And I can't bear it either.

CONCERN FOR THE KING

Isla

"WE NEED TO TALK," I say to Poppy, and she stops fluffing the pillows on my bed long enough to look over at me.

"Oh? Now you would like to talk?" She sits down on the edge of my bed and crosses one leg over the other one so that her foot is dangling. She kicks it around in a circle, her hands folded over her knee. "All right. What would you like to discuss? What do you think about the rain we got last night? Oh, did you hear that Barbie in the kitchen found her true mate? Do you think Beta Seth plucks his eyebrows?"

Letting out a sigh, I walk over and sit next to her. "Stop it, Poppy. I understand that you're upset. You feel like I should've told you what was going on, and you're not wrong. I just… I didn't know anything until last night. And after I talked to Maddox about it, I was so exhausted, I just wanted to go to sleep."

"I understand." She pops up off of the bed and crosses to where she left her duster earlier. Picking it up, she begins her aggressive dusting motion again. "You didn't want to talk to me about it. I get it. After all, you're a princess, apparently, and I'm just… a stupid maid."

"Poppy!" I exclaim, going over to her and taking hold of the duster so she either has to stop or jerk it away from me. I can see her contemplating the latter but she doesn't. "I would've told you this morning, but my brother got here first, and I thought he should know. He's family."

"And what am I?" she barks at me. "Just a servant? Some stupid girl who that the king assigned to you?"

"Of course not!" I wrap my arms around her. "You're the best friend I've ever had!"

She is stiff in my grasp for a moment before she begins to relax. "I am?"

"You are!" I tell her. "You are more of a sister to me than any of my actual sisters. But Ben and I grew up together. We used to be the only confidant the other had, and when he was so sick, he used to tell me how afraid he was, and I used to tell him about the struggles of helping mom and dad keep the family afloat."

I release her now and see that she's relaxed a bit in understanding. She really has been acting like a jealous brat, but I guess it's a bit flattering to see that she cares so much about me that she's upset that I didn't tell her my secret first.

"Well, next time you have a major secret, you'd better tell me first!" she says dusting me with the duster. I almost laugh, but the dust tickles my nose, and I sneeze instead. She hands me a tissue, but she's not done berating me yet. "Seriously! You're pregnant, and you are a princess, for sure, even the king admits it, and you don't tell me?"

"I know, I'm sorry," I say again.

She laughs and shakes her head. "Really, Princess Isla!" She sounds mad, but she's not anymore. She's just giving me a hard time. "I don't know what I'm going to do with you!"

Before I can respond at all, the door comes flying open. "I can tell you what you're going to do, Poppy!" Maddox's voice shakes the room, he's so mad. "You can pack up your fucking stuff and move yourself right back to the servants' quarters, you ungrateful little bitch!"

"Maddox!" I say, stepping between them. He's so mad, his face is red, and maybe for the first time since I've met her, Poppy actually looks frightened. "Calm down!" I tell him, but he jerks away from me, stepping closer to her, his hand in her face, and for a second I have visions of Seth knocking the living shit out of Mrs. W.

"Let me handle this, Isla! You're too soft on the servants!"

I leap between them, putting myself in front of Poppy. I don't think Maddox would really strike her, but I don't know. "Listen!" I scream at him. "We're fine!" Poppy is trembling behind me. I can actually feel her body shaking. "You have got to get a grip on yourself, Your Majesty!"

His eyes meet mine then, and he lowers his hand. "You were arguing!" he insists. "I heard you through the door!"

"While I'm not sure what I think about you admitting you were eavesdropping just now," I begin, "I can assure you that I have it under control. The last thing I need is for you to come storming in here to save me from Poppy of all people! Have you already forgotten the lengths she went to to help you save my life when I was missing?" Fury shoots through me as well, and I can't help but wonder when this is all going to end. When is he going to stop trying to control every little fucking aspect of my life?

But I don't have an answer for that as he stands there staring at me, and I suppose that there is no answer. Maddox has never been one to listen to reason before he goes flying off the hook, not when it comes to me anyway.

He takes a step back and lowers his hand for a moment before raising it again to drag down his chin. "I thought that the two of you were having a disagreement," he says.

"Even if we were, that doesn't give you the right to storm in here and scare the shit out of us!" I tell him. My hand instinctively goes to cradle my abdomen, "Do you honestly think I'm so weak and fragile that I can't even stand up for myself against Poppy?"

"Hey," Poppy says behind me, clearly calmer now. "I can be tough."

I turn and look at her, shaking my head. "I know you can, but you're also my friend, not an axe murderer." Back to Maddox, I say, "You have got to stop coming into the room like that!"

He hasn't actually said he was sorry yet, and I'm beginning to wonder if he is even capable of it at the moment. I know he's under a lot of stress lately, and that's probably why he is out of control. I don't think it's a very good excuse for losing his shit every five minutes, but I can only imagine that it takes a toll on a person.

I get it now—the reputation he's always had for being unhinged. I can see that now, and the longer I stare at him without him even moving to apologize to me or to Poppy, I can understand why everyone uses words like cruel, unyielding, heartless, and savage to describe him.

"Beg your pardon," is the best I'm going to get. He takes a step toward the door. "We need to be outside in about an hour."

I want to tell him he can go without me, that I don't want to go anywhere with him, but I understand he needs me there. "Fine." That's the best he's going to get from me.

He moves to open the door, to step out, and I see that he has that haunted look in his eyes, like he does when he's thinking of Rebecca.

I can only imagine what a wreck he must've been back then, when she died. He must've been shouting at everyone all the time.

I turn back to Poppy. "Are you all right?" I ask her.

She sighs loudly and says, "Yep. I will be. As soon as I change my underwear."

It's too much for me, and we both begin to laugh uncontrollably, grabbing onto one another as we shake with hiccups and the kind of laughter that starts low in our bellies and rocks our entire bodies.

When we finally recover the ability to breathe, she says, "I'm so sorry, Princess Isla. I didn't mean to behave that way. I was just afraid that you didn't need me anymore."

I pull her close to me and hug her tightly, and she hugs me back. "I will always need you, Poppy," I assure her. "But please, don't ever yell at me again. I can't handle King Maddox's storming the castle antics."

"I won't," she says, but I believe it about as much as I believe that he won't ever lose his cool again.

Letting her go, I begin to get ready for the execution, an event I don't want to attend to begin with, but I know I must be there. I need to show my support to Maddox. It means a lot to him. As I shower, my mind goes back over the way he's been acting lately. I wish I could do something to help him, but it seems like all I do is make it worse.

We can't agree on anything. He doesn't like any of my ideas, and he doesn't want to let me do any of the things I feel I need to do to help our child. It seems like every day he grows more and more out of control, and I have to wonder how long this will go on.

I hope that this execution will ease things a bit and he'll start to relax a bit, but when I run my hand over my abdomen, knowing that there's life there, I have to think that the next several months, while I carry his child, King Maddox is only going to grow more and more unsettled. He'll be angry more frequently, and he'll yell at everyone more often.

I don't know what to do about any of this. He's not the man I fell in love with when he acts like this, but abandoning him now isn't an option. Not only am I carrying his child, but I also love him.

I get dressed in a purple gown that matches the royal colors of the land, and Poppy does my hair and makeup. All the while, I am praying to the Moon Goddess that nothing unfortunate happens at the execution. If something does, it just might be the last straw for Maddox.

Something tells me we will not be that lucky, though....

"You look beautiful," Poppy tells me as she slips some earrings in my ears. "Are you nervous?"

I'd be lying if I said I wasn't, so I nod at her.

"It'll be all right," she assures me, but she looks a bit apprehensive herself. "It'll all be over soon, and then, you won't have to worry about that wicked Zabrina ever again.

"I know," I tell her, but I'm not so sure. I have a feeling Zabrina is one of those people who can haunt someone long after she's gone.

THE EXECUTION

Maddox

IT'S DRIZZLING as Isla and I step outside to begin our walk to the stage that is set up behind the gallows. My father used to give his declarations from inside of the castle. He'd simply step outside onto a balcony and address everyone before he ordered the execution. Sometimes, he'd do that right before going back to bed. Other times, he'd sit in a chair near the balcony and sip a whiskey while he contemplated the world.

I never knew what to think of him in those moments. Did he feel at all guilty for what he'd just done or did he feel like the most powerful man in the world? I have a feeling, now that I am in that position myself, he might have had a bit of each of those sensations.

Isla looks beautiful in a purple gown and cloak that remind me slightly of the one she'd been wearing when she first arrived at the castle. Not that I'd seen much of her in it that day, but I'd seen it hanging in her closet later. This one is the same style, but it is made of much nicer material and is a bit longer. She glances over at me, and I consider taking her hand, but most of the people in attendance aren't sure who she is, and I don't want the announcement of our expected child to come on the same day that we are putting to death four criminals.

They can make assumptions if they like, but plenty of other people are walking along with us, including Seth, Beta Ian and his wife Alaina from

Duster pack, Gail and Cody who were there when we discovered the bodies of Alpha Hayes and his wife, and a representative from Hill Country pack who had her child taken from her in the night.

All of us walk solemnly across the courtyard, me in the lead, except for the guards that flank us on all sides, toward the stairs that lead to the stage.

The crowd of thousands of onlookers is silent as we go. Not a single word can be heard from any of them. Not even a cough or sneeze.

They lined the area in front of the dais where the guards had set up a perimeter, and they stretched all the way back to the castle wall, a good fifty yards away. But they didn't stop there. Lots of people are sitting atop the ten-foot stone structure, and as we ascend to the stage, I can see the crowd stretching beyond that as well, off to the tree line where people are seated on the branches of the first several trees as far across the expanse as I can see from left to right.

If I had to guess, I would say there were over two hundred thousand people here....

I don't have enough guards to stop them if they riot. Thankfully, only about five thousand of them are actually inside the castle walls at the moment, but even then, I probably have a hundred palace guards as well as two thousand soldiers from the army standing by in rank and file over on the far north of the courtyard. If the people try to organize and make their will known, we will be screwed.

I have to hope that this will go peacefully, but I have no idea what will happen. Zabrina had made her threats, telling me that she had allies who will not sit idly by and watch her be put to death.

We are about to find out if that is true.

At the top of the steps, I moved into position in front of the railing that came just above my waist. The wood is slightly wet from the drizzle, but it's not soaked through yet. Only small puddles are beginning to form on some of the lower surfaces nearby.

I look down at the ground in front of me and note that it is at least a fifteen-foot leap to the cobblestone below. My wolf has handled harder jumps, but it will be painful when I land. Again, all of this is hypothetical. I don't want to have to leap.

A small crowd of dignitaries from the castle are positioned in front of the stage. They won't have a view of the front of the execution, but it doesn't really matter since the condemned will have bags over their faces anyway.

I scan this crowd to see if I can read the expressions of the people standing there. Most of them look satisfied with my decision. I see very few shaking heads of disapproval.

I also see Isla's brother, Ben, waving up at her, as well as Poppy and a few of the other important servants. Mystica is stationed over by the gallows in case something goes wrong.

I hope that our hangmen are good at their jobs this time because I really have no desire to see any accidental beheadings.

Isla doesn't wave back at Ben, but she acknowledges him with a head nod, which I think is more suitable. She does the same to Poppy, and I remember that I owe everyone a better apology for my behavior earlier that day.

Perhaps when all of this is over, I will be able to relax a bit more and stop acting so ridiculous.

But I doubt it. Ridiculousness seemed to be my new normal.

Once I am in place, I look around me to make sure everyone else is settled, and then I shout the words I have been dreading saying for most of my life. "Guards, bring out the condemned!"

The crowd breaks into a murmur at that point as the guards stationed near the castle door closest to our location turn and pull open the doors so that their fellow prison guards can bring out the four wolves who are about to meet their maker.

The three men are brought out first. All of them have their hands tied, two guards on each side of them, but the hoods are not yet on their heads. They are dressed in standard-issue prison uniforms that are clean and neat. I don't want anyone accusing me of mistreating the prisoners.

One of them is crying, another is looking around frantically, and the third walks with his chin up, looking straight ahead. The one who is crying wants his mother. I wonder if the one searching the crowd is also looking for his mother or perhaps for his wife.

Zabrina is at the end. She isn't wearing a prison uniform. She is wearing a black gown. I don't know who made that decision, but it seems fitting. She is the mistress of death as far as I am concerned, so she may as well look the part.

Alpha Jordan's daughter isn't actually walking under her own power either. I'd hoped that the drugs she'd been given to sedate her would have worn off by now enough for her to be able to walk by herself, but she is either still in a drugged-up state or she is refusing to walk by herself. I'm guessing it's not the latter since she isn't screaming or carrying on.

Part of me is disappointed to know that she's likely going to miss out on her own execution.

Once the prisoners are all positioned behind their nooses, it is my turn to speak again. The crowd falls silent so that they can hear me as I lift a hand for them to listen. I have rehearsed this speech a thousand times in my head since I set the date for the execution, but I am still nervous. I have to sound authoritative, strong, and convincing.

"Ladies and Gentlemen, today is a solemn day for all of us as we gather together today to see a fitting punishment meted out for crimes committed against our pack, our people, and our crown. As you may know, three of these citizens have been accused of willfully committing murder when they stormed the home of Alpha Hayes of Duster pack and his family, slaughtering nine people and leaving two children orphans."

Behind me I hear weeping as Alaina, Beta Ian's wife, thinks of her poor sister and the others who were murdered in her pack just days ago.

I do not let it distract me as I continue. "Through investigation, it was determined that these men followed the unjust orders of their acting Alpha, Vinny, who is now deceased, and attacked men and women as they slept in their beds as well as other servants who were going about their assigned tasks for the day. Because of their willful disregard for the laws of our land, they are condemned to death!"

I recite the names of the three men, and hear a woman begin to sob loudly from the crowd. She falls to the ground, and the guards quickly step in to remove her. From the looks of her, I'd say she's one of the mothers.

I get the answer to that question when the man who had been yelling for his mom when he was walking in shouts, "Mama! Mama! Please, help me!" One of the guards moves in to silence him with a gag.

It's unfortunate, but if that is the only hiccup we encounter, I will count this as a success.

But then I have to move on to the other prisoner....

"Zabrina, Alpha Jordan's daughter, has been found guilty of two counts of murder, one count of attempted murder, and one count of conspiracy to commit a terrorist act on our people. For these crimes against our pack, she has been sentenced to death."

I pause for only a moment to see if there is a reaction, but I don't hear one.

"By my authority as the Alpha King, I order the four of these citizens to be hung by the neck until dead!"

With that the guards move forward to place the prisoners in the proper position, put the bags over their heads, and slip the nooses onto their necks.

In a few moments, this will all be over. The four of them will be dead, and the world will be a safer place for my baby, and everyone else, to live in.

As Zabrina is moved forward and the bag is about to go down over her head, she shouts, "I curse you, Alpha Maddox! I curse you and your breeder, Isla Moon! I curse your children and your families for all of the generations to come!"

One of the guards hits her hard enough to shut her up, but then, an eruption in the crowd draws my attention to the right side of the gallows where another woman is screaming, "No! Not my daughter!" and a man starts shouting, "That's my mate! No!"

My guards are slightly thin on that side because of the collapsing mother, and it takes them a moment to get there.

A ripple races through the crowd as people begin to question whether or not a woman should be hanged for these crimes, and I know that we have to act fast if we are to keep them subdued.

As the nooses are placed in position, I give the signal, and then… someone in the back of the crowd shouts, "Now!"

STABBED

Isla

MADDOX GIVES the signal for the condemned prisoners to be killed, and someone in the back of the crowd watching shouts, "Now!"

Immediately, chaos erupts in front of the gallows as dozens of shifters leap up and change into their wolf forms. Women, children, and some men scream and try to get out of the way, but the wolves plow through them, trying to get to the gallows.

The guards react immediately, also shifting to fight back. I hear Maddox shout. "Drop them!" and the hangmen do their job even as the wolves that are either from Hill Country pack or Zabrina's pack–Maple pack storm the gallows.

"Seth! Get Isla inside, now!" Maddox shouts over his shoulder just as he shifts and takes off down the stairs toward the fray.

Seth turns to look at me, obviously upset that he's not running, too. I want to tell him to go on, that I've got this, but then I remember I am carrying a baby, and I'm not so brave anymore. It looks like the wolves that have started the chaos are not just in front of the gallows, but they are running in different directions, too, possibly trying to get into the castle, and the guards are doing their best to try and stop them.

"Stay with me!" Seth says and grabs hold of my arm. I have no intention of straying from him, but then I remember that my brother is here, and panic sets in.

"Ben!" I shout, pulling back slightly to get Seth's attention. "Where's my brother?"

Seth sighs and looks around, but neither one of us sees him.

"Ben!" I shout both with my mouth and the min-link.

"I'm over here!" he says, throwing up an arm, and I see him then in a crowd of people that are being protected by some of the guards that were stationed between the gallows and the stage.

With my arm firmly in his grasp, Seth takes off running again, and I have trouble keeping up.

As we are running, a wolf comes flying at us, and Seth pulls out a knife, pushing me behind him. The claws from the wolf slash at his face, but Seth plunges the blade into its neck, giving it a hard push. The wolf is no match for the powerful Beta and his weapon, and it tumbles backward onto the ground, bleeding from its neck.

"Come on!" he says again, but this time, I am moving ahead of him, as my brother comes running toward me. I take a quick look over my shoulder, but I can't see Maddox anywhere, and there's not enough time for me to truly stop and look.

Seth gets us to the closest door, unscathed, and pulls out a ring of keys. While he's fumbling for the right one, Ben and I bang on the door. Surely, someone inside has to have heard the commotion and will let us in.

Either that, or everyone inside ran to hide.

Before Seth gets the right key in the lock, the door opens. An older woman I've never seen before, wearing a servant's uniform, opens the door only a foot and looks out at us.

"Oh, good. Let them in," Seth says, and she pulls the door open a bit more. He thrusts his knife into my hand, for what reason, I'm not sure. Maybe because he's about to shift and he won't need it.

When others see that the door is unlocked, they come running, but as soon as Ben and I are inside, the woman turns and locks the door again. I want to protest that she should let those other people in, but I don't know who is friend and who is foe. It's best to let those decisions be made by someone else. Besides, it looked to me like there were more guards than rebels.

I take a step back, trying to catch my breath, about to thank the woman for unlocking the door when I see a flash of silver from her hand.

Ben jumps in front of me, trying to protect me, and in that split second, I see that she is holding a knife.

Right before she plunges it deep into my brother's stomach.

"No!" I scream, remembering I'm holding a knife, too. I've never used one on a person before, but my instincts kick in, and I lash out at her the same way that I saw Seth stab that wolf. I slash across her throat before she can move aside, and blood spurts everywhere. She raises a hand to try to contain it, but her fingers are nothing against the red, sticky flow. She collapses onto the ground.

I have no time to think about what's just happened, why this woman would let me into the castle and then try to kill me. All I know is that Ben is grievously injured. The knife she carried was large, and she buried it up to the hilt in his gut. It was obvious she was trying to stab me, but my sweet brother got in the way to save me.

"Ben!"

He is on the floor, and blood is pouring from the wound, flowing around the knife that is still protruding from his abdomen. I'm not sure if I should pull it out or leave it. "It'll be okay, Ben," I tell him, but I can see how quickly his face is turning pale, and I am afraid I'm lying to him. I lift his head and put it on my lap. I'm not even sure what to do. The only person I can think of who can help is Mystica, and I don't think she'll be able to because of the fight outside, and I'm not even sure my mind-link can reach her.

Maddox is too busy. I don't even know where Poppy is.

I start doing the only thing I can think of—screaming.

"Help! Help! Someone help us!"

"Isla, Isla!" Ben says, his blood-covered hand coming up to rest on mine. "It's okay."

"It's not okay!" I tell him. "You're dy–bleeding everywhere."

He actually grins at me. "I am dying, Isla. I know that. You can say it. It's… not a secret."

The tears are streaming down my cheeks now, running almost as thick as the blood seeping from him. "No, you can't," I tell him. "I can't do this without you."

"Isla, you already are," he says. "Besides… I saved you… and the baby, and that's all that matters."

I shake my head and use the mind-link to call for help. Maybe someone from Willow pack will be close enough and be able to help. "Someone! Please, send a healer! My brother is dying!"

No one answers.

Ben is still smiling up at me. "I'm so glad… I… got… to… s-s-see you," he says.

"Ben, please, try to hang on. Please," I beg him.

He does his best to squeeze my hand. "You always were the b-best one," he says. "I l-l-love you so m-m-much."

"I love you, too. Ben! Please!"

I hear him inhale one more time before his eyes close, and he goes still.

Not knowing what else to do, I drop my head on his chest and begin to weep.

~

Maddox

I should have been better prepared for this, but I never really thought that anyone would be so stupid as to try to save these worthless criminals. Now, as I charge through the crowd, ripping apart everyone who tries to stop me, I only have two things on my mind.

One, make sure that Isla get back in the castle safely and two, make sure that Zabrina dies.

She is not leaving these castle walls alive ever again.

The hangmen did their job. As I run toward the gallows, my wolf teeth dripping blood down my chin, I see that the four criminals are hanging. Zabrina's body swings frantically in the air as she tries her best to find purchase, but there's nothing beneath her to stand on.

The other three are not struggling as hard, probably because they know that the uprising has nothing to do with them.

I see a large black wolf leap onto the gallows. He is trying to get to her, to get beneath her, so that she has something to stand on. One of my guards jumps in front of him and tries to fight him off, but the black wolf is too big, and he manages to rip at his throat before tossing him into the crowd.

Well, he won't have that kind of luck with me.

A smaller brown wolf gets in front of me, his fangs dripping with saliva. I go low, sweeping his feet out from under him, and knocking him aside. Then, I leap up onto the gallows in one bound to see that the black wolf has given Zabrina a place to stand. She is doing her best to keep her footing, to pull herself to an upright position with her hands bound, and I see other wolves coming to try to help her. If one of them shifts into his human form, he could potentially get her free.

I won't be having any of that.

Rather than leaping for the snarling black wolf that is trying to keep the Alpha's daughter standing, I aim for her. She's so high up, I can't reach her neck, but I can sink my teeth into her torso. As I jump up over the black wolf, he tries to snap at me, but I manage to lock my teeth into Zabrina's gut and rip as I fall onto the other side of the gallows. She can't scream because of the noose, but blood and entrails spill everywhere, and the black wolf's eyes enlarge with horror as he sees he cannot save her now.

"No!"

He shifts into his human form and stands there, naked, trying to put her back together. "No! She's my mate!" he says.

I snarl at him and come back for seconds, not above taking him out when he's in his human form, but he shouts. "You'll pay for this, Maddox!" and turns and leaps off of the gallows, shifting into his wolf form before he lands.

I don't know who he was, but I do know that Alpha Jordan mentioned her finding her mate that must have been him.

With his departure, the other wolves that have attacked us quickly fall apart. I see the black wolf leap over the castle wall, but I can't chase him right now because I hear Isla's voice in my head.

"Maddox! Help me! It's Ben!"

TEARS AND BLOOD

Isla

BEN ISN'T BREATHING, and I don't know what to do. He's bleeding everywhere. I feel lost, hopeless, and alone.

"Maddox! Help me! It's Ben!" I shout for the hundredth time using the mind-link. I don't expect him to answer me this time either, but I hear his voice saying, "Isla? Where are you?"

I feel my heart begin to pound just from hearing his response. "We went in through the door closest to the stage, and some woman stabbed him! He's not breathing. Where's Mystica?"

"Are you safe, Isla? Where's the woman?" he asks me.

I wish he wouldn't always do that, answer my questions with his own questions. "She's dead!" I shout at him, still unable to believe that I've killed someone. "Maddox, what do I do!"

"I'm coming," he says, but that doesn't help me any, and I know that if we don't do something soon, there will be no getting Ben back.

My tears have soaked his shirt right above the wound, and he's starting to turn blue because he hasn't been breathing. I think about doing that thing where you blow into someone's mouth and pound on their heart, but I don't think I can do it.

I've never seen anyone die before....

Oh, yes, I have....

I've seen two people die recently. One of them, Sydney, even Mystica couldn't save. She'd lost too much blood.

But the other one, Maddy, she had come back to life when I had held her in my arms… and cried.

I look down at Ben. I've already soaked him with my tears, but not right over the wound. Do I have to get my tears on his would for him to come back to life?

Even thinking about it sounds ridiculous, but it's worth a chance. After all, he can't be any more dead than he already is.

I grab hold of the knife and yank it out. It feels so gross sliding out, but the sound it makes, a wet, squishing sound, is even worse. It's not hard for me to continue to cry. I just lean down close to his wound and let my tears roll onto his broken, bleeding flesh. The blood is only leaking out slowly now, and I imagine that's probably because my brother's heart is either no longer beating at all or the beats are so shallow, they aren't doing anything to move the blood through his veins.

I can't believe this is happening. I can't believe I let this happen. I should've kept him inside. I should've made him go home! Whenever I think of all of the things I could've done differently, my tears increase until the wound is completely soaked, and I am beginning to think that whatever happened with Maddy was just a coincidence, a miracle unrelated to me, or some kind of a fluke. Whatever it was, I'm not seeing any signs of life in Ben, and that just makes me cry harder.

The door beside us opens carefully, and I realize that it's Maddox. How he got in, I don't know. I don't see a key, but maybe someone else let him in. He's careful as he steps inside, not wanting to hit us with the door. He's only wearing a pair of shorts so I think he must've just shifted. He's coated with blood, but then, we are all coated in blood.

"Mystica is on her way. She'll be here in a few minutes," he says as he gets down on his knees across from me. He glances around and sees the woman's body. "Klara?" he whispers. "What the hell?"

I don't know her, so I don't know why she's made this decision, but it's not important to me right now. What's important is figuring out what to do with my brother.

Maddox leans down and listens to his heart and then shakes his head. "I don't think he's got a heartbeat, baby," he says.

My tears fall faster. "Fix him!" I demand, knowing that Maddox can't just do that.

"I'll do what I can." He begins to press on Ben's heart, trying to pump it for him, I think.

"Should I breathe for him?" I ask him.

"No, unless his heart is beating, it won't matter." Maddox seems to know what he's talking about, probably because of all of the battles he's been in.

He continues to work on his heart while I cry and beg and plead, and then Mystica comes in. She's got her medical bag, but I know there's not much she can do.

Ben's already been dead for almost ten minutes.

"Let's get out of the way and let her work," Maddox suggests as other healers show up from inside of the castle.

"No, leave her here," Mystica says as she listens to Ben's heart with a stethoscope. "He's not dead."

"What?" Maddox and I both ask at the same time.

"I can hear his heartbeat. It's faint, but it's there," she explains. "You remember, don't you?" she asks me. "With the baby?"

I nod. "Yeah, I remember. But… it doesn't seem to be working."

"Of course, it's working," she says. "It's just… he's a lot bigger than Maddy. And… I think it might take something more powerful than tears."

I raise an eyebrow. "More powerful?"

Her head rocks back and forth. At the moment, another healer is attempting to sew up the bleeding veins inside of Ben while he's lying on the floor, something they would usually do in a surgery, and it's so gross, I almost think I would be happy to supply them with a different kind of bodily flood–vomit–but I'm not going to throw up on my brother's body.

"Blood, honey," she explains. "Take the knife. Slice your hand, and squeeze it over the wound. I think… I think the healing powers you have will be even stronger in your blood than in your tears."

I reach for the knife, but Maddox grabs it before I can. "Wait a minute!" he says. "I don't know why you think that will work, Mystica, but I'm not going to have Isla hurting herself for no reason."

I don't have time to explain to my beloved that I will try anything to try and save my brother's life. Since he has the knife I yanked from my brother's body, I slide my hand across the stone floor to grab the knife Seth gave me, the one I used to slash the woman's neck, and while Maddox and Mystica are still arguing about it, I do exactly what she said.

My hand screams in pain as I slice across it, but the pain in my heart is worse than the one in my hand as I move my hand over to drip blood into the wound.

"Just let her try!" Mystica is shouting, and Maddox is ready to argue when he sees that I'm already doing it.

"Damn it, Isla!" he says, trying to pull my hand away. "Bandage her up!"

"No!" I yell at him. "Let me try!"

Maddox leans back slightly, his eyes widening, and I realize there's something strange going on with me when I say those words, but I don't have enough time at the moment to think about it.

My hand is dripping blood into the wound, mingling with Ben's, and as I continue to squeeze, I can feel something happening. I can feel some sort of power surging through me. I close my eyes and pray to the Moon Goddess begging her to help my brother.

The more I pray, the more I squeeze, the more I bleed, the dizzier I become until I feel the world swaying around me, and I am falling backward into Maddox's arms.

"All right, that's enough," he says. "We can't take a chance on hurting the baby!"

I know he's right, but I want to help my brother.

Sitting back, I stare at Ben's face as Mystica and the others continue to work on him, but I don't know what to think. Is his face a little less pale? Can I hear his heartbeat, faintly, or is that someone else's?

"Ben, please, come back to me," I repeat over and over again. "Please!"

It seems like forever passes before I hear the sound I've been waiting for. Ben gasps deeply, like he's just come up from being underwater, and he even tries to sit up. Mystica won't let him, though. "What happened?" he asks, looking around. He sees my face, and I see a bit of relief wash over him that I'm here.

"You died," she tells him.

"What?" I see the confusion on his face. "What do you mean I died?"

"You died, and your sister brought you back to life with her magical powers." Mystica speaks as if it is all matter-of-fact.

His forehead crinkles, but he nods in acceptance before he says, "Thank you for saving me, Isla."

"I love you, Ben," I say, and I don't even have to look at Maddox's face to know that he doesn't believe what he's hearing, that I did anything magical.

Mystica and the other healers finish patching Ben up and give him some medicine for the pain. Some guards come and move the dead woman. I don't know where they're taking her, and I don't care. I've never killed before, but I'm glad that that woman is dead.

After a few minutes, they get Ben up and put him on a stretcher so they can move him to a bedroom nearby. I go along with him, a bandage on my hand, which isn't bleeding any more.

When we get into the bedroom, Mystica does her best to make him comfortable, and then everyone leaves except for a nurse who is stationed outside of the door and Maddox and me.

"I'm so sorry, Ben," I tell him. "I should've made you leave."

"Don't be sorry, sis," he says. "You didn't know. It could've happened anywhere."

"Still… I almost lost you. And Mom and Dad probably will kill you." That makes him laugh.

"Probably," he says. "But… if I'm honest… I'm not sure I was ready to come back, Isla."

"What do you mean?" I ask him. "You wanted to die?"

He shakes his head. "No, no. Not that. I just… I wanted to stay there. It was so beautiful and peaceful."

"Where were you?" Maddox asks him directly.

Ben shifts his eyes to look at Maddox and says, "On the island. On Maatua."

THE AFTERMATH

Maddox

It's too much.

I have too much to take care of right now, too many things to think about and do, to sit here and consider the possibility that Isla's brother has just died, gone to the island of Maatua, and then been brought back by her tears or blood or both. No, with the uprising that just happened in the courtyard, I can't even begin to process it right now.

I know that I will come across as an absolute jackass if I even try it at the moment. Isla is staring at me, waiting for me to acknowledge what Ben has just said, but all I can do is nod my head. "Is there anything you need now?" I ask instead. "Are you hungry?"

"Hungry?" Mystica repeats. "I think he'd better stick to IV fluids for a while, Your Majesty. We did just sew his stomach back together."

I have no idea which parts of him were split apart. What I do know is I can't comment on his adventure to the isles at the moment.

Isla games my arm. "Are you okay?" she asks me, looking concerned.

"I'm fine," I tell her. "And I want to make sure that you and your brother are well before I go back off to check on the situation outside."

"Ben is settled now. He needs to get some rest," she says, pointing out the obvious, but then, I probably look like that's what I need her to do since I'm not making sense to her at the moment. "I will stay with him at least until he's sleeping. I need to call my parents, though."

"Of course," I tell her, taking her gently by the arms. I'm sure she's not looking forward to making that phone call. "You can use whichever phone you want."

She raises an eyebrow at me, and I recall the fact that we have had an argument about that before. "I think I'll stick to the one in my bedroom, thank you," she says, a hint of a smile forming in the corners of her lips.

I want to kiss her. I'm so glad that she's all right that I just want to take her in my arms and never let her go. But there hasn't been time for even a quick peck since I found her in the hallway covered in blood, and I doubt there will be much time for it for a while. She killed someone a little while ago, and even though I know it was the only way to protect herself and our baby, she has to feel bad about that.

I need to find out what the hell turned a loyal servant of over twenty years against me. It really seems like this place is descending into chaos, and I am in the center of it, about to be picked up into the air and toss me a thousand miles away.

My first stop is to get some proper clothing, and then I will head back out to the courtyard to see the aftermath. I want to know who the ringleader was, that large black wolf, and I want to see how many casualties we had.

Most importantly, I want to make sure that Zabrina is dead.

"I will leave him to you, dear," Mystica says to Isla as she packs up her bag. "He's fine now, but I'll have one of my nurses, Heather, stay here with you as well."

Isla nods and thanks Mystica, embracing her like they are long lost family, and it makes me shake my head. I don't know how it is that Mystica has managed to convince Isla that everything she says is the gospel truth, but it gets old. I feel like Mystica could tell her that the sky is green and the grass is blue, and Isla would reply that she'd never really noticed that before, but now that Mystica mentions it, that does appear to be the case.

I take a few deep breaths before I kiss Isla's cheek, thank Mystica for her help, and then head down the hallway. I am in a rush now, as I want to look more official. It seems quite clear to me now that the problem I thought I had before is a full blown crisis. I've got to make the citizens of the kingdom know that I am the Alpha King, the rightful conduit of power, and they cannot displace me.

When they find out about the baby, that should help. In order to make sure no one can claim my power, I need to present the kingdom with an heir. I have done that now. It's just… early on. It would be best to wait until Isla is at least into the second trimester in case something goes wrong, but I might not have the luxury of waiting that long.

Lots of people are running through the halls, mostly soldiers and other staff members, trying to be of some use, I'm sure. Occasionally, I see a lost citizen, someone who probably came into the castle seeking refuge from the attack. No one approaches me, either because they still recognize me even in just a pair of shorts or because I am covered in blood. Either way, I make it to my room and manage to take a quick shower before I get dressed in an official uniform similar to the outfit I had on before this all went wrong, and then I head back out to check on the situation.

The ground is covered in blood. The courtyard looks like the scene of a battle, and I suppose, for all intents and purposes, it is a battle. Over by one wall, there's a small stack of bodies. Along another section of the wall is a bigger stack. Most of the bodies in this larger stack are in their wolf form, and I think these must be the rebels who caused the uprising to begin with. The other stack consists mostly of wolves as well, but I also see the body of a woman dressed in the clothing of a commoner and a few men in guards' uniforms whom I'm guessing were attacked before they had a chance to shift.

Seth comes over to me, dressed in a pair of black slacks and a gray shirt but disheveled. I know he hasn't left the courtyard since the attack began. He looked exhausted, but I saw no signs of him slowing as he came over to me.

"How many of them got away?" I ask as we meet near the gallows.

"As far as I know, just the one, the big black wolf that you were fighting near Zabrina." He looks around, his mouth, opening slowly, like he has something else he wants to tell me but isn't sure how.

I don't have time for him to mull things over so I bark out another question. "How many people did we lose?"

"Six guards, two citizens, and one of the hangmen," he says. "But–"

"Damn it," I yell, stomping my foot. I put my hands on my hips and take a few deep breaths. "All of these innocent people need to be given proper burials. Make sure their bodies are correctly identified and their families are notified."

"Of course, Sir," he says.

"Are the injured being tended to?" I look around and see some healers I recognize working on civilians who are injured, though nothing looks too life threatening. And I see Mystica over with the injured soldiers, as well as some other healers. A few of them look more critical. I contemplate going to get Isla's blood for just a second and then roll my eyes at my own ridiculousness.

"We need to figure out who that black wolf was, how he got in here without anyone knowing he was dangerous, and squash whatever this movement might be." I look around at the scene, wondering how this has even transpired.

"Yes, Sir. We are working on all of that. But there is one more thing you should know about–"

"Really, Seth!" I exclaim. "This was the worst case scenario. We should've been on top of this." I shake my head. "Well, at least the prisoners were all hung before they could be saved, right?"

"The three men from Hill Country pack were dead when the rebels tried to get them down," he tells me, nodding his head. "Their bodies have been taken back to the prisoners graveyard where they will be dumped in an unmarked grave."

"Very good," I say. "And none of the other people on the stage were harmed, were they?" I think of what the representatives from Duster pack have already been through. Thank goodness they didn't bring the Alpha's children with them.

"Any other people, Sir?" he asks, confused.

"Yes, Isla's brother was injured. Although, technically, I guess he wasn't on the stage. Still, he was over there with us." He looks more confused the longer I speak.

"But I escorted Miss Isla and her brother back to the castle myself," he tells me.

"Yes, that's right. He wasn't wounded until after he got in the castle then… he was attacked by one of the maids."

"What?" Seth is as puzzled by the situation as I am.

"We need to figure out what's going on, if the castle has been infiltrated as well," I tell him. "All right. I guess that's all. I'm going to go talk to the men, make sure to keep their morale up."

"But Sire," he says, "there's one more thing."

I sigh, not wanting to hear one more thing. "What is it, Seth?" I ask him.

He has that apprehensive look on his face. "It's Zabrina," he tells me.

"What about her?" I ask. "I killed her myself."

It takes him a moment as he ponders his response and then blurts out, "She's gone."

DEATH DREAM

Isla

"It felt so real, Isla," Ben says to me from his position in bed. "It was like we were really there."

I smile at him from my chair near the window. I was really hoping he'd fall asleep, but he hasn't, and even after I went and cleaned up and checked on Poppy, who was fine and helping the injured, Ben is still wide awake.

I even asked the nurse to put something in his IV, and I think she did, but he's still chatting about his dream, and I know he wants me to ask him exactly what his dream was about, but I am hesitant. It's clear to me that Maddox doesn't think there's anything special about the dream Ben had when he was dead–if dream is even the right word–and it's probably silly of me to even ponder asking him.

But Ben isn't going to rest until I tell him. "What happened, Ben? In your dream. Or vision. Or whatever it was?"

He takes a deep breath, and his eyes glass over a little bit so that he is looking off in the distance. "We were standing on the island, you and me," he begins. "Your belly was a lot bigger, too, like you were almost ready to have the baby."

I try to smile, but the idea of having the baby makes me so nervous. What if there's something wrong with the baby because of the drugs I was given? Maybe Ben is about to tell me something that's meant to make me feel better about it, and even if what he says ends up seeming like a vision and not a dream, I think I will never feel completely comfortable thinking that everything is okay with my child until the baby is born and in my arms, safe, sound, and whole.

"We were by this mountain," he continues. "Everything was so green. The grass beneath our feet was soft and velvety. The vines growing up the trees and the side of the mountain were lush and emerald green. Bright flowers grew all over everything, too. They were like sunshine–yellow and orange. Some of them were a bright red color, like fire. It was amazing! And the trees were so tall. It was like a mix between the forest and the jungle."

I nod and force a smile, rubbing my stomach, even though it's not big enough to seem like I'm pregnant yet, I know there's a baby in there.

"We stood there, looking at this brilliant blue waterfall that cascaded down the side of the mountain and spilled into this big pool at the bottom. The water was blue, but it was also clear, and we could see the rocks at the bottom. They looked like volcanic rocks, they were black and dark gray. But they weren't sharp. Like the water had dulled them or something, and there were all of these big, beautiful fish in a rainbow of colors swimming around. It was amazing!"

"It all sounds really pretty," I say, trying to sound more enthusiastic than I feel. I don't remember Mystica saying anything about a waterfall flowing into this magical pool, so I don't know if she just left that out or if that's not what Ben saw when he was dead. Or maybe the whole thing is just made up.

"Anyway, we were standing there, taking it all in, but you started having pains in your belly, so you finally got into the water. You were wearing this long flowing dress in bright blue with red and orange flowers all over it. You got in the water, and after a few minutes of you being in pain and shouting, this baby just floated up to the top of the water. You picked him up, and he was perfect. He was crying, but when you held him close, he stopped. He wasn't hurt at all."

I give him a moment to bask at the end of his story, smiling back at him, but then I have to ask, "Were we the only two there, Ben?"

He shrugs. "I'm not sure. I didn't see anyone else around us, but they might've been behind me or something. I was just paying attention to you–and how beautiful it was. It was so peaceful. I just wanted to stay there forever. But then, I heard you crying, and I felt like I needed to leave. It wasn't you in the water that was crying, though. It was like you were far away and crying, but I could hear you, so I turned around and walked away, through the forest, and it got really dark, and then I opened my eyes, and I was back here, in the castle."

It is an interesting story, and in a lot of ways, it reminds me of my visions, the ones I've had in my sleep about Zabrina, Private Wylie, and even the man and woman in the meadow, whom I have to wonder about. Could that boy who reminded me of Maddox have been my son? Was the woman he was with his fated mate? I hadn't spent too much time considering it because I am so worried that something will happen to my baby.

But I want to believe Ben's story. I want to think that if I go to Maatua and have my baby in the magical pool, he will be okay. I don't know if I could stay here and have him in the castle and use my own blood and tears to save him if something is wrong, but I'm not really willing to take the chance. Maddox doesn't want to believe it, though, and if he won't let me go, I'm not sure what I will do. I could end up making him angry again. And I don't think I can sneak out. I promised I wouldn't try again, and that would be dangerous, as I've learned.

"You should rest," I tell Ben for the hundredth time.

"I know," he says. "But it's hard to sleep when I keep going over all of it in my mind."

I nod in understanding. I feel the same way when I have a vivid dream that seems to be real–and often ends up being real. "But if you don't sleep, you won't heal. You didn't heal completely, you know."

"I feel fine," he argues.

I laugh at him. "You have an IV with Mystica's best pain medicine in it. Of course, you feel fine."

He shrugs. "That's a good point."

"Listen, I need to go try calling Mom and Dad again," I tell him, even though I don't want to. The last time I'd tried calling them, they hadn't answered. I hope that they didn't hear about the uprising at the castle because that will worry them, and I don't want them to be scared about anything. I'm fine, and Ben is, too, now. They don't need to freak out, but I am sure they will be upset that he came all the way to the castle without telling them he was leaving.

"All right," he says with a sigh, and for the first time since he opened his eyes, I can see that apprehension is his primary emotion. "Do you think they'll be mad enough to kill me again?"

I laugh at him. "I hope not. But they probably won't be happy. You can't do this again. It's almost fall break–don't think you're going to come back here for that on your own."

"You know, if there hadn't been an execution at the castle while I was here, if there hadn't been an uprising, if I hadn't been stabbed, I would've been able to pull this off." He seems pretty proud of himself for someone who literally managed to get himself killed doing something his parents would've told him he wasn't allowed to do.

"Yes, it sounds like the Moon Goddess was conspiring against you," I say with a chuckle. As I start to get up, he stops me with his hand on my leg.

"What?" I ask him. The look on his face tells me that whatever he's going to say is serious.

"Are you okay about what happened with that woman, Isla? That lady who stabbed me?" His eyes are wide, and I can tell he's curious but doesn't want to upset me.

I take a deep breath, not sure how to answer that. "I don't feel good about it," I tell him. "But I know that I did what had to be done. I couldn't let her stab you again or hurt me and the baby."

"Who was she?" he asks me.

I shake my head. "I asked Poppy, and she said she's worked here for a really long time, and she has no idea why she would suddenly start acting that way, but she didn't know what pack she was from. Poppy was going to try and find out. Maybe she was from Zabrina's pack or something."

"Or Hill Country pack?" he asks me.

I nod. "I guess so, but I don't even know that the rebels were from one of those two packs. I haven't found out anything since Maddox left. He's been so busy with everyone out in the courtyard." I was hoping to see him soon, and not just because I wanted to see if he could answer my questions. I just wanted to hold him.

"Well, I think it was really odd that she acted that way. I remember the look in her eyes, vividly," he continues. "She looked... crazed."

I didn't get too good of a look at her face because I was trying to make sure she didn't stab me, but I believe him. "Maybe she had problems and no one knew." I can still picture her body lying on the stone floor, her throat bleeding everywhere. I never would've thought I was capable of something like that, cutting someone's neck, killing someone, but I guess it shows what a mama will do to protect her young, and that includes both Ben and my baby.

"Now, get some rest while I go try Mom and Dad again," I tell him. He withdraws his hand and I push out of the chair.

But I don't make it more than a step when there's a soft knock on the door, and Poppy sticks her head in.

Immediately, I can tell by her face that something's wrong. "What is it?" I ask her.

She clears her throat. "Sorry to disturb the pair of you," she says. "But... you have company." She steps aside and I lock eyes with a very pissed woman who looks like she wants to kill me.

ALPHA JORDAN KNOWS

Maddox

"WHAT DO you mean Zabrina is gone?"

The words leaving my mouth sound like they can't possibly be true, like there's no way in hell that Seth is accurate with his description to me of what the situation is at the moment.

Zabrina can't be gone. I killed her myself! I can still taste her entrails in my mouth from when I leaped up and grabbed hold of her with my teeth and tore her middle apart so that that black wolf who was trying to save her would be unsuccessful.

"We've looked everywhere for her," Seth says, shrugging and shaking his head. "We have no idea what happened to her."

"But she's dead," I tell him. "I took care of her myself. I know she has to be dead." I have a very vivid picture in my mind of her guts spilling out of her body as it continued to swing on the noose. "The black wolf ran off the moment he saw that she was dead. It's clear to me that she was the reason that he was here, that the riot started to begin with. They were trying to keep her from being killed."

"We seem to have gotten the same understanding from the witnesses we've interviewed," Seth says.

"Did you get any of the rioters alive, though?" I ask him.

He shakes his head no again. "We didn't. All of them either got away or were killed. We think only a few actually escaped, and I've got soldiers out looking for them now."

I make a fist and ram it into my other palm. I don't know what to say to that. It seems like we can't fucking do anything right. "That big black wolf... he is memorable. Someone has to have recognized him."

"Yes, some of the people in the crowd say they know who he is, that they saw him before he shifted and recognized him, and that they've heard rumors of him, a large black wolf who is notorious in battle, but I've never heard those types of stories about him," Seth says, rambling a bit.

"About who?" I have to know. "Who is he?"

"He's the son of Alpha Henry from Southern pack, Sir," he tells me. "His name is Austin."

"Why would he be after Zabrina?" I have to know. "Her pack lands are far from Southern pack."

"I don't know, but... do you think... Alpha Jordan would tell us?"

Seth finally has something intelligent to say. "Yeah, maybe, but we'll have to torture it out of him. He's so frail right now, we'll have to be careful or we'll kill him."

"It might be that the reason we can't find Zabrina's mother is because she went to Southern pack. We were looking for her in her own pack and her neighboring packs, mostly in the north, so we wouldn't have found her down there." Seth seems to be thinking aloud as he speaks.

"Let's start with Alpha Jordan," I suggest. "Maybe he can tell us why Austin would be after Zabrina, and then we can see if his father, Alpha Henry is smart enough to cooperate with us or if he's going to make bad choices like his son."

"Yes, Sir," Seth says as I turn to head inside to speak to Alpha Jordan. I still don't understand how Zabrina's body could be gone. Who would've snuck her out of here? And toward what end? It's not like she could have left under her own power. She was definitely dead, and since I don't believe in bringing dead people back to life, regardless of what Isla may claim happened with her brother, I know she's still dead.

Which means someone took her from here while all of my guards were in the process of making sure that the rebels who had started the fighting were either dead or being chased out of the courtyard.

We have cameras in the courtyard. We can go back and look at those. They were installed after Zabrina kidnapped Isla and no one knew what had happened to her. Perhaps that will lend us some sort of a clue as to what has gone on here.

But for now, I want to know why Austin, the son of Alpha Henry of Southern pack, was here trying to rescue Zabrina.

Seth and I head down the stairs to the dungeon. When we arrive at the cell and I see the broken, skeletal-looking Alpha, I think this might be helpless. He's not going to cooperate with us.

Still, I have to try. I walk inside, and he looks into my face. "Is she dead?"

"I think so," I tell him, and his face falls, but then a look of confusion settles in. "What do you mean you think so?"

"I mean, I'm pretty sure she's dead, Alpha Jordan, but there was an uprising at the hanging, and now, Zabrina's body is missing." I don't even like saying the words.

His expression shifts again, and he looks like he is hopeful that she may still be alive. I want to be able to squash that look right off of his face, but I can't. "Why would Austin from Southern pack be here?" I ask him.

His eyebrows raise as his tongue lashes out to wet his dry, cracked lips. He has streaks of dried blood on both sides of his face. He's filthy and reeks of body odor. Perhaps if I offer him a shower, he'll speak...

"You don't know?" he asks me, and a low chuckle rumbles out of his dry throat.

"If we knew, we wouldn't be fucking asking you," Seth says, obviously irritated.

He chuckles again, this time at Seth, I believe. I put a hand out and tap my Beta on the arm, trying to remind him he needs to be nice to the half-dead asshole we need information from.

"Well, this is rich." Jordan turns his head so that his eyes are focused on the ceiling of his cell. It's so dark in here, with only one bare bulb swinging overhead, and the shadows cast over his face make it impossible to tell what he's thinking. "I guess you really aren't in touch with the far reaches of your kingdom."

I'm not sure what to say to that, but it seems pretty clear to me that he does know the answer to my question.

"Jordan," I begin, "I know you've got to be tired. You've been in here for a while now. You look like hell. Why don't you tell me what you know, and I'll move you to a room upstairs, someplace where you'll be more comfortable while you–"

"While I wait to die?" he asks me, shaking his head slowly. "What makes you think I care where I die?"

"There's a chance you might recover," I tell him. "I can get your medical attention."

"What would be the point?" he asks me. "I have nothing else to live for. I'll never leave this castle again, not unless by some miracle I am saved by another band of rogues during an uprising. No, I don't see the point in trying to prolong a life without my family, with my daughter likely dead, and my pack stripped from me."

I bite back the urge to tell him that this is all his fault, that if he hadn't attempted to organize against me, he could still be the alpha of his pack. His daughter would be alive, and he could be back there in his own home, relaxing in front of the fireplace with a good book.

But I see no reason to bring all of that up now, and I think that Seth is about to say something until I give him a look.

"Do you remember what I told you the first night I came to the castle?" Alpha Jordan asks me. "Or were you so blinded by your emotions for that damn breeder at the time that you didn't hear a damn thing I had to say?"

I think back over the conversation we had when he first arrived. I remember he was trying to tempt me with Zabrina, saying she would make a good Luna, that I should consider marrying her and having a baby before my time ran out and I reached my thirtieth birthday without an heir. At the time, I didn't know that I would fall in love with Isla, who had just arrived on the same day.

I did know that I wasn't at all interested in Zabrina, not even a little bit, and that was the case even before I met her when her father was just telling me about her. When I met her, it was confirmed that she was a terrible person, and I wanted nothing to do with her.

Yet, I don't think that's what he's talking about now, so I go back over that conversation. He'd wanted me about Duster pack and Hill Country pack, as well as some of the other packs where there had been attacks.

None of those attacks and uprisings were anywhere near Southern pack, though. They were all in the far west, away from Alpha Henry's territory.

I am at a loss when I look at him again, and Alpha Jordan has an expression in his eyes that tells me he thinks I am dumber than the stones that make up the walls of this building. "You asked me a question about my daughter, remember? If you can pull that information out of your ass, then you'll have the answer to the question you're asking now, but unless you do, I can't help you. One of these days, King Maddox, you're going to learn that listening to other people is important."

I want to punch him for making that remark. I absolutely know that listening to other people is important. If I wasn't a good listener, this place would've fallen apart a long time ago.

Although, in fairness, it does seem like we've had an awful lot of problems lately…

Turning to Seth, I say, "He's not going to tell us anything else."

I can tell my Beta is reluctant to go with me, but we are wasting our time here, so we step back toward the door of the cell.

"I can't feel her," Alpha Jordan says, and I don't know if he's talking to me or just talking in general.

Glancing back at him over my shoulder, I see that his eyes are glassed over, and it seems that he is really concentrating. "I can't reach her at all. I do believe she is dead."

My mouth drops open, and I intend to say something respectful because even if he's a traitor, there's no reason to be a jerk now, but Seth says, "Good. She deserved to die," and that's that.

Alpha Jordan's gaze narrows, and we turn to walk away.

"What the hell is he talking about?" Seth asks me.

I continue to go over the conversation I'd had with him again and again in my mind, but I can't remember all of it.

"Why would Austin want to save her? Does Jordan owe Henry money? Do they have an alliance? Are they friends?" Seth asks all the right questions, but I have no answer.

And then we walk back outside and the notion strikes me, something I should've figured out from the beginning. I feel stupid and want to blame it on being distracted, but I have no excuse as I gasp and put my hand on Seth's arm to steady myself.

"What is it?" he asks me.

I have only one word for him as a response: "Mates."

SHE'S ANGRY

Isla

"Mom? Dad?" I say as my parents come charging into the room. "What are you doing here?"

"Oh, thank the Moon Goddess!" Mom says, ignoring my question as she practically runs across the room to Ben. She wraps her arms around him and cradles his head like he is a small child. "We were so terrified!"

Dad stays back a bit, but he has a worried look on his face as he surveys my brother and Mom.

"Mom, I'm fine," Ben says as he struggles to get himself free of Mom's grasp. "Seriously, you can let go."

Mom relaxes her grip, taking him by the shoulders as tears stream down her cheeks. "When we heard you were hurt in the uprising, we were so scared. We got here as quickly as we could."

"Thank goodness I just bought that new car," my dad says. "We would've had to take the train."

My dad doesn't seem nearly as upset or even surprised as my mom, but then, perhaps he has always been a little more chill than she is.

My mom whirls around to look at me. "Isla!" she says in a stern voice. "What in the world were you thinking? As soon as Ben got here, you should've called us! He could've been killed, and he isn't even supposed to be here!"

"I'm sorry, Mom." I'm not sure what else to say. She's got that look on her face that makes me know she's not going to listen to anything that I say.

"You should be sorry!" she shouts at me. "I can't believe you would act so irresponsibly! We raised you better than that, Isla. Perhaps working in the castle is having a bad influence on you. Is there some other servant around here who is making you act this way?"

"No," I say quickly. "No, not at all, Mom. I was going to call you, but–"

"I told her not to, Mom," Ben says quickly. "I knew you'd be mad and worried about me, but I wanted to show that I could do this, that I could come to the castle by myself, that I'm capable of it. I'm not just a sick little boy anymore."

"But you are only fifteen!" Mom shouts. "You are a little boy, as far as I'm concerned. It doesn't matter whether you're sick or well, Ben. This is a dangerous journey, and you should never have come here all on your own!"

"I'm sorry, Mom," Ben begins, but she doesn't let him get much out before she's interrupting him again.

"Why in the world didn't you just ask us to come with you? Your father and I would've been happy to come with you to see Isla, if it was all right with her. We've been talking about coming for a visit anyway. But with everything going on at the castle, with the prisoners and the attacks in other packs, it just didn't seem like a good time for us to be leaving Willow pack."

"I understand, Mom," Ben says. "I came because… I missed her so much."

Ben is still trying to keep what we've discovered a secret from my parents, and I don't think that's a good idea. I think it's time to tell them the truth. They might be mad at us for snooping, but they can't stay that way when they've been keeping unbelievably important information from us, not to mention my mother point blank lied to me the other day when I asked her about where we were from.

"Mom, Ben came here to ask me some questions about where we came from," I begin. "You should know that we are both well aware of the truth now, that we are from Maatua, that you and Dad were the queen and king. We know a lot, but we don't know everything."

"Isla!" It's my dad's voice that cuts through the room with an angry tone this time. "Why are you filling Ben's head with such nonsense? You know that's not true, not a word of it!"

Frustrated, I let out a loud sigh. "Dad! It is true! I have proof–in more ways than one. And, I'm going to need your help!"

"It's not true," Mom says, but she has a waiver in her voice that tells me she's lying. "We're from the south. We're from–"

"I found Isla's birth certificate," Ben cuts in. "I found a lot of stuff–in the floor in your bedroom. We know that her last name isn't really Moon. We know that she was born on the island. I have the picture of the two of you on your wedding day, and we know that it was held in Maatua."

My mother's mouth is left hanging agape for several moments as she tries to figure out what to say. She is shaking her head, like she wants to deny it, but how can she?

Tears begin to stream down my mom's face. "You shouldn't have been snooping, Benjamin."

"I told him to," I say, taking responsibility for the situation. "I knew that you used to hide Dad's birthday gifts in a secret spot in your room, so I told him to look around, and he found your hiding spot."

"But why?" Dad asks. "Why is it all so important to you? Why can't you just accept the fact that we live in Willow pack now, and assume that everything else isn't important?"

"We want to know the truth of where we came from for a lot of reasons, Dad, but when I was kidnapped, I almost died, and I had vivid dreams about boarding a boat in the middle of the night. I wanted to know if it was just a dream or if it was a memory." I hoped my explanation would help them begin to see why I had gone to such great lengths to find the truth. I had a lot more to tell them, but I needed to let them process this statement first.

"I didn't realize it was so serious, Isla," my dad says. "You almost died?"

I nod. "Mystica, the pack healer, was able to save me, but since then, I've had a lot of vivid dreams, and some of them have already been proven to be prophetic. I had to know why this keeps happening. I had to know why."

"What sort of vivid dreams?" my father asks.

I tell him about the dream I had about Private Wylie before he died and how he ended up dying the same way that I dreamed it would be almost at the same time that I was dreaming it. I told him about the dream I had of Zabrina walking out of the water and into a trap. And I told him about the man and woman in the meadow. "That one, as far as I know, hasn't happened yet."

My parents look at one another, and I can't read their expressions exactly, but I do recognize the look. They are having an internal dialogue, probably not even through the mind-link, debating whether or not to tell us something.

Eventually, my mom says, "I have those kinds of dreams, too, Isla. That's how I knew Ben had been hurt. I called the castle, and they confirmed that he'd been injured in the uprising."

I stare at my mother, not sure what to say. I had no idea she was also capable of having these kinds of dreams. She's never told me that before.

"Mom, I wasn't just injured," Ben says, "I was dead. I died."

"What?" my dad asks, a skeptical look on his face as he shuffles from one foot to the other. "What do you mean you died?"

"I died!" he says again. "I was dead. I had this vision…"

"You're having them, too?" Mom looks confused. "You shouldn't be able to."

"Only when I was dead," he clarifies.

"I don't know how you can be alive now if you died," my dad says. He seems as skeptical of the situation as Maddox is.

"Isla brought me back to life," Ben says.

I take a deep breath. I didn't want to get into all of that so quickly because it is so hard to believe that I was actually able to save Ben from death's grasp, and we've already unloaded so much on them.

But it seems that we're in it up to our elbows now. "I know it sounds crazy," I say. "But… a few days ago, a baby was born here in the castle, and she wasn't breathing. I was helping with the delivery because it was this girl I know having the baby. Anyway, when I saw that the baby wasn't breathing, I started crying. My tears fell on her, and she started breathing. Mystica, the healer, she's from Maatua–she says that it was my tears that saved her."

My mom just stares at me, stunned, but my dad says, "Honey, I don't think that crying on a baby can bring them back to life. It must've just been a coincidence."

Ben says, "She saved me, too, though, Dad. I was dead, and Isla cried, but then, she also cut her hand, and her blood dripped down on my wound, and then, I started breathing again."

Both of my parents look shocked now, but my dad still looks a bit skeptical.

Mom turns and looks at him and says, "You know why."

"But–" Dad stutters.

"Daniel! You know why! It's true. It's the same reason I have the dreams that I have, the visions. Isla has the gift, and you know exactly why she has it!"

"But Constance," he begins.

I have to cut him off, though. "Mom, what are you talking about?"

She looks at me with tears in her eyes and says, "In Maatua, there's a magical pool of water that can bring people back to life."

I nod. "Mystica told us all about it." I haven't told them about the baby yet, and now doesn't seem like the right time, so I don't mention that I want to go there to have my baby–yet.

"Well, one day, we were picnicking near the pond. Your older sisters were running around chasing butterflies. I was with them, and I thought your dad was with you, but he wasn't, and when I came back–you were gone."

"We looked everywhere for you," my dad says, "but it took forever to find you. When we finally caught up to where you'd crawled off to, you were bleeding."

"You'd been bitten by a snake," my mom says. "I saw it slithering away. It was a poisonous snake, and you were so little…."

"Your mother scooped you up and took you into that pool of water," Dad continues.

"By the time I got you there, you weren't breathing anymore. You were blue, and your little body was so swollen. I prayed to the Moon Goddess to spare you," Mom says with tears rolling down her cheeks.

"And… then, you started breathing again," Dad says.

"You were fine! Just like so many people before you, the pool saved your life." Mom wipes at her tears.

"But none of those other people have been able to save other people who had died," my father points out.

"That's true," Mom agrees, " but Isla, you do know our true last name, don't you?"

I nod. "Masina."

"That's right, and it means moon—because… you are a direct descendant from the Moon Goddess. Coupled together, I think that's why you are able to use your powers to save lives."

"Which means…" Ben continues, "you don't have to go to Maatua to save him."

My mom is puzzled as she looks between my brother and me. "Save who?"

I look from my mom to my dad and then back again before I say, "My son."

THEY FOUND A BODY

Maddox

"MATES."

The word hangs in the air between Seth and me, both of us trying to process what this means for Austin, assuming he's escaped. Zabrina was obviously his fated mate. He came here to try to save her, even though she was acting as if she had absolutely no intention whatsoever to be with him. She was here, trying to become my Luna queen, yet he was willing to risk his life, and actually sacrifice the lives of some of his pack members, to try to free her ass.

And from the sound of things, there's a chance it just might have worked…. How can her body be gone if she's not alive? But how can she be alive when I ripped her intestines out?

None of it is making any sense to me.

"She has to be dead," Seth says. "If you did as you say you did, and I believe that you did, then there's no way she could be alive."

"I would say you're probably right, but seeing as though Isla's brother Ben died a few hours ago, but he's alive now." I can't imagine there's anyone else in this palace who has the healing powers Isla allegedly has. In fact, it's hard for me to accept that even Isla is capable of bringing people back to life. But it does seem like it's too much of a coincidence that Isla cried over two people who were dead and then suddenly they were not dead anymore.

"What do you think we should do next?" Seth asks me, drawing me out of my thoughts.

"We need to get to Southern pack and see if Alpha Henry has any idea where his son might be. We will need to find Austin and make sure that whatever his force's intentions are, they aren't able to attack again. I'd like to think that now that the execution is over, there would be no reason for any of them to attack us again, but who knows?"

I continue to walk until I am outside, but then, I see a warrior running over to me. He's dressed in his uniform and covered with dirt, and from the look of things, he's been running for a while. I don't remember seeing him inside of the courtyard during the fight. In fact, I'm pretty sure he's one of the guards that is usually stationed near the gates. "What's going on?" I ask him.

"Sir!" he says, out of breath. I have to wonder why he didn't shift to run over to talk to me. "We've just gotten word from the village. Apparently, someone has strung up a body in the town's square, and the citizens are pummeling it with rocks!"

My eyes widen as I look at Seth. "A body?" I ask. He nods.

"Male or female?" Seth asks.

He shrugs. "I'm not sure. They say it's hard to tell at this point, the body is so badly beaten."

Confusion washes over me as I think about the possibilities. It has to be Zabrina, doesn't it? But she was wearing a skirt when she was strung up, which means it should be obvious she's a woman whether she's dressed or not. I did tear her guts out, but the rest of her body should be intact.

But then… if it's her body in the village, I have no idea how it got there, so who knows what someone might've done to her to get her there.

"Do you know why they are throwing rocks at the body?" I ask him.

"No, only that they are shouting, 'Goddess save the king!' as they do it," the warrior tells me.

"Shit," I mutter. So… it seems that this crowd is in support of me, even if they have no idea who the person is that they are pelting with rocks.

Turning my attention to Seth, I say, "We should go."

He nods, and the two of us run off to the garage, knowing we need to get to the village and find out what is happening there, but also why it is happening. How did this body get there? If it's not Zabrina, or if it's not one of the rogues that attacked the castle, then who the fuck is it, and what do we need to do to find out who killed the person?

In the garage, we get in the closest SUV, and Seth starts the car. We tear off, watching out for citizens who are still milling around outside where they fled to escape the turmoil at the execution.

"It has to be Zabrina," Seth says as he steers around a family walking back to the village. "Who else could it be?"

"I don't know," I admit. "I think it's probably her, too, but that doesn't clear up all of the mystery. We have to figure out how the hell she got out of the castle grounds and into the village."

"That's true," he says. "And why."

The why part might be as simple as someone wanting to take their frustration out on someone, but it could be something more.

Another thought occurs to me. "If Zabrina's body is being pummeled in the square at the village, we may draw in the attention of the rebels who started the uprising in the first place."

"So you think Austin might be there?" Seth asks me.

I nod. "I think that's a good possibility."

It doesn't take long before we arrive at the village. We roll up on quite a large crowd of people who are acting unruly. As I step out of my vehicle, I see a few of my guards trying to control the crowd, but there aren't enough of them, and it seems like everyone wants to get a rock thrown at the body.

The corpse is strung up on a flagpole, about eight feet off of the ground, and I can see why others might not know who it is. Though naked, there are rips and tears in the torso, innards hanging, twisted limbs, and a bag still covering the upper half of the head.

I know exactly who it is, though. The bag is a good tip-off, but then, so is the narrow waist.

It's Zabrina, all right.

And she is most definitely dead.

But how she got here, I have no idea. Someone in this crowd has to know something. I doubt that a person would go to all of the trouble to steal her body from the courtyard and drag her down here but then leave before they got to see the aftermath of their decisions. They have to be here somewhere, and if that's the case, I want to talk to them.

But the crowd is out of control, and the few guards are not going to be able to stop the madness. Using the mind-link, I call back to the castle to let them know they need to transport at least a hundred warriors to the village right away.

Then, I start surveying the crowd.

Who here looks like they know how this all got started and will speak to me about it without causing too much trouble?

I look through the myriad of faces, trying to determine who my best bet is. My eyes fall on an older gentleman standing toward the back of the crowd, his arms folded across his muscular chest. His gray hair lets me know he's mature enough to know he needs to answer my questions, and his clothing tells me he's probably a respectable member of the citizenry and not someone who is going to balk at seeing me.

"Excuse me," I say, walking over to him.

His eyes widen slightly as he realizes who I am.

"Yes, Your Majesty!" He tips his head to me, and I make a waving motion with my hands, not thinking that his formality is necessary.

"Do you happen to know how that body got here?" I ask him, point blank.

He says, "By the time I came out of my store, it was already strung up, but I believe that man over there in the black shirt had something to do with it. His name is Preston, and he is a bit... off-balanced, but also a big proponent of yours."

I turn and look at the man who is dancing around, picking up rocks and throwing them at Zabrina's body with ardor. He has a big grin on his face, and his eyes are wild as he does his best to rile up the crowd.

He does look like he's a little off. I have no idea how he would've managed to get that body out of the courtyard without any of my warriors noticing, though.

"Thank you, sir," I say to the man, and he nods.

"Of course, Your Majesty. I'm just glad you finally killed the bitch who wanted to poison all of us."

I realize then that the villagers know that Zabrina had intended to poison the water. It's no wonder they are continuing to stone her long after she's dead.

"It's that guy over there," Seth says to me as I walk back over to him. It seems most people in the crowd haven't noticed me yet, so I can walk freely. Seth is pointing at Preston as well.

"Yeah, that's what I've heard. Let's wait until the backup soldiers from the castle get here, and then we can move in and get him under our control."

Seth nods, so we wait, and I wonder which way the crowd is going to break when the soldiers get here. I want to position myself to be able to stop Preston from getting away. Something tells me, even if he does break away from us, there are enough people in the village who will know where to find him.

Still, it would be easier to just catch him to begin with....

I hear the approaching vehicles and watch faces as some of the citizens realize they are about to have company. The ones in the back who are mostly just watching take off for their homes, but Preston is too busy dancing around to notice until it's too late. When he sees the warriors pouring out of the black transport vehicles, he turns to run and hits his head on my chest. I grab hold of him. "Where you going, Preston?"

He opens his mouth to respond, but I'm not listening to him. Over his shoulder, I see a flicker of movement down the alley that catches my attention. As quickly as I can, I hand Preston off to the closest soldier, and then, I shift and take off running as Austin shifts and darts between the trees. I shift, too, hoping my wolf is faster than his.

I'm not going to let him get away this time.

WHY DID HE DO IT?

Maddox

IT'S TAKEN me far too long to accept what Austin already told me in those few moments when he was trying to save Zabrina. He said he was her mate, but I didn't think that was possible. His pack is so far from hers. Even though they were mates, it made little sense to me that he would want to save her. It's not as if they were lovers–were they?

I need to catch up to Austin to find out the truth. He has started quite an uprising by even being at the hanging, so there has to be something I am missing.

Zabrina told me about the mate bond herself. She told me that it hadn't meant much of anything for her to walk away from her mate, so why would Austin go to so much trouble to try and spare her life? If she died, it would be painful for him, but not for long, not without a true relationship like I had with Rebecca to increase the pull I had to her. I didn't just feel a mate pull to Rebecca, I loved her as my wife and Luna.

So why is Austin running through the woods from me now after having tried to save her from a death she so very much deserved? Why would he be willing to risk everything to try and save someone who didn't care about him at all?

There has to be more to it than a simple mate bond!

I see him up ahead of me and know that I am gaining on him. He is large and fast, but I am bigger and faster. Being the Alpha King has given me the ability to run faster than a lot of other wolves, even those who aren't quite as... mature... as I am. When he has to slow to leap over a tall hedge, I can ground on him. He takes a corner too fast, and I am literally nipping at his heels. I bite down on his back leg and grab hold of him, tugging him toward me.

He yelps but then turns his head to face me, attempting to bite the top of my head while I am clamped down on his leg. I'm having none of it, though as I lash out and hit him across the face with my claws, instantly drawing blood from his snout. He yelps again, this time falling backward onto the forest floor as I shift my position and move to hold him down by his shoulders.

I hear some of my guards coming up behind me and know that he's not going to be able to get away from us now. Maybe he'll be smart enough to start answering some of my questions.

Using the mind-link, I say, "You know this is over, Austin. What the hell are you doing? You can't possibly love Zabrina after she walked away from you."

He glares at me. "Fuck you, Maddox!" he says back to me in my head, his wolf face still bleeding from where I swiped my claws across his snout. "You don't know a damn thing about love! You fucking killed her, and all she ever wanted to do was to love you!"

I stare down at him, confused about what the hell he's even talking about. Is he talking about the same Zabrina that I knew? The one that kidnapped Isla? The one that killed Private Parker and seduced Private Wylie and sent him to his death?

"You need some time to get your shit together," I tell him. "At the moment, you're in big trouble for starting an uprising at an execution. You and your band of assholes killed some of my guards and some innocent people. You're going to be the next one to swing from the gallows, Austin, unless you cooperate."

"Fuck you!" he says and attempts to spit blood in my face, but I dodge out of the way, and then, my troops are there, and I release him into their custody and trot back toward the village, thinking I still need to know why someone brought Zabrina's body to the village.

When I get back to the square in the center of the village, I see that Seth has Preston, the man who apparently brought Zabrina's body here, in his custody, and they are both in their human forms, which means he didn't have to shift to track him down. I am handed some pants by an aide, and then I head over to see what's going on with Preston.

"It's a revolution, man," he's saying to Seth, clearly nervous but also hyped up. "If we don't nip this shit in the bud right away, it's going down, and it's going down faster than you can even think about it, man!"

I look from Seth to Preston and then back again, not sure if I should ask Seth to interpret this for me while the man is still standing here, babbling on, or if I should just shut this down and take them both to the castle.

Seth seems to be on the same wavelength as me. "Preston is concerned about Austin's motives. He believes he's trying to gain sympathy through claiming Zabrina is his mate, but he believes there's another woman who is actually Austin's mate, and this is all political."

All of that makes sense to me, somehow, and it's the first time in a long time that I feel that way, the first time I've heard something related to this situation.

But Zabrina does have a mate. Her father told me so, and he alluded to it being Austin when I talked to him in the dungeon before we heard that Zabrina's body was in the village.

I am missing something… I am missing something important.

"Let's take him back to the castle, and we'll sort this all out there," I say.

"But I didn't do anything wrong!" Preston protests.

"You stole the body of an executed prisoner, brought her to a second location, and encouraged a mob to stone her, Preston," I explain to him. "How is that not doing anything wrong?"

"Because! I was doing it to help you!" he replies, with his arms splayed at his sides. "I needed to encourage the people of the village to remember why we hate Zabrina and why we love you, Your Majesty!"

I was beginning to think the man had been smoking something pretty potent.

"If you were truly trying to help, the sentiment is appreciated, but this wasn't the way to go about it, Preston. You've riled everyone up and potentially put people in danger. With Austin still hanging around here, there's a good chance that other people from his rebellion might still be here, too. Citizens could've been injured, Preston. This is not the way that we handle things in a civilized village."

"No offense, Sir," he begins, his eyes not quite focusing on my face. "But I'm pretty sure society frowns upon hangings these days, too. Public executions are a bit barbaric, don't you think?"

I open my mouth to attempt to explain myself, but then I remember that I'm talking to someone who is probably so stoned he won't even remember having had this conversation with me later, let alone what he told me.

"Get him the fuck out of here," I tell Seth.

My Beta doesn't have to be told twice. He takes hold of Preston while he continues to shout and hauls him to one of the transport vehicles. He's not the only one who is being placed in custody. Several other people who were vigorously tossing rocks at Zabrina are also being loaded up.

And then there's the body itself.

I don't want to bring Zabrina back to the castle yet one more time. I'd really rather just bury her here in the village and be done with it. But I won't have her body continuing to stir up trouble. I order the guards to have her taken back and buried in the criminals' cemetery in an unmarked grave, hoping that this is enough to finally put all of this behind us.

But I know that it's not the end of the problems.

Clearly, Austin's pack is unhappy and ready to march against the throne. I have to think that there are other packs out there that are willing to do the same. I need to find out for certain if Austin really is Zabrina's mate or if my first hunch that that couldn't be the truth was right.

Several townspeople want to speak to me. "Do you think there will be a war?" a woman clutching a small child to her bosom asks me.

"What are the chances that this is the end of all of it, now that the witch is dead?" an older man wants to know.

"I assure you, our soldiers are ready to stomp out any uprising," I tell them. "As you can see, we are fully capable of protecting you and your families."

"But what about the heir?" another woman asks. She looks to be about my age, and judging by her clothing, she is one of the more affluent citizens of the building. "Until you have a child, won't there always be the threat of an uprising?"

Shaking my head, I try to choose my words carefully. "Nothing will stop some people from lusting for power. Unfortunately, that's just how some people are. But the fact that I don't have an heir shouldn't be seen as an extra reason for these uprisings."

"I heard a baby was born at the castle a few weeks ago. Is it true?" another man asks.

"A baby was born, but she wasn't mine," I say, watching their faces fall. "I promise, all of these issues are being addressed."

"So you are working on having an heir?" the affluent woman asks.

I don't want to answer that question. I smile at her. "All I can say is, you needn't worry. Trust me. Trust the Moon Goddess. You are all in good hands."

"No offense, Your Majesty," the younger gentleman says, "but it seems like we don't have a lot of reason to believe that's true after what happened during the executions and knowing that something like this can happen under your watch. How did that woman's body get out from the castle walls?"

I need to get out of here before I lose my cool and begin to yell at these innocent people who have done nothing wrong. "We are investigating the situation," I tell them. "Now, if you'll excuse me, there are people back at the castle who need my attention."

"Wounded?" the woman shouts after me, but I pretend not to hear her.

I am beginning to lose my grip on the kingdom, and I'm going to have to do something to fix this. Having a baby will help, but it won't do everything. No, I'm going to have to figure out exactly where this most current uprising was sparked and nip it in the bud.

TELLING THEM THE TRUTH

Isla

"Your son?" my mom repeats. "Isla, what in the world are you speaking about?" Her face is even paler than Ben's as she stares up at me.

I have to think carefully about how to answer that question because Maddox probably doesn't want the entire kingdom to know our business just yet, but Ben knows, and if he knows, it's only a matter of time until my parents know.

Besides, I've never been one to keep information from my parents–unlike them. They are, apparently, very used to keeping information from me and my siblings.

Until recently, when I became a breeder, I didn't keep anything from them at all.

With one hand still hovering over my abdomen, I begin to try and explain the situation to them. I want to call out to Maddox and ask him to come and be here with me when I tell my parents the situation, but I know he is busy with the aftermath of the uprising, and I can't tell them to just wait until he returns.

With a deep breath, I say, "I'm pregnant."

My parents exchange a look, and I can see disappointment settling over both of their faces. I've always been the responsible one, the one who would never do anything that might make the Moon Goddess feel dishonored or my parents feel disrespected. They instilled good moral values in me from the time that I was a little girl. So for them to think that I could go against the Moon Goddess's wishes and have sexual relations with a man outside of a proper marking and marriage ceremony has to be disappointing.

"Is he your mate?" my father asks, his voice laced with tension.

"I don't know," I tell them. "I'm not old enough to know that." It was almost my twenty-first birthday, but I wasn't there yet.

"Do you love him?" my mother asks me.

That was much easier. I nod. "Yes, I love him very much."

"And does this… guy… love you?" I can hear my father's disappointment morphing into anger.

I almost laugh. My father has no idea he's just called the Alpha King a "guy" like he's just some common butler or something. "He says he loves me." That's true–he has recently let that bit of information slide out of his mouth. It makes me giddy to say that, but I keep my joy inside of me.

"Isla… I'm sorry, honey. I want to be happy for you. I really do. I am glad that you're going to have a baby. We'd love to have another grandchild!" my mom says, forcing a smile, but she has tears in her eyes.

"Maybe this one we'll actually get to see," my father mutters, and I hear the pain of being cut out of my sisters' lives in his voice.

"It's just… what about your mate?" my mom asks me. "Most women who get pregnant before they meet their mate are never blessed to meet him. They end up mateless, sometimes even wolfless, as a punishment from the Moon Goddess for not obeying her wishes."

I can feel tears in my own eyes as well. I have so many questions I want to ask them about Maatua and me being in that pool and coming back to life, but instead, we are discussing whether or not I've disappointed the Moon Goddess.

"Mom, Dad, I'm pregnant… because it's my job to be pregnant," I tell them.

Both of them look at me with expressions of utter confusion etched into their faces, brows furrowed, mouths agape. "You… what?" Dad asks for both of them.

"It's my job to be pregnant. That doesn't dispute the fact that I love him, and he loves me, but… when Alpha Ernest brought me here, it wasn't to take the job of a maid. Maids don't make the kind of money I do, and they don't make the kind of money Alpha King Maddox gave you when he came to visit you in the village either."

My mom stands, taking a few steps away from the bed where she'd been sitting next to Ben. Now, her mouth is hanging open, but rather than it being in surprise, she appears to be in awe. "Is it…. Are you… Isla, are you a breeder?"

Slowly, my head nods up and down. "Yes, Mom. I'm a breeder."

"What?" my dad asks, still not getting it. "A breeder?" He is shocked, and not in a happy way like my mom. "For who?"

"For… the king?" my mom asks.

Again, I am nodding. "That's right." My hands protectively cover my abdomen. "And this baby… is the heir to the throne."

"Ohh!" My mom covers her face as tears fill her eyes. She rushes to me and pulls me against her chest, stroking my hair as she says, "My baby! My baby is giving birth to a king!"

I can't help but smile as she holds me close. It feels so nice to be back in my mother's arms. Even though, I do think it's kind of surprising that she's so proud of me to be giving birth to a king when technically, so has she. My oldest brother, Chris, would have been the king of Maatua.

Maybe that's why. Maybe because she gave up her opportunity to have one of her children become a king, she is proud of me that I have managed to find a way to bring royalty back to our family.

"What is happening?" my father asks, and I'm not sure if he's asking me or Ben.

"Isla's the king's lady," Ben says. "They're like… in love and stuff. She's carrying his baby. But she's only a few weeks pregnant, so I'm not exactly sure why she knows it's a boy. Is it because you saw it in a dream, Isla?"

"I was going to ask how far along you are, baby," my mom says, pulling back and patting me on the cheek.

"I'm not exactly sure," I admit. "But not too far along."

"And what did you mean about saving the baby?" my dad asks. "Is something wrong with him?"

They were asking me so many questions all at the same time, and all I wanted to do was ask them my questions.

"Uhm, well, I did have a dream, and even though I'm not quite sure, I think it was a vision or a premonition. I've been having a few of them recently. Some of them have already come true. This one was far in the future, though, if it was my son. I just… feel like the baby is a boy. I don't know how far along I am exactly, but I know I was pregnant when I was kidnapped and poisoned by that awful Zabrina that was put to death today. So Mystica, the pack healer, is afraid that the baby might have complications because of it."

"Mystica?" Mom repeats.

I nod. "Yes. She's from Maatua. Do you know her?"

My mom turns and looks at my dad, and he sort of shrugs.

"Not exactly. I know of her," my mom says.

"I'm sorry, Mom and Dad. I know we got off topic, but listen, I really want to know about what happened back there. You said I died? And I came back to life? Do you think that's why my tears and blood were able to save Ben and Maddy? Or bring them back from the dead or whatever?"

Once again, my parents are exchanging glances that I can't read, and it is very frustrating to me. I wish that they could simply answer my questions. But they don't seem capable of it, not without this facial expression exchange that seems to be some sort of a replacement for the mind-link they could be using instead.

Eventually, my father says, "It probably has a lot to do with it, Isla. But we aren't sure. We've never heard of anyone else who died and came back to life from the pool having any kind of powers."

"It might be because of your ancestry," Mom says.

I look from her to my dad, to Ben, and then back to mom again. "Because we are related to the Moon Goddess?"

"That's right," my mom says. "It's all so complicated, dear, and without you knowing all of the secrets of Maatua, it will be difficult to explain."

"Will you at least try?" I ask, feeling overwhelmed. My mom sits down in a chair next to the window, and I do the same, and Dad comes around the bed and sits near Ben's feet. I can see them looking at one another again, but this time, I think my parents are using the mind-link, trying to sort out who is going to tell the story and how much exactly they are going to say.

"After you came back to life, we took you home and told everyone in our family about what had happened. A few people didn't believe us; some did. We tried to put it behind us and just be thankful that you were all right," my mother begins.

"But then, something strange happened," my father chimes in. "Something we were unsure about."

"Something we couldn't explain," my mom adds with a nod.

"What was it?" Ben asks.

My father sighs and pulls out his wallet, which I think is peculiar, but we are both hanging on their every word. He opens it up and pulls out a photograph, which he hands over to me.

The picture is of me when I was a little girl. I've seen the photo before, but it's been a long time. I'm standing in a field of some kind, holding an orange cat in my arms and smiling at the camera. It could be any back yard anywhere. I had no idea that it was on Maatua, but when I look at the trees behind me now, I do notice they look tropical.

"What am I looking at?" I ask, studying my face. Was this before or after I had died?

"The cat," my father says. "Do you remember the cat?"

I look closely at the kitty, and suddenly, I feel a slight twitch in my heart, and I smile. "Ginger," I say.

"That's right." Mom takes the picture from me and hands it to my brother so he can see it before he gives it back to dad. "That cat was your best friend when you were little. You loved her so much."

"What happened to her?" Ben asks, and I want to know the same thing because I don't remember.

"She got hit by a car," my dad says, and I feel my heart break. I don't remember that at all.

"It was awful," Mom says, shaking her head. "You were beside yourself, Isla, crying so hard."

"Your nanny had put the cat in a box on a pillow," Dad explains, "and we were going to have a funeral for her. We'd had the pack healers try to help her, but she was dead. Not bloody and gross, but dead nonetheless. So… when the nanny brought her in for you to say goodbye, you held the box and cried and cried."

"I don't remember," I admit.

"You wouldn't. You were so little," Mom says.

"So… you probably don't remember what happened next," my dad says, eying my mom to see if she wants to tell me or if he should say.

They don't need to tell me. Before my mother even opens her mouth, I know what she's going to say.

"Just as we were about to take Ginger from you and put her in her grave… something unusual and unexpected happened, " Mom begins, pausing for dramatic effect.

'She got up and ran away?" I ask.

My parents nod. Mom says, "You'd brought her back to life with your tears."

TRUE MOTIVATION

Maddox

I AM GROWING leery of interrogating prisoners in the dungeon, but I have no choice since I don't trust anyone else to speak to Austin. He's still bleeding from the injuries he sustained when he ran from me. All he has on is a pair of ratty old shorts, and he's sitting on the dirty dungeon floor, both arms chained to the wall behind him so that he can't even lower his arms.

I stare at him for a moment. He's breathing heavily, and I'm not exactly sure why. I don't see any new injuries, so I can't imagine he's been beaten by my guards, though if they did lay their paws upon him, I'm certain it would be for good reason. So... why is he so out of breath?

"Austin," I begin, "explain to me why you began the uprising during the executions." I use my Alpha voice and command him to answer me. It doesn't always work. Some people are so disloyal, so criminal in nature, they can simply ignore me when I compel them to do something.

I can see that he is struggling with it, though. He wants to tell me to fuck off again, but at the same time, he feels the need to answer me because I am his Alpha King.

"I already told you," he finally gets out between pants for air. "Zabrina was my mate."

"I don't believe you," I tell him, straight up. "Alpha Jordan tried to tell me the same thing, but it didn't make any sense to me then, and it doesn't make any sense to me now. Your packs are nowhere near one another, and she had already rejected her mate long ago. So if she'd rejected you, then, you wouldn't still be longing for her."

"How would you have any idea about the pangs of rejection, Your Majesty?" His chin is thrust into the air in defiance as he stares at me. "You were blessed to have your mate as your wife, your queen, your Luna. Most of us are not as blessed as you are."

I think that his second statement has nothing to do with my mate; he is just making a general statement.

I shrug. "Perhaps you are right and all counts. I am blessed to have had my true mate as my wife, and perhaps many people are not as blessed as I am, and though I've never suffered the pain of rejection, I do know the pain of losing my mate. I know it quite well." Even thinking about Rebecca now has my heart feeling heavy in my chest like a stone at the bottom of the sea. "So… what is it, then? What is it that would drive a man with as much to gain as you have to declare war on the Alpha King?"

"I didn't declare war on you." He's breathing more easily now, and his eyes drop to the floor for the first time since I've entered his cell. Could it be that he is feeling a bit upset about the way that he has acted?

Somehow, I doubt it.

"Didn't you, though? You attacked my troops in my courtyard of my castle during a ceremony I was leading. How is that not an attack on me? How is that not a declaration of war?" I lift a hand to stroke my chin, and he raises his eyes to my face again.

"If I had wanted to wage war, Sir, I would've brought all of my warriors, but I brought only a handful. And honestly… it wasn't our intention to attack, but then, when I saw Zabrina hanging there… I had no choice."

"What you are saying is all lies!" Seth shouts from behind me, stepping forward and banging his hand into his fist. "First of all, Zabrina wasn't hanging until after you shouted 'Now!' as I recall. Secondly, the fact that you even had a signal to declare to your waiting men lets us all know that this was planned. Finally, of course, you had a choice! You could have simply chosen to not attack!"

I put a hand out to try and silence Seth, but it's clear he's worked up now. When I turn to look at him, his face is red, and he is sweating. I almost find something comical in it, but I say nothing, choosing instead to return my attention to the traitor before me.

"She's not your mate," I tell him. "She never was your mate. So… what else could be your motivation?"

"I loved her," he says, and his voice sounds solemn enough that I almost believe it for a moment.

"You've never even met her," Seth barks. "The only way anyone could ever think they loved Zabrina would be if they'd never even met the horrific bitch!"

Again, I move to silence him, though I am biting back a chuckle at the truth of his statement.

I have to think over the possibilities of why Austin might've moved against us. He had an organized attack ready to go in the courtyard during an execution, which he had to have thought would fail. He knew I would recognize his wolf, and he had to think his chances of getting out of here were slim to none.

Beyond that, I had to find out who Zabrina's true mate had been. Jordan wouldn't be helpful with that, and I still wasn't precisely sure how reliable her mother would be. I didn't want to drag her back to the castle when she was innocent and had lost so much, but I might need to.

But then, another thought occurred to me.

Zabrina had killed her own maid for implementing her in the scheme to drug me. What if I were able to find one of Zabrina's former maids? Would she be able to tell me who Zabrina's mate was?

Not that finding out who he was would necessarily help with all of this, but it was worth a try to see if maybe it could point me in the right direction.

Austin looked pathetic, sitting there on the floor with his arms hung up over his head. "What does your father think of all of this?" I asked him. "Does he know the son he's raised?"

Austin grumbles at me, but he doesn't tell me where I can go, and I wonder if he regrets his actions at all. He is a large man, with a strong, powerful wolf, and a capable warrior. Why would he put himself into a situation where I could capture him? Especially when any outside forces were so far away?

All of these questions need answers, but I won't be getting them from him. "It's a pity you didn't approach me and ask if I was in need of the services of someone like you," I tell him. "I know you think that you're a badass and that you should remain on the dark side of the law, but I think I might've been able to find a place for you as an advisor. Now, well, the only ones you'll be advising are the rats."

He smirks at me, and for a moment a bit of that cocky attitude he'd taken with me back before I had him under arrest, when we were in the woods, is back. "You'd be surprised to see how a man like me can get by in a place like this." He looks around like he's checking out the accommodations on a luxury retreat.

"I guess you'd better get used to concrete, mildew, feces, and rodents," I tell him. "We all know that your pack has its fair share of miscreants, but even that place isn't as dirty as this hovel."

He only grins at me in response, and I see a hint of lunacy in his eyes.

I've grown weary of talking to him and not getting any answers. "When you're ready to speak to me, to tell me the truth about all of this, you know where to find me."

"Yes, I do," he says with a devilish twinkle in his eye. "All I need to do is go up to the breeder's room to find you. I'll find you buried up to your hilt in her pussy, and then I can kill you both."

I want to step over and kick him in the groin for insulting my Isla that way, but that's what he wants from me. He wants to upset me, to throw me off my game, to make me lash out irrationally.

"Why you son of a bitch–" Seth is already flying toward him before he even finishes his insult, but I put out a hand.

"Stop, Seth. He won't be able to get out of here to do anything of that nature," I remind him.

"Are you sure about that?" Austin taunts. "I've heard you've had a few escapees recently."

I shake my head. "I'm afraid you've heard wrong. You simply don't know the details of the situation."

A low groan escapes his throat, and I'm pretty sure he knows I'm lying.

I'm done with this conversation, though. I need to check on the wounded, and then I will head up to speak to Isla. I need to make sure that she, and our baby, are doing well.

I bid Austin goodbye, and he shouts at me to fuck off again, which seems about right, and then I go to the infirmary, but all along the path, I can't help but think about what Austin is really up to. Anything that seems simple, cut and dry, is usually worth looking further into because life is rarely as uncomplicated as he is trying to make it, which really only means one thing.

He's lying. He has to be.

SOMETHING ABOUT MARY

Isla

Ginger.

The story of my cat gave me pause to think about everything that I'd learned about myself. I distinctly remembered that cat now that my parents had reminded me. I didn't have many memories at all from my childhood, and most of the ones I did have were vague. A flicker of a face, laughing on a swing, standing outside and staring up at a large tree, opening a present. Those types of memories didn't give me much context for where I was, who I was, or what I was doing.

But seeing this picture had jarred memories in me that hadn't entered my mind for so long. They were still there, though. I remembered the cat. I remembered playing with her, how sweet she was, how her fur felt beneath my fingers.

I didn't remember her dying, though. And I certainly didn't remember her coming back to life.

"After that," Mom continues, tears beginning to stream down her cheeks. "After that, everything sort of fell apart."

My dad reaches over and squeezes her hand, and I can see that he is emotional, too.

"What do you mean?" I have to ask. "After the cat came back to life, everything fell apart?"

I see the look my parents are exchanging, and it makes me confused. I can see that they are discussing whether or not they want to tell Ben and me the truth about what happened.

We are into this story deep now. They need to tell us everything. And they need to tell us now.

"What happened after Ginger came back to life?" I ask, my tone more demanding now. I lean forward in my chair, making my stance more pointed.

"The cat ran away," my father says. "I have no idea what happened to the cat herself."

"But… it was the miracle that had occurred with the cat that started everything in a downward spiral," Mom says.

"We don't want you to feel like any of this was your fault." Dad looks right into my eyes and shakes his hands back and forth over the top of one another, stressing his words. "It wasn't. You didn't do anything wrong, Isla."

My brow wrinkles in confusion as I try to guess what they might be talking about. "Oookay," I say. "What is it that you think I might infer is my fault?"

"The war," my mom says. "The war and the deaths that preceded them."

"Deaths?" I wasn't sure if I should continue to lean forward to let them know I was serious about them telling me what they were talking about or lean back in my chair because I was beginning to feel nauseated.

My father didn't even bother to look at mom this time. He just launched into telling us what had happened, all the while staring at a spot on the floor, only sparing a few glances up at me or Ben from time to time.

"After the cat came back to life, we tried not to tell anyone what had happened. We hadn't told many people about the incident at the pool to begin with, and we certainly didn't want people to think that the pool was capable of working miracles. We were aware that other people had had similar incidents happen there, but we didn't know of anyone who had had the experience of bringing something else back to life after their resurrection."

Dad pauses to take a breath. "We told the staff that the cat must not have been dead, that it must've just been in a coma or something, and most everyone believed that because the alternative was impossible to accept. Everyone except for the healer. She was certain that the cat had been dead, so we told her about the incident with the snake and the pool. She called it a miracle of the Moon Goddess, and she was probably right."

Mom sniffles a bit and wipes at her eyes, and I am still lost, not understanding what the healer has to do with the war.

"We knew that the story was safe with the healer, but there was someone else who had been there when the cat came back to life that was full of questions, and I couldn't do anything to dissuade him from discovering the full truth of the matter."

Taking a deep breath, my father meets my eyes for just a moment, and I so even without knowing where he's going with the story, I have enough pieces of the puzzle to put together to know what he's going to say before he begins talking again.

"My brother, your uncle, was there when the cat came back to life. Tony was always hanging around you kids. He loved you all like you were his own, or at least, I thought he did...." He has a vacant look in his eyes for a moment before he shakes his head and drags a hand down his face. "But it was from that moment on that we lost all chance of having any peace in the kingdom."

"Why is that?" I can't help the question that comes from my mouth, even though I'm trying to keep Dad talking before he clams up, and I end up without the entire story.

"Because... he saw what you could do, the power that you had, and he wanted it for himself," Dad explains. "He began to ask me questions about what had happened at the pool, and at first, I was honest with him. I didn't see any reason why I shouldn't tell him. He was my younger brother, and he obviously cared about you. But... the more questions he asked, the more I realized a storm was brewing."

"Then... he did the unthinkable." Mom's tears are flowing thicker now. Ben pulls some tissues from the box next to him on the nightstand and hands them to her, and Mom dabs at her cheeks.

"Tony wanted to have the power of granting life. He thought that he could create an army of people that wouldn't be able to die. For some reason, he thought that you wouldn't be able to die because your tears could bring you back to life. He thought that anyone who died and came back to life in the pool was indestructible, but we have no reason to suspect that."

"I believe you're right to think that I can die. I'm pretty sure I was very close to dying, if I didn't actually die and come back thanks to the healer, when I was poisoned," I explain.

"Yes, well, he also thought that having someone who could bring others back to life at his beck and call would bring him immense power," Mom explains, shaking her head. "I never knew how power hungry that man was until I saw his eyes enlarge thinking of what he could do if he could gain some sort of influence over a person who had been brought back from the dead."

My mind was boggled. I couldn't quite grasp why Uncle Tony would think that having someone like me close to him would bring him power. But then, from the sounds of it, the man was clearly mentally unbalanced in some ways to even go that far to begin with.

"The first person he decided to try was his best friend, a guy I grew up with, named Will. That guy would've done anything for Tony. We were all very close. Tony went to great lengths to hide what he had done from all of us at first, and if he had done all of it in secret, perhaps we never would've found out, but he had to make a big production out of it, and that's where the true horror began."

"What do you mean?" I ask my dad.

"I mean, he killed Will one evening. No one knew it. He rolled him up in a carpet and put him in the trunk. The next day, he took his wife on a picnic. Your Aunt Mary, do you remember her?"

He pauses, and I realize that I do. The face of a beautiful woman with dark hair and big blue eyes comes to mind. "Aunt Mary…." I nod. "It's been so long since I even thought of her. Wh-what happened to her?"

Dad sucks in a deep breath and continues. "Well, he took her out there to the pool on this alleged picnic because he wanted her to see what he was capable of, that he could bring the dead back to life or some bullshit. He drags Will out and dumps him in the pool, and Mary is mortified, screaming and crying, but Tony assures her, if they just give it time, Will's heart will start beating again, and he'd come back to life."

I can hardly believe what my dad is saying. My own uncle would do something so harsh? Kill his best friend and take his body out to the jungle just to show his wife he was powerful?

"What happened to the guy?" Ben asks.

Dad shakes his head. "Nothing. He just… floated. Tony waited and waited, but Will was dead. The pool wasn't bringing him back to life."

"Why not?" I ask, wondering how the pool decides who to save and who not to.

"Too much time had passed," Mom says. "We had gathered enough information from other people who knew of the pool's power and had tried to revive people there to know that there was a limit on how much time could've passed before the person was put into the water. If it was more than a couple of hours, the pool didn't work."

"It had to be almost instantaneous," my father agrees. "So Will was dead, and Tony had been the one to kill him."

"And that did not impress his wife?" I say, assuming that had to be the case. I couldn't remember Aunt Mary much, but I knew she was not the type of person who would be happy about that.

"No, she wasn't, but she didn't have a lot of time to think about it," Dad explains.

My brow furrows. "What do you mean?"

"Well, Mary tried to tell Tony that what he had done was awful and that he should've known it would never work because too much time had passed. She told him that it had to be sooner, that not so much time could have passed, but she also told him that what he was doing was madness. He had to let that notion go. He would have to come back to the castle and tell me what he had done and pay for his crimes."

A chill goes down my spine as I think about my beautiful aunt telling Uncle Tony exactly what my father has just said. "I'm guessing he didn't listen?" I ask.

My mom is crying again, harder this time. "No, he didn't listen."

"He decided to try again." My father's teeth are gritted together as he speaks, and I don't think I've ever seen him so angry before in my life. "With your aunt."

"What?" All of the blood seems to leave my face as I realize what my dad is saying. "He killed Aunt Mary?"

Dad nods. "Shoved a knife right through her heart, watched her die, and then pulled her body into the water."

THE PUPPET MASTER

Maddox

IN MY OFFICE, I sit by myself and ponder what to do. I have a few options, but mostly, I need to do whatever I can to shore up my defenses. It seems quite clear that I'm beginning to lose control of the kingdom.

I can't even keep people safe in my own fucking backyard.

Finding one of the maids who was in Zabrina's service shouldn't be too hard. I believe she abandoned all of them when she left here. I know none of them left the castle with her, and I doubt that her mother would have taken many of the maids that serviced her daughter with her when she left since she had her own maids. And Zabrina's friends. She had brought a couple of her cronies along. I'm pretty sure they left with their Luna.

So… what would we have done with extra maids? I'm guessing they would probably have just been assigned to tasks within my household.

I pick up the phone and call the number that goes to the head maid's room. I have no fucking idea who it is now since Mrs. Whateverthefuckhernameis was fired and the replacement was locked up for unlocking every door anyone asked her to.

"Yes, Alpha King Maddox, Sir?" a female voice answers. "How may I help you?"

"Hello—who is this?" I ask.

"This is Gretchin, Sir. The new head of maids."

I know who she is, and I'm a little surprised that she was placed in that position because she hadn't been here for very long.

"Gretchin, do you happen to know if any of Zabrina's maids are still in the castle? Did they all leave when the Luna left? Or are some of them still here?"

"Oh, yes, Sir," she says. "A couple of them are still here. One called Maude and one called Heidi."

"Perfect," I tell her. "Can you send them to my office, please?"

"Yes, sir."

I thank her and hang up, and my mind continues to wander. Perhaps I should call Alpha Henry and see if he knows about his son's plan, but I don't know if I have time for that, and less than ten minutes after I requested the presence of the maids, they show up, knocking hesitantly on my partially open door.

I look up to see that one of them is quite old–maybe in her sixties–and the other looks to be younger than Isla. They stand there in maids' uniforms, their heads tipped, but the older one has a scowl on her face.

"Come in, ladies," I say, gesturing toward the chairs across from me. "Be seated, please."

"Yes, Sir," they both say at the same time.

"I have a quick question for both of you," I begin, folding my hands in front of me. "I hope that you will both be willing to tell me anything that you may know that will help with solving the problem I'm currently working on."

"Of course, Sir," the younger one says.

I have an idea that she is Heidi just because Maude is a bit of an old-fashioned name, but I'm not sure. "Which one are you?"

"This is Heidi," the older one says, hooking her thumb at the other girl. "I'm Maude, Sir."

I nod–just as I'd suspected. "Do either of you happen to know who Zabrina's fated mate was?"

I have blurted the question out there, and it seems to have taken them by surprise as they exchange glances with one another, eyebrows raised. "Sir?" Maude asks me. "You mean... the man she was fated to that she rejected so that she could come here and try to be your mate instead?"

I scoff. I can't help it. It's not because of what Maude has said but because it angers me that Zabrina would even think that was possible. "Yes, I suppose that is what I'm asking," I say.

They look at one another again before Heidi speaks up. "She told me very little about him, Sir. I only know that she met him at a Moon Goddess Ball when she was twenty-one. Her father instantly told her to reject him as his pack lands were far away, he wasn't very powerful, and he had it in his mind that she could be the next Luna Queen."

I nod along with what Heidi is telling me. "Who was he?" I ask.

"We don't know," Maude answers quickly, that scowl back on her face from earlier. "She never told us his name or what pack he was from."

She seems dismissive, like that's that, and she doesn't expect me to ask any more questions.

Unfortunately for her, I've never been one to give up so easily. "Oh," I say. "Nothing at all? Only that the pack was far away? I was under the impression the two of you were close with Zabrina, that she would've trusted you."

"She did trust us," Maude says quickly, obviously irritated that I would suggest otherwise. "But we don't know the details. She didn't like to talk about it."

"Why is that?" I ask, more curious now than conniving.

"She didn't like that her father had made her go to such great lengths. And she was superstitious. She was afraid that rejecting her true mate would bring bad luck to her life," Maude is telling me. "Turns out she must've been right."

"Why do you say that?" I ask her, thinking I already know what she will say, but I want to hear it from her mouth.

"Well, because! Look at her now! She's dead! If she hadn't been forced to reject her mate and come here to seek you out, been told that she had no choice but to succeed or forget about ever coming home, well, perhaps she would've made other choices."

Listening to Maude talk makes me feel slightly bad for Zabrina at first, but then, I remember how horrid that bitch was, and any hint of sympathy that was beginning to bubble up inside of me is squashed.

"Are you saying that Alpha Jordan forced his daughter to come here and wreak havoc on my life, try to kill my breeder, kill a couple of my guards, and one of your own?" I ask them, lacing my fingers together.

The two of them exchange glances, but Heidi is the one who speaks next. "We feel that Zabrina let the pressure get to her, and she made some terrible decisions, sir. But it was all fueled by the insistence that she could not fail. I personally believe it drove her a bit mad."

"So really Alpha Jordan is to blame for all of this?" I ask them.

"No," Maude says quickly, shaking her head dismissively. "It wasn't the Alpha who caused all of the trouble, sir."

I am confused. "But you just told me that he was making Zabrina act the way that she was, didn't you?"

"We said someone was forcing her, Sir, but we didn't say who," Heidi explains.

"Well, who else could it have possibly been?" I am confused and beginning to feel like they are messing with me.

The answer comes from Maude. "Luna Elaine, Sir. She was the one who wanted her daughter to come after you so hard. She was the one who insisted that Zabrina could not fail in becoming the next Luna Queen."

I try not to stare at them too hard or let my mouth drop open, but I am shocked. I never would've dreamt that was the case. Lune Elaine always seemed like a bystander in all of this. But these women seem very clear on the idea that Luna Elaine is to blame for much of this.

I clear my throat and then ask the question I most need an answer to before I let them go, even though they've already tried to tell me that they don't know. "Who was the mate?"

"You'd have to ask Luna Elaine," Maude tells me. "She would know."

"Do you know where she's hiding?"

They look at one another again, but neither is asking.

"She left you here, you realize? She didn't take you with her when she fled. She took others but not you, and even if you say it's because you were her daughter's maids and not hers, that doesn't change the facts."

"Beach Front pack, Sir," Heidi blurts out. "That's where they went."

Maude groans. "Heidi! We don't know that for sure!"

"We do," Heidi says, shaking her head. "We do know it, Sir."

"Very well, thank you. You may both go."

As soon as the two maids leave my office, I pick up the phone Beach Front pack is one of the most remote packs from the castle, and though I've never had a problem with them, I also don't know their Alpha, Alpha Geoffrey, very well.

It takes a few rings for anyone to answer, but when I hear a secretary's voice, I ask for the Alpha. Again, I must wait, and then, I begin to think about all of the facts I've been given from the two maids, and the situation becomes a bit clearer to me.

Alpha Geofrey has three sons. One is my age. One is about Isla's age, and one is about Ben's age.... Could one of his two oldest sons be Zabrina's mate? His Luna passed away about five years ago, so Alpha Geofrey might be a little lonely out there along the coast by himself.... Perhaps Elaine had more reasons to tell her daughter to reject her mate than she let on.

"Alpha King Maddox," Geofrey says in my ear. "I'm surprised you would have time to call today with so much going on at the castle."

It's evident from his attitude that he's not got my back. "Cut the bullshit, Geofrey," I snarl at him. "I need to talk to Luna Elaine."

"What makes you think she's here?" he asks, but I can tell by his tone that he is mocking me.

"Don't make me use my Alpha voice," I tell him, which makes him chuckle under his breath.

"Fine, she is here, but I have no idea why you would need to speak to her, Sir. Haven't you done enough to damage her today? You killed her daughter yourself, I've heard."

"What I do to prisoners who have been sentenced to death is none of your affair, Alpha Geofrey. Now, put her on, or I will send my warriors to fetch her from you."

"You would send warriors into a peaceful pack? That sounds like an act of war," he snarls.

"And you refusing your Alpha King seems like an act of treason!" I wish I could reach through the phone and shake him.

The phone goes eerily quiet, so I wait, growing angrier and angrier with each passing moment.

Finally, I hear someone pick up the receiver, and then, in a breathy, feminine voice that reminds me too much of her daughter, Luna Elaine says, "So… you finally figured it out?"

And it's all I can do to keep from slamming the phone down on my desk and shattering it.

NO ONE CAN STOP ME

Maddox

"You're the mastermind behind all of this?" I ask Luna Elaine.

"That's right," she says, "and while you may have killed my daughter today, don't think that it's enough to stop me. If you want to keep your kingdom, you're going to have to figure out who else is the enemy, Alpha King Maddox, and my revelation as the bad guy probably isn't going to be the most shocking event related to this uprising."

Her words have me seething, and I wish I could reach through the phone and smack her in the face. "If you honestly think that you can bring me down, you're wrong," I tell her. "You're not capable of it, Elaine."

She laughs, and it reminds me of her daughter's witch's cackle. Just when I thought I'd never hear that sound again, here it is, in my ear. "You are very confident, Maddox." She says my name with a disrespectful lilt, and while I'm sure that's because I've used her first name without her title, and she's just trying to get me back, I don't appreciate it.

"I am confident," I tell her.

"Listen, I gave you the opportunity to prevent this from happening. You could have simply accepted my daughter as your next Luna Queen. You could have bedded her, which would've been enjoyable to you–she was very well trained in the art of lovemaking–and you could have an heir on the way right now. Your weakness would have been disposed of, and the other pack leaders would've recognized you as a strong, capable king. But now... well, she's out of the picture, your breeder is nothing but a woman-child of unaffluent bloodlines, and even if she does manage to give you a child after all her body has been through, no one will accept that child as your heir to the throne. They'll call the child a bastard and say he or she is not worthy of the throne. As they will not be because her parents are mere peasants. Who would want a child of such meager ancestry as the next ruler of our kingdom?"

My teeth grind together as I wish to tell her how wrong she is about everything she's just said to me. But I can't. Telling her the truth about Isla, that she's actually a princess, that she's already pregnant, none of those pieces of information are necessary for me to disclose at this juncture, and the last thing I want to do is give Luna Elaine more reason to come after Isla.

"You are wrong." That's all I can say, and it's enough. "You will regret going against me, Elaine. Trust me, by the time this is over, you are going to be reunited with your daughter, but before you go, you're going to wish you'd never ever crossed me."

As her laughter begins to fill my ear again, I am ready to slam the phone down, but I have to ask the question I called in an effort to find the answer to. "Tell me the truth, Elaine. Zabrina's true mate–it was Geofrey's oldest son–wasn't it?"

"I won't tell you jack shit," she says, no longer laughing.

"I am still your Alpha King, and you will!" I demand.

She scoffs at me, a chuckle escaping into my ear before she says. "It doesn't matter. Zabrina had fooled many men in many packs into thinking they were her true love. You found that out today. Our reach is long and wide. You cannot stop all of us."

"Tell. Me."

"Fine," she says. "Yes, her true mate was Thomas, Geofrey's oldest son. It doesn't matter now. All of her suitors are coming for you. All of the men that taught her how to pleasure a man so that she would have a chance to be your Luna Queen."

"You will regret this." Those are the last words I say to her before I slam the phone down and drop my head, rage and disgust flowing through me.

I sit there, seething, trying to decide what to do. She says there are enemies everywhere, ones I don't even know about yet. This kingdom I love so much, one I've sworn my life to protect, is falling apart all around me. For the first time since I was a boy, I'm starting to doubt my abilities to do this.

Can I remain king?

"Sir?"

"Not now, Seth," I say, not even looking up at my Beta who is standing in the doorway.

"It's important, Your Majesty."

I sigh deeply and lift my head to see him standing with his hands folded in front of him, and by his face, I can tell that he has something to tell me I'm not going to want to hear.

"What is it?"

He takes a deep breath, lets it out slowly, and then, in a voice so quiet I can hardly hear it, he says, "She was pregnant."

My first instinct is to ask him who he's talking about, but I already know. "How did we miss that?" Didn't we examine her when she was in the prison?

"She was only a couple of weeks along," he explains. "But in her current condition, Mystica was able to tell."

"Shit," I mutter. "So she didn't even know?"

"No, she didn't. But if anyone finds out–"

"No one will find out!" I bang my fist on the desk. "See to it."

"Yes, sir," he says. "But if they were… whoever the father is, well, it could be a problem."

I almost laugh. If the news he'd just given me wasn't so somber, I would have. Zabrina deserved to die, but the growing life within her did not. I would've spared her until the child was born if I had known, even though it was clearly dangerous to keep her alive. Now, I have killed a prisoner but also a child.

"We have more enemies than you could possibly imagine," I attempt to explain.

Seth has a forlorn look on his face and asks, "We can do this, can't we?"

For the first time in my life, I have to admit, "I don't know."

～

Isla

"What happened to Aunt Mary?" I ask. "Did she die?"

"She did die," my mom says, but quickly enough, she adds, "but then she came right back to life."

"And… she had powers," my father tells me. "That became the true problem."

"Powers?" I ask. "What sort of powers?"

"Your aunt was originally from an island near Maatua. It was a small island, a peaceful island, but that wasn't because of how kind the people there were. No, it was because many of them had magic. People were afraid to mess with the inhabitants of KiloKilo because it never ended well for anyone who crossed them."

"Many mages and wizards lived there," my father says, and my forehead wrinkles into a crease. I hadn't known that mages and wizards were real. "They were also shifters."

"So your aunt already had some powers," Mom continues. "Nothing too powerful. Just a bit of clairvoyance, not enough to help her predict her death, some ability to ward off evil spirits–except for her husband."

"Are you saying that after she died and came back her powers were stronger?" I ask for clarification.

"That's right. She could do many things she couldn't before, like tell the future, control the weather, and even cause intense pain," Dad tells us.

"That's wicked cool!" Ben proclaims, but I'm not sure I agree with him.

"It was wicked," Mom clarifies. "And when your uncle had control of her, he forced Mary to do many things she didn't want to do."

"Why would she listen to him?" I ask. "Why didn't she just do something to hurt him?"

"Because he was her husband," Dad reminds us. "She loved him. Even though he killed her, she felt the need to protect him, to help him, to work with him to get him what he wanted."

"And what did he want?" Ben asks, but I already know the answer to that.

"Maatua," I say, my voice just a whisper.

"Yes, he wanted to be king, but not just of the island–of the world," Mom says.

"Eventually, Mary realized what he was doing was wrong," Dad continues. "He waged war, and she helped him at first, but when he ordered her to kill a bunch of innocent women and children, she said no. They argued, and in a fit of rage, Mary caused a major earthquake."

"It shook the entire island." Mom has tears streaming down her cheeks as she speaks. "Buildings toppled. Thousands died. Mary was devastated."

"It was then that she decided she had to do something to stop Tony," Dad says. "So… she killed him."

"She didn't just kill him," Mom says. "We were gone by then. We left right before the war began, but one of my close friends stayed until the bitter end. And according to Carol, Mary took Tony out to the pool and used her new powers to drop a large boulder on him. She stabbed him in the heart and let him lie right next to the pool, trapped by the boulder, until he died."

My mouth is hanging open, listening to the story. It sounds awful, but it also sounds to me like Uncle Tony deserved to die a horrible death for what he'd done.

"Then… Mary cursed the island and disappeared. No one has seen her since." Dad has a somber look on his face as he shakes his head, staring at the floor.

I let all of that settle into me, and I think about how much of it must be true and how much of it might just be an exaggeration.

If I were to go back to the island, maybe I could find Mary. Maybe I could get her to reverse the curse.

I don't have any idea if my powers will allow me to save my baby on my own, but if there's a chance that I can get to the pool and use the water to save my son's life, then I will do it.

Even if Maddox forbids it.

"Do you think Mary will know who I am if she sees me?" I ask my parents.

They exchange confused looks. "What do you mean?" Mom asks. "She's somewhere on the island, most likely. Or she went to her own island. When would she see you?"

I take a deep breath and answer her question. "When I go back to the island."

"No," Dad says. "Honey, you can't do that, and there's no need to. You saved Ben and that baby. You don't need to go there to save the baby, and there's nothing left of Maatua to save."

I think he's wrong. It's my land, my ancestors' legacy. I do need to go back and reverse the curse, bring back the people, make Maatua a home again. Not just for me, but for my baby.

Pushing up off of the chair, I stand near the bed as the door opens, and I don't even have to look to see who is standing there. It's just as well. He needs to hear this, too.

"I am going back," I say. "I'm going to save Maatua from the curse, restore our family to the throne, and make sure my baby is safe." Turning my face to look at Maddox, I add, "And no one is going to stop me."

Thank you for reading! Book 3, *Lost By The Alpha*, starts now! Read chapter 1!

LOST BY THE ALPHA CHAPTER 1:
FANTASTIC VOYAGE

Isla

Water laps at the boat as we glide across the water. The larger waves we encountered a couple of days ago, waves that made me question my decision to do this and think that there was a good chance I was going to end up in the ocean, have died down, and now, it's just a calm, rolling motion that makes me want to fall asleep.

But I can't do that.

I haven't been able to sleep for days, weeks, not since I had decided that this was something I had to do, even when Maddox had forbidden me to leave the castle.

Fighting with him absolutely breaks my heart, but I have my reasons for being here. He didn't understand that. He didn't want to listen to me.

I'd taken advantage of the problems he was having, and now, I am here... even though he may never forgive me for what I've done.

Rubbing my hand along my abdomen, I stare out at the ocean, pressing my aching back to the bench behind me. Traveling while so very pregnant is just as uncomfortable as Mystica had warned me that it would be stressful, difficult, unpleasant, even painful.

She hadn't been wrong, but to me, the importance of coming was far more important than staying at home. I will survive being uncomfortable, but I wouldn't be able to live with myself if something happened to my baby.

"Are you still sitting up here?" Ben asks me as he comes up from the lower deck. The ship we've hired isn't large, but it's big enough for the five of us and the two crew members. The sleeping quarters downstairs are pretty comfortable, not that I've actually slept any at all, but my youngest brother has seemed cozy enough.

"I am still sitting here," I tell him, as if he hasn't figured as much out. "Captain Dave says we should be spotting land within a few hours."

"Captain Dave has been spotting the gin for a few hours now," Ben mutters, and I chuckle, but it takes a lot of effort, so I don't let it linger. "Is your back still bothering you?"

"Yeah," I tell him, arching it so that I can try to stretch out some of the lower muscles in my back, but it's hard because the baby is so big these days.

"Do you want me to rub it?" My brother has been nothing but kind to me ever since he snuck out of the house to come with me.

"No, thank you." I give him a half-smile. "I'll have Mystica give me some more of those herbs when she gets up." Everyone else is still sleeping this early in the morning. I wish that I was, too, but I'm still fretting, hurting, and wondering what's about to happen to us.

"I can go get them if you want," he offers.

"No, it's okay. I'm all right." I'm not sure what I would do without Ben. He's helped me so much, getting away from the castle, to the train, to the dock, and now… here on the boat.

It's been a whirlwind week, and I'll be happy when we get this over with and can get back home, but I have to take it all one step at a time.

I hear footsteps echoing off the stairs again, and I can tell by the footfalls who it is. I grimace a bit and brace myself. Ben slides over and holds my hand. I don't want to see him. I don't want to talk to him. I wish he wasn't even here, but there was no escaping him, not from the moment he'd shown up at the castle and began making demands.

Glowing amber eyes meet mine as I glance over to see him standing there, his blond hair messy from sleep. His clothing is wrinkled, and he has a scowl on what some women may describe as a handsome face, though I can't think of him that way.

Not after everything he's said to me.

"Oh, good. Look who's awake. Mr. Sunshine. Good morning, Antony," Ben mumbles.

He glares at us and walks over to the railing, staring out at the ocean. "We'll be home in an hour or so," he says. "Then, the real work begins. If you think you're uncomfortable now, on this boat, Princess, just wait until you hit the jungles."

I am not looking forward to it. I'm not looking forward to seeing the destruction of our homeland, trekking across uneven land, dodging who knows who might be out to get us. No, nothing about what lies ahead of me has me excited to disembark.

But I am curious to see the land of my birth. Mystica insists that there's nothing there we can't handle. I'm not so sure. I might have some sort of magical powers that allows me to heal people and maybe even bring them back from the dead, but that doesn't mean I'll always be in a situation where I can do that if something happens.

And what if something happens to me?

I doubt I'm going to come back to life again.

Poppy's tone is almost as disagreeable as Antony's when she emerges from down below deck. "You'd better have some sort of an idea where the hell your mother is when we get there or else, you're going to be the next who has to rely on that damn waterfall to bring you back to life."

Antony turns around and glares at her, and I say, "Poppy—that's not very nice, considering what happened there."

"I know!" she spits, coming over to sit next to me, folding her arms across her chest. "That's exactly why I said it. Your cousin is an asshole, and I'm tired of putting up with his shit. If he's going to keep being so fucking rude to everyone, I'm going to be rude right back to him."

"Poppy, has anyone ever told you that you need to be more assertive?" my brother jokes, and I backhand him in the bicep.

Antony doesn't even turn around. His eyes are fixed on the horizon.

I can't imagine how all of this is for him. Sure, he's a bit of an asshole, like Poppy just said, but he's been through so much in his life. It's no wonder he's bitter and angry at everyone.

But his attitude had almost been enough reason for me not to come with him either.

Almost.

Now, as he mumbles, "Land, ho…." I take a deep breath. We will be there soon, and he's right… that's where the real trouble begins.

I stand, my back aching, as I walk over to the railing near my cousin and look out.

I can hardly see it, but it's there, off in the distance. It's just a green dot on the horizon, my first glimpse of Maatua in almost twenty years. From here, it doesn't look as big as I expected, but then, perhaps it will get bigger when we are closer. Then, perhaps I'll get a better indication of exactly what it is I am getting into here.

I just hope we don't end up having to travel to that other island, my Aunt Mary's homeland, KiloKilo, the land of wizards and mages, according to everything I could find in the library in the castle before I left home.

"We'll be arriving at Maatua in two hours," Jude, the captain's assistant, says, coming around from the other side of the boat. "We will drop all of you, but as we stated, we will not be staying. We'll be back in two weeks."

Two weeks. My hand runs over my abdomen. I'm not due for another month. I hope they aren't late. I really don't want my son to be born on the island.

Jude continues, "We will stay for five hours. If you are not there, you will have to hope another ship drops by."

"And how often does that happen?" Poppy asks him.

He looks her up and down, something I've noticed him doing before. He's probably ten years older than her, but it's pretty clear, the short sailor with greasy black hair is interested in Poppy.

A grunt from next to me makes me wonder if he's not the only one, though I can't imagine Antony being interested in anyone but himself—and his mother.

"Not often," Jude tells Poppy. "That being said, we have seen another boat on our radar that seems to be headed in the same direction. It's a couple of hours behind us now, so it could change courses. At any rate, be ready to get off when we land because we will not be hanging around."

"Another boat?" Ben repeats, turning to look at me. My breath catches in my throat. Surely, he doesn't know already? We have been so careful….

I say nothing in response, and neither does anyone else. But my cousin mumbles, "So fucking stupid. Everyone is so goddessdamn scared of the island. There's nothing to be scared of. I keep telling all of you, the war is over. There's hardly anyone even on the island!"

"While that may be true, you can't say that it's not dangerous," I say to him. "If it was safe, you wouldn't have come for me."

"I already told you, Princess, my mother refuses to speak to anyone but you. That's the only reason I had to track you down. I want this over with more than anyone, but you won't be in any danger. My father's dead; he has been for over a decade. The war is over. Most of his followers are dead. Those that aren't have left the island and moved to areas of the mainland like your family did. We'll be perfectly fine."

I want to believe what he's saying, but I can see in his eyes that even he doesn't fully believe that.

"Two weeks," I repeat. "And four days until the Blood Moon."

"That's right," he says. "We'll have time."

I shake my head but focus my eyes on the green dot in the distance that is growing bigger by the moment.

I hope he's right. Otherwise, I've potentially ruined my relationship with the king to try to save my family's homeland from permanent destruction based on second-hand information from the son of a mad woman. My own family didn't even know Antony had survived the earthquake. They thought he'd been killed all of those years ago. His showing up to speak to me had been shocking.

My agreeing to this mission had been a huge risk, and a hundred times a day, I ask myself what the hell I'm doing.

When Maddox finds out what I'm up to, I have a feeling he'll be asking me the exact same thing—if he will ever even speak to me again.…

Find *Lost by the Alpha: The Alpha King's Breeder Book 3 here.*

Follow Bella on Facebook here.